Loving a Girl
Like You

Loving a Girl
Like You

Sequaia

www.urbanbooks.net

Urban Books, LLC
300 Farmingdale Road, NY-Route 109
Farmingdale, NY 11735

ISBN 13: 978-1-64556-457-7
ISBN 10: 1-64556-457-6

First Mass Market Printing May 2023
First Trade Paperback Printing May 2022
Printed in the United States of America

10 9 8 7 6 5 4 3 2 1

Distributed by Kensington Publishing Corp.
Submit Orders to:
Customer Service
400 Hahn Road
Westminster, MD 21157-4627
Phone: 1-800-733-3000
Fax: 1-800-659-2436

Acknowledgments

First, as always, I must thank God for all that He has done and continues to do for me and my family. To my children, I love you all so much! Rique, Riqo, and Lyri, you all mean the world to me. To my Hubs, thank you for your continued support. To my friends and family who support me, thank you. To Bri, thank you. To my super agents, Diane and N'Tyse, words cannot express how much I appreciate you all. Thank you to the Urban Books team. I appreciate you all. And last but certainly not least, thank you to my readers. You all are the reason I keep going. Your support means everything to me. I hope you all enjoy Lemere and Amree's story.

Chapter 1

The original "Before I Let Go" by the legendary Frankie Beverly and Maze blared through the speakers of the enormous MGM Grand conference room in Las Vegas, Nevada. Amree Haylin, journalist for *Extraordinaire Magazine,* stood off to the side, watching most of the guests in attendance dance and mingle as she nursed a now-watered-down coconut martini. Generally, she'd never drink on the job, but her nerves were getting the best of her. She was the only journalist from *Extraordinaire Magazine* in attendance, and as the only one from the team there, she was under so much pressure. *Extraordinaire Magazine*'s motto stated that every journalist on their team was extraordinary, yet Amree felt that in her case she had yet to prove it. This was her very first time attending such a huge event, and she felt totally out of place and had a good mind to leave. However, there were three things her conscience reminded her of that stopped her from doing so: losing her job, looking as if she couldn't handle working with the big dogs, and how this was the opportunity to prove she was an extraordinary journalist.

And that was exactly whom she was among currently—a roomful of big dogs. There were well-known journalists, athletes, musicians, actors, and actresses all around her as she stood in a dimly lit corner like a child afraid to enter the cafeteria as the new kid in school. Her eyes wandered around the room, hoping to locate someone looking as lonely as she felt. Then maybe she could at least begin to mingle. In her peripheral vision, she noticed a light flashing from her clutch. Withdrawing her attention from the people in the room, Amree retrieved her cell from her clutch.

Erynn: Why are you texting me when you are supposed to be working? Unless it's to tell me Trey is there and you got his number for me, I shouldn't be hearing from you until after the event is over.

She read the message and rolled her eyes. Erynn wasn't saying anything she cared to hear, and her reply was going to prove it.

Amree: Why did you take so long to text me back? I could've been dealing with a real crisis!

Erynn: Girl, you're in a roomful of success, and you look bomb as fuck! Do your job and stop being afraid to let your Black Girl Magic rock. You are there for a reason, regardless of what doubts you're allowing to play on insecurities you should not have. So act like it. If you'd walk around and quit standing in one place, you wouldn't even have to approach anyone. They'd come to you. I'd bet my last dollar on it. Now get.

Amree: Ugh, you don't know me like that. Fine.

Erynn: Actually, I do. Just read yo' ass like a book. Lol. Now get to work, but have fun, too. Love you. You got this.

Not bothering to reply, Amree put her phone back inside of her clutch. Then she scanned the area once more. One thing she could be positive about that Erynn had mentioned was that she did look stunning tonight. The black knee-length spaghetti-strap dress fit her size-nine, five-foot-six frame perfectly, putting emphasis on her inherited hips and handful-sized ass. Not for any sized hands either, but the size of hands on a man who wore at least a size-twelve shoe. Only a man with those kinds of hands would be able to properly grip what she had back there.

Her makeup was done naturally with golden highlights that accentuated her smooth brown skin. Her brown orbs sparkled beneath the MAC "I Like 2 Watch" eyeshadow: a mid-tone brown with gold sparkles. The gloss on her lips added a minor illusion to how plump and pink they really were.

Nonetheless, there were certainly women in the room who paid for injections to have lips even comparable to hers. Even with a ton of beautiful features, it was her hair that drew attention to her beautifully framed face. This evening, she wore her dark brown and orange-dyed tips bone straight with a small part down the middle and pushed behind her diamond-studded ears.

"Fuck it," she mumbled, downing the last of her drink as if it were a shot. She placed two white Tic Tacs on her tongue, allowing them to sit there briefly before biting down on them so that the minty flavor would hit quicker. She then put a piece of gum into her mouth, refusing to be known as the pretty journalist with the bad breath. Rubbing her hands against the fabric of her dress, she moved them in a swift downward motion, smoothing out invisible wrinkles, and she made sure her badge displaying PRESS was in perfect view. Then she gradually walked away from the back corner she had become comfortable in. Erynn was right, and because her goal was to earn the title of being an extraordinary journalist, she had to step away from that corner and get to work.

"Would you like for me to take that?" She ended her slow stride to smile at the young waiter who paused in front of her, offering to dispose of the empty cup in her hand.

"Yes, please. Thank you," she spoke, handing it to him.

"No problem. Uh, I know this may not be appropriate, but I just wanted to compliment your beauty. There's a ton of famous women in this room, and you shine a little brighter." He grinned at her, and she couldn't help blushing.

"Thank you," she replied, her smile still very present.

"No problem. Be careful. There are some vultures in this room."

"I'm tougher than I may look. Don't let the pretty face fool you."

"Good to know." He winked before walking off.

"Oh, my God," she muttered, feeling her cheeks heat up again and not believing she'd flirted with a damn waiter, which meant the martini she drank had kicked in. He wasn't an ugly guy. In fact, he was quite handsome. He was a shade darker than her, with his hair cut low into a fade. He reminded her of the actor Mack Wilds, only darker. Though handsome, he wasn't her type, and not because of his occupation. She wasn't too big on occupations as long as he did his part and didn't put her in danger or jeopardize her livelihood. As far as the waiter was concerned, he just looked young. She desired a man her age or older. She wasn't into the youngsters.

Okay, time to keep moving, she silently encouraged herself as she started again with no actual destination in mind. She unintentionally bumped shoulders as she walked, receiving the stank face from a few, which only assisted in making her feel further discouraged and ready to fight. The rudeness she received each time she said, "Pardon me," or, "My apologies," merely to be looked at as a peasant or rudely dismissed, made her angry enough to want to physically defend herself. She was always courteous of others, and unfortunately, she felt people took that as her being a punk, a character flaw she definitely didn't have.

"Ugh," she grunted, stopping right where she was for no reason. She just paused, needing to calm down, needing a second to remember where she was and what she was there for to keep from spazzing. At least she hoped that was what she would gain from the brief intermission.

"If you're trying to hear our conversation to post something on one of those little blogs without clearance, I will sue you and whoever you work for." A tone that sounded like one she'd heard on the radio caught her off guard. Amree's face scrunched in confusion as she made a slight turn toward the voice coming from her left side. When her eyes landed on who she assumed was the person speaking to her, shock shot through her, consuming her so much she felt her mouth fall open. Literally, she felt her jaw drop.

"So, you *were* listening?" the woman queried, staring at Amree as if she was disgusted.

Apparently, her reaction equated to guilt. "Uh, no, no, I wasn't," she finally expressed, shaking her head vehemently.

"Sure you weren't. Why would you just stop near us if you weren't?" The pompous look spoke volumes and showed exactly how she assumed Amree was lying.

Amree glared at her blankly. She never imagined her first time meeting one of her favorite singer-actresses would be like this. Mary stood in front of her looking as fabulous as ever, and all she wanted to do was turn and run away or cuss her out if she didn't quit speaking to her like some anybody-ass ho. She would only be starstruck for so long. Eventually, Amree from the south side would appear, and she was not the one to play with.

"Because I just stopped, okay? Trust me, if I wanted your conversations on paper, I'd ask. I'm the most private person in the world, so trust, I know how to not invade anyone else's privacy. I was not listening to you. No clue what you two were talking about. To be honest, I don't care." Her shell shock and fan phase diminished. She'd be a fool to continue to stand there and be scolded like a child. A reply from the woman she once couldn't wait to meet wasn't important as she stormed off, frustrated. Had things gone differently, that could have been a huge win for her, being able to interview someone so iconic. Amree, on the brink of tears, headed for the nearest secluded area.

Removing her phone from her clutch, she started texting Erynn with so much force one would've thought she was pressing an actual keypad instead of the touch screen of the iPhone. She was so in tune with what she was typing that she didn't notice anyone heading in her direction, not until the heat from the closeness radiated to her.

"I hope whoever he is, you're telling him it's over."

She shook her head before rolling her eyes as she turned around to see who was invading her personal space.

Lemere sat in the booth reserved for him and his small entourage consisting of his bodyguard and manager and his cousin, who was pissing him off with his groupie antics. Usually, it wouldn't have bothered him, but this wasn't that kind of gathering. Tonight was an opportunity for him to rub elbows and create connections to help further his career. Granted, he was already very famous. Still, there were a few areas of the industry he wanted his hand in, areas of the game that were untouched by him. Tonight, that would change. It had to, and that was why he was there, ready and eager for advancement. And there were more than a few people in the room who could help make it happen.

His only issue was that he hadn't moved from his spot to see anything work for him. His manager walked off not too long ago, claiming to be headed to work in his favor. Yet each time he looked up, the dude was grinning in the face of a female, mostly ones they already knew, which did nothing for him. Or he was in the face of a pretty regular nobody. It was bad enough that he was bored, on top of being two seconds from cussing out his "unable to sit his ass still" cousin, Mason. Mason wanted so badly to get up and introduce himself to anyone who would listen and ask for photos for his social media, and Lemere wasn't having it.

"Nigga, if you don't stop shaking like a fiend dying for a hit, I'm gon' send yo' ass up out of here." Lemere cut his eyes at him, causing his bodyguard, Shakil, to laugh.

"I ain't bouncing that hard, nigga. Plus, I gotta piss," he voiced.

Both Lemere and Shakil squinted at him like he'd said the dumbest shit they'd ever heard coming from a grown-ass man. It was.

"Nigga. Go piss. You seriously gon' sit here 'til yo' shit explode?" Lemere fussed.

"Yo, punk ass, the one ain't want me moving like I'm gon' embarrass yo' ass," Mason fired back.

"You embarrassing yo'self, my nigga. Especially if you piss yo' pants like a three-year-old. Take yo' ass on. Just come right back. Shit, you worried 'bout me bein' embarrassed," Lemere scoffed before continuing. He wanted Mason to know exactly how he felt. "I'm past that. Over here fuckin' mortified. Yo' ass," Lemere griped, shaking his head, wholly regretting letting Mason roll with him.

"Nigga become a rap star and wanna learn big words. I'll be back," Mason spat as he stood with a face contorted in discomfort.

"You wanna go follow that nigga, make sure he don't talk to nobody?" Lemere asked Shakil.

"Nah, I ain't paid to watch him. He'll be back. The worst thing that can happen is they throw his ass outta here." Shakil laughed.

"That nigga simple than a mothafucka. Can't believe my mama sister birthed him."

"Fame changes everybody, even those around you, whether you like it or not," Shakil added.

"Unfortunately," Lemere mumbled, knowing Shakil hadn't told one lie. "Where this nigga Thomas at? I'm 'bout to move around on my own. Shit, I'm bored as hell sitting here and probably giving off an arrogant-ass impression."

Lemere wasn't really into the crowd, mainly because he wasn't the center of attention as he liked to be, even though he'd never admit it out loud. Still, he knew by not at least attempting to mingle, it would give people an idea about him that either wasn't true, or he wasn't cool with. He didn't want even the artists he already collaborated with thinking that he chose today of all days to be a whole different nigga. If he continued to wait there sipping rosé and staring into the crowd, he would absolutely portray that.

"*Man,* Thomas over there talking to a badass bitch, boy. She ain't a celebrity or video ho, 'cause I'd know. She must be a reporter, A&R, or some shit. Finer than a mothafucka, though," Mason delivered dramatically, walking back into the booth.

"That was quick. The way you were shaking, I just knew you was gon' flood us out this bitch," Shakil joked.

"Fuck yo' swoll ass," he scoffed.

"Long as that nigga out there working for me like he supposed to be, I couldn't care less who he talking to."

"You ain't seen her," Mason said breathlessly, eyes wide, looking like a lovesick puppy.

"You acting like niggas ain't ever seen a bad bitch before," Shakil commented, glancing at Mason skeptically.

"I'm done talking to you niggas. Specifically you, old hefty-ass bodyguard. The last time you probably even came close to a bad bitch was to stand out of the way for her to speak to Mere," Mason huffed, relaxing back in his seat.

"Ditto, my nigga." Shakil nodded, smirking.

"You a liar, homeboy. I sleep with one every night. What you call my baby mother? At least I got a girl."

"Yet you lusting over the broads in this room. Both y'all niggas giving me a headache with the bickering," Lemere finally cut in. They were getting on his nerves, and Mason was embarrassing himself. He hoped shutting them up would help Mason save face, if only for a little bit.

"A real nigga still gon' look," Mason advised both men, having to have the last word.

"Ay, Lemere." Thomas's voice broke the tension as he strode back into their booth with a guest. Though Thomas drew their attention, it was the woman standing next to him who secured it.

"Damn." The soft whisper departed from both Lemere's and Shakil's lips.

"I told y'all," Mason shot, causing both men to shoot daggers at him.

"What's up, Tom?" Lemere asked, regaining his cool.

"Good thing you're still here. This is Stephanie from *Media at Large* magazine and blog. They're interested in interviewing you and featuring you in their issue 'Top 10 New MCs,'" Thomas informed him with a broad smile on his face as if he'd just scored him a major endorsement deal.

"That's what's up. Thomas will make sure the meeting is set up." Lemere stood and shook her hand. "Ay, let me holla at you." He turned his attention back to his manager.

"What's up?"

"This interview is cool and all, but there's a whole lot of money to be made in this room. You need to get out there and do better and not use my clout to get yo' dick wet."

There was no mistaking the seriousness in Lemere's tone, and whether he said it or not, Thomas was aware he'd better get on his shit before he found himself jobless.

"I . . . I got you, man. You should mingle too. Show your face more." His voice shook even with him trying to be and sound assertive, not wanting to be embarrassed by the other men in the area or the woman he was indeed trying to bed.

"Go do yo' job, man," Lemere demanded once more before turning his back to Thomas. Tonight was going every way but how he expected, and to say he was over it already was exactly how he felt.

"Ay, Shakil, I'm about to go bump shoulders with a few folks."

"Finally. I've *been* tired of just sitting here with you niggas. Ain't never seen a star scared to interact," Mason spoke, standing and dusting imaginary dust from his suit.

"You not coming with me," he spoke before turning toward Shakil. "I'm good. This is the last place I need protection. Stay with my lame-ass cousin. Y'all eat, drink, sightsee, and I'll meet you back here in no longer than an hour. By then, I'll be ready to dip."

"All right." Shakil shook hands with Lemere. Mason wasn't horrible. In fact, it wouldn't feel like he was working roaming the room with him.

"I don't need no babysitter. Plus, this dude won't put me in the face of no one important," Mason protested.

"You came with somebody important. Let that be enough. Or sit yo' ass in timeout. I'm not playing with you, Mase. You betta be on yo' best behavior like you at Sunday service with Auntie, or I'm on yo' head," Lemere chastised him, meaning every word.

"All right, man." Mason shrugged him off, sucking his teeth.

"Ay, just drag his ass out of here if he becomes too much," Lemere told Shakil with his eyes on an anxious Mason. He couldn't believe the desperation being revealed by his cousin.

Lemere left them there, moving as far off into the crowd as possible, even though he knew Shakil would spot him at some point. Shakil was outstanding at his job, always keeping his eyes on Lemere even when it didn't seem as such. As he strolled through the crowd, he could hardly get through as he continued to be stopped for hugs and brief conversation, making him regret sitting in his booth as long as he had. In such a short amount of time, he'd established a few connections he hadn't had before, and he looked forward to seeing if some would actually pan out or if people were just doing a whole lot of talking. He continued his stride, heading in the direction of rapper's excellence. That wasn't what the area was called. It was what he saw when he saw the men across the room, men whose level he one day hoped to reach by favorites and accolades.

"Damn," he mumbled as he was mesmerized by the curves rushing past him, forcing him to do a double take. He turned on his heels completely, watching her ass jiggle in the dress she wore. He hadn't seen her face, but her body was enough to redirect his initial destination. Luckily for him, she'd stepped out of the way of the crowd, giving the two of them privacy she had no clue they'd need. He observed as she tapped forcefully at her phone as he crept up behind her.

"I hope whoever he is, you're telling him it's over," he spoke over her shoulder.

"Excuse me?" she challenged with much attitude, turning around to see who was all up in her business and personal space.

"You heard me," Lemere informed her as his lips took on a mind of their own, stretching into his million-dollar smile. Her facial expression said it all. She was shocked to see it was he who'd interrupted her text rant. Lemere was more than happy to see that her face was just as banging as her body, if not more. When he'd followed her, he didn't expect her to be breathtakingly gorgeous. Most women he encountered didn't have a ten for a body and a ten for a face.

"Uh, no, I wasn't texting a boyfriend. I don't have one of those. Um, how can I help you?" she spoke, watching him with bouncing eyes, indicating he had her nervous.

"What's your name?"

"Amree. I didn't mean to be rude. Just having a rough night," she admitted.

"Oh, so you not having fun?"

"Not really. I'm not here for that anyway. I'm working," she advised him, lightening up some and nodding toward her badge.

"Oh, that's what's up. So you know who I am?"

"Yes. Would have to live under a rock not to," she kidded.

"Nah, I ain't that famous." He shrugged, smiling.

"If you say so." She smirked.

"Amree, I think you're beautiful and would like to take you—"

"Oh, no, I can't," she cut him off, though his offer was flattering. He stood before her, fine as hell in a black tailored suit and gray dress shirt, with a dia-mond-encrusted L around his neck and a diamond as big as his knuckles in his ear. His caramel skin looked just as good as the string of caramel one would see spilling from a Twix when broken in half. His beard and sideburns, as well as his curl-enhanced fade, were lined to perfection. His videos and IG posts did him absolutely no justice compared to seeing him in person.

"Why not?" he asked, feeling rejected, something he didn't take well.

"Because I'm here for work, and anything outside of that would be inappropriate."

"Who you work for?"

"*Extraordinaire Magazine*. I'm also an entertainment writer."

"That's what's up. So, I'm saying, I'm not famous enough to be interviewed by your magazine or to even collaborate with you on some entertainment writing?" He cocked his head to the side, peering at her as if he dared her to deny him.

"Oh, no. Interviewing you . . . working with you would be awesome. I just didn't think—"

"Set it up," he cut her off.

"Excuse me?"

"I said, set . . . it . . . up."

"Oh, okay. Um, do I contact your people by email? An office number?"

"Nah, you pull out yo' phone, check your calendar, and give me a date and contact info so we can confirm."

"I could do that, but I'm positive your schedule is far less open than mine. It would probably work best by you telling me a date."

Lemere released a low chuckle as he removed his phone from his pocket. "How about in a few weeks? But the meeting would have to be in person. I don't trust the phone shit."

"Th . . . that's fine."

"All right. A few weeks from today in L.A. Give me your details so I can confirm the place and time with you." He extended his arm, giving her his phone. Quickly she gave him the number to her office and her email, which linked to her cell.

"Cool, what number is this?" he inquired, taking his phone back.

"My office."

"All right." Lemere chuckled while nodding.

"Well, thank you. You kind of saved my job," she tittered.

"I doubt it. You're a good look. I'll see you soon, though."

"Thank you." She blushed as he slowly began to move away from her.

"Ay." He turned back to her.

"Yes?"

"Remember, if someone else approaches you, you're here for work purposes only, all right?" He winked at her, then walked into the crowd before she could respond. Unbeknownst to her, Lemere had just staked his claim.

Chapter 2

Amree stood on the other side of the tall wire fence, impatiently tapping her foot and waiting for the buzzer to sound and the gate to open. The groans coming from behind her let her know she wasn't the only person tired of waiting. She understood everyone's plight, but she also knew the gate wouldn't be opening until whoever was on the other side decided to open it.

"I can't stand when they do this bullshit," someone spoke from behind her, sucking her teeth loudly. From the tone and antics, she knew the person was a woman. Who the woman was or what she looked like she couldn't care less about. So, looking back to see hadn't even crossed her mind.

"Well, we'll be waiting until they ready. It's nothing new. I wish y'all would back up, though. It makes no sense to be all up on me or anybody else. Can't get the damn gate open if we all up on it anyway," another woman spoke up. This one Amree could see, as she was in front of her. She was also familiar with this woman.

Bekah.

They'd crossed paths more than a few times at this very location.

"Thank you," Amree spoke, releasing a low chuckle. She was glad Bekah stated the obvious, because apparently there were still some people who needed clarity.

"Girl, not only do the people on the other side of this gate get on my nerves, but those on this side do too," Bekah replied, shaking her head. Amree looked at her and nodded, feeling the exact same way.

"You look cute," Bekah complimented her as she always did when they saw one another. Amree was casually dressed in black jeggings and a gray tunic long enough to cover her ass, her hair was pulled in a high ponytail, and diamond studs adorned her ears. On her feet were a pair of Balenciaga sneakers. Her outfit was simple yet very cute and within the dress code.

"You always have him dressed so nice." Bekah smiled, moving her attention from Amree to the young boy holding her hand and being as patient as possible.

"Thank you." Amree smiled and looked down, admiring the cute Abercrombie & Fitch denim jeans and blue and gray crew-neck sweater. "And so do you," Amree said, returning the compliment and glad that, this time, she meant the compliment. Usually, Bekah's hair looked crazy because she never pulled her wigs all the way down. They always lifted in the front like she had a molehill in the center of her head tacked around the edges and floating at the top. Today, though, her hair was laid. An indication of a new hairstylist who could iron and lay a good quick weave, the part down the middle proved there wasn't a wig on Bekah's head today.

"Thank you. I do what I can with this wack-ass dress code they have." She rolled her eyes in annoyance. Bekah, who favored Kim Fields in her *Living Single* days, was dressed in a purple and pink plaid maxi dress that hugged her wide hips effortlessly.

"Single line, please," a voice called out, gathering everyone's attention as the buzzer of the gate rang and opened.

"Finally," Amree breathed out and headed through, doing her best to not become irritated by the impatient people bumping into her.

"Daddy!" The sweet tone of a little boy rang through her ears. Amree smiled wildly as she watched the curly-haired boy run into the arms of the man he favored. Actually, favored was putting it lightly. He was the spitting image of the man who now held him in his arms, planting kisses on his cheek. As they embraced, the little boy giggled uncontrollably, and Amree was reminded of the first and most important reason she always took this trip, no matter how annoying or hard it was at times. The other reason she kept coming back was for herself. Each time she came, she left with something she didn't know she needed. She watched and waited until the handsome little boy was put down yet secured next to the man before she started walking.

"Am-E, what's up?" he sang, greeting her with a one-arm hug, which she reciprocated using both arms and squeezing tightly.

"You know how crazy that sounds coming from a grown man?" she teased, dropping her arms and backing away.

"I don't give a damn. That's what I've called you yo' whole life and gon' continue to do so," he exaggerated.

"I know," she laughed. Am-E was a nickname given to her by and reserved for one person. The one in front of her.

"Let's go sit down." He gestured toward the wooden picnic tables. She followed him as he led the way a few tables down for them to sit.

"How have you been? And don't lie either," she spoke as soon as they were seated.

"Last time I checked, I'm the oldest. Yo' big brother. If anyone gon' be demanding sh . . . stuff around here, it's me."

"Whatever, Maksym. Answer my question." She waved him off, dismissing the authority they both knew he had.

"I've been good. Maintaining. Looking forward to days like these until I'm out this bi . . . piece," he spoke honestly.

"You know we'd come more often if we could."

"Auntie, can I get snacks?"

"Tyler Maksym, what are you supposed to say before you interrupt when people are talking?" she asked him with a smile. Yes, she was correcting him, but it was always so hard to do angrily because he was so adorable. Not only that, but she hated to be too stern in front of her brother. She knew he didn't care since she was the one currently raising his son. Still, she didn't want to seem like she was being mean to the child or seem more authoritative in his presence. When the three of them were together, she usually took a back seat and let her brother parent his son.

"Sorry. Excuse me. Now can I get a snack?" he asked with a smile and raised eyebrows, then quickly shifted his expression to a pout and batting his eyes, causing them both to laugh.

"I swear you taught him that shi . . . stuff the last time we were here." Amree turned her attention to her brother, who was still laughing.

"Nah, he's his daddy's son," Maksym boasted like the proud father he was. Not only did Tyler

look like him, but it was also apparent he'd inherited his father's charming ways.

"Whatever." She rolled her eyes as she opened
the giant picnic basket and removed Ritz peanut
butter crackers for her nephew.

"Thank you." Tyler smiled, tearing into the pack.

"Why you still calling him Tyler Maksym? You
know first and middle names are only called when
the kid is in trouble," he queried.

"Because y'all didn't want to name him Maksym
Jr. like I suggested. And I like the way they sound
together. He doesn't associate my calling him both
with being in trouble. He doesn't even get into
trouble," she told him.

"Am-E, I know raising my son for me and his
worthless-ass m-o-t-h-e-r isn't a walk in the park,
and you know I appreciate all you do. I also know
he's not an angel. He's a four-year-old boy, and I'm
sure he gets into some bad stuff. Don't ever not get
in his butt if he needs it. I appreciate you not trying
to overstep boundaries, but ain't much I can do for
him from here, and you're raising him. I'd rather
you do what you need to do so he don't end up on
the wrong side of the law and have people who
don't give a damn about him teaching him about
consequences."

"Whoa, whoa." Amree smiled, putting her hands
up. "I get on him, trust me. But he's four. He does
stuff four-year-olds do. And you know I get him

together quick if I have to, but he doesn't give me any issues. Look at that face," she gushed. "He's good for his auntie. Huh, Tyler Maksym?" she asked.

"Yup, and I the man like you said, Daddy." He grinned proudly.

"All right, I'm just making sure," he spoke with a raised brow as if he was still skeptical.

"I got this, Maksym, you know that." She looked him in the eyes, the same eyes she and Tyler had. It was a beautiful trait passed on from their mother. Everything else of Maksym and Tyler was their father. While she was the spitting image of their mother, her brother and nephew were the clones of her father. Maksym and Tyler were a shade lighter than her, with beautiful honey complexions, broad noses, full lips, and wild, curly hair. Her brother was always a pretty boy with a little thug swagger and was a ladies' man through and through.

She lost count of how many confrontations she'd gotten into behind either her brother playing a female or a female getting a little too disrespectful with him for her liking. Hell, she even tore into her nephew's mother's ass more than once. With all the trouble Maksym's looks got him into, she could only imagine the problems Tyler's would cause.

"I do. So, can you get the food set up now? I'm hungry, and I don't want cold food."

"You get on my nerves." She shook her head but did as she was told. Although Amree hated that her brother was incarcerated, for reasons like today she was grateful he was in a camp instead of a regular prison. His visits were usually outdoors in a picnic area that made it easy for the kids visiting their family members to be kids and not feel restricted. They were able to run, jump, and play as if they were spending a day at the park with Dad, Uncle, Grandpa, whoever they were visiting. Another perk was being able to bring in outside food. Of course, it was thoroughly checked, but having the option was amazing. Today, she brought Spanish rice, macaroni salad she learned to make from her Hispanic neighbor, flour and corn tortillas, chicken, steak, and shrimp for fajitas, and a few slices of pound cake. Pulling everything out, she began placing it all on the table.

"This 'bout to be so good. You cooked it all, right?" Maksym asked, rubbing his hands together as his mouth watered.

"Quit playing with me." She rolled her eyes.

"What? I was just checkin'. You may have been too tired to cook." He shrugged as he waited for her to fill his plate. That was one of the rules inmates had to follow. They couldn't make their own food nor touch money or go up to the snack bar alone.

Amree gave him a nice amount of everything, made her and Tyler's plates, and still had enough left for each of them to have thirds. The visit lasted about eight hours, and they all tended to want to eat again before it ended, so she always stocked up.

"So, tell me, what's up with work? How did that big event you were so nervous about go?"

"It started out blah, and then after Erynn cussed me out and I moved around the room, it got better. I don't know why I can't shake feeling like I only got the job because Ashley and I went to college together. Anyway, I have an interview coming up with a well-known rapper. If it goes well, it could be my big break."

"Yeah, you need to shake that shit. You and I both know she put you on the team because if you can't beat 'em, join 'em. The entire time you two were in college together you said you always felt she tried to copy your style of writing and she always asked you for tips. You're on that magazine because you're an asset, a damn good one. Believe that. And since you didn't say what rapper, I assume you don't want me to know—right now. And how is Erynn? Her ass ain't wrote me back yet."

"No offense, but you know how I am. I never want to jinx anything. I slipped up and told Erynn. Having the news in more than one ear, I . . . I'll tell you who *after* the interview, as long as he doesn't fake. And she's good. I really wish y'all would stop. Both of you are some hoes, and I don't want to be in the middle of drama or watch either of you get hurt. I don't know why y'all like each other anyway." She pouted as he laughed.

"Mayne, we just friends. She cool, and no lie, I'd hit that. But out of respect for you, we won't take it there. Plus, I got a little shorty who writes and visits me. . . ."

"Uh, who? I'm telling my friend," she said, making him laugh again.

"You'd sell yo' own brother out?" he questioned, tears in his eyes from laughing so hard.

"Maybe." She shrugged before laughing herself. They both knew she wouldn't, which was another reason she'd never want them to be together. She'd be "Bennett and not in it," feeling bad as hell knowing one was playing the other.

"Yeah, she knows. I keep it just as real with her as I do with you. Which is why you should know that if I'm not giving Erynn my last name, I ain't fuckin with her like that. Erynn's out living her life as she should be. Being tied down to me while I'm in here is an option I'm not giving her. The caliber of woman Erynn is is not to be a jailhouse girlfriend. She's wife material. If I can't give her that, then friendship is all either of us will be offering the other until the time is right." He shrugged like he'd said nothing when he really said a mouthful.

"Ay," she sang dramatically. "Well, talk yo' shit . . . stuff, brother," she giggled, covering her mouth at the curse word she let slip. Cussing in front of Tyler was a no-no, though she always slipped.

"Man, let me live." Maksym blushed.

"Nah, when you talk like that, y'all have my blessing any day of the week. Especially 'cause I know if you were to get married, it'd be forever. Neither of you believes in divorce. I can approve of y'all getting married, but not just fu . . . messing around," she spoke honestly.

Had Maksym given her this speech a long time ago, she would've stopped gagging each and every time he and Erynn flirted and showed interest in each other. Well, maybe a little. Either way, it would've made it easier for her to disregard her feelings that they weren't right for one another.

"All right, time to change the subject. Why you not dating anyone?"

"Um, you and Erynn can stop discussing me and my business in y'all little correspondences." She smacked her lips, and Maksym laughed.

"Yeah, yeah." He waved her off. "Answer my question."

"I don't know. I guess the obvious reason would be that no one who has tried has sparked my interest."

"I hope you don't have single mom syndrome," he teased.

"Single mom syndrome?" She looked at him with a scrunched face, utterly confused as to what he meant. As far as she knew, single moms were out doin' the damn thang.

"Too focused on the kid to live a little. In your case, to live a lot."

"Well, I definitely don't have that. I am living, loving, and focusing on myself *and* my nephew. Doing that isn't stopping me from dating. I've been on a few dates since you must know. All in my business. The dates I've gone on, the guys haven't panned out for me. And I'm not looking for a man. The one I'm supposed to have will come to me, period."

"All right, sis. Damn, my bad," he chuckled, throwing his hands up in surrender.

"Can I go play ball with Christian?" Tyler asked, cutting in on the awkward silence that came once Maksym's laughter ceased.

"Sure, go 'head, and remember what I told you," Maksym said, looking him in the eyes.

"I know: don't let them punk me, be just as tough, don't cry, fight back," Tyler said, reciting the rules his father had taught him about interacting with other kids.

"All right, go have fun. Stay where you can see us and we can see you."

"Okay, Daddy," he agreed before rushing off to play with Christian, a kid he'd bonded with over visits, and a few other kids.

"That boy worships the ground you walk on," Amree commented with a smile.

"That's my little man. I can't wait to get out of here so me and him can do all the things I wanted to do with Pops growing up."

"You could've been home if—"

"Don't go there, Am-E. You know why I'm still here. I wasn't 'bout to leave, be on parole or probation, and be limited to how I can move as a free man. I'm limited enough in here. When I get out, I don't want to check in with nobody or have any limitations with how I move."

"All right, geesh," she relented.

Although she hated her brother serving additional time, she understood Maksym's reasons. He could've been released this year with one year of probation, but he decided to complete the additional year in jail to come home without the extra stipulations.

"He's gon' need a shower as soon as y'all walk through the door." Maksym chuckled, changing the subject and looking over to Tyler rolling in the grass.

"I'm sure. I'm okay with it. At least he isn't fighting."

"I didn't tell him to fight, only to defend himself and not take shit from these badass kids. Some of 'em think they tough, have little chips on they shoulder. Plus, it's better that Ty beat the kids up if necessary than for me to get on one of the daddies or somebody, 'cause that's exactly what I'm doin' if my son get beat up," he spoke honestly, and he and Amree laughed.

"I know, 'cause I'm slapping grannies and mamas about my nephew."

"Speaking of mamas, I heard Colene is getting out soon."

"Her mother called me. Although I know how you feel about her, she should be able to see her son. I won't keep her from him, even though it'll be a cold day in hell before she takes him from me."

"You don't even gotta let her ass see him," Maksym scoffed.

"I do and I will. That's not right. I don't like her ass either, yet I won't be the one to keep her son from her, communication-wise anyway."

"She kept herself from her son. Nobody told her dumb ass to get hooked on drugs, prostitute, traffic shit, and sign her rights as a mother over. She ain't want Ty. She can keep that same energy."

Amree sighed. It was apparent her brother still harbored ill feelings against his baby mother. She did too, but she also firmly believed in not keeping a child from a parent who was trying. Yes, Colene made mistakes, even signed over her rights to Tyler. But the only way it would be too late for her to make things right with her child was if he decided he didn't want anything to do with her. It would be decided on his own recognizance, not due to persuasion from her or his father if she could talk enough sense into him to not do so.

"Do I have your blessing to supervise him with his mom if she asks to see him? I won't leave her alone with him, but I'll allow her to see him with your blessing."

Maksym stared at her, looking as if he was deeply considering the answer, and he was. Colene had done so much and caused so much pain that he was still trying to get over. She betrayed him in multiple ways, but the ultimate pain was her saying fuck their son and leaving him on his sister's porch in nothing other than thin pajamas. He had every right to be angry and say fuck her, but Amree was right. Tyler should be the one to decide what happened between him and his mother.

"Don't let that ho take my son nowhere. She don't need to ask him about me, either. Whole convo needs to be PG, and I'd prefer she start with an apology to him," Maksym stated matter-of-factly.

"I already said she's not taking him anywhere, and everything else I got. Don't worry. Besides, it's a big question mark if she'll even come see him. I've heard from her mother, not her."

"All right, man." He sighed.

"Maksym, I've had Tyler for two years, almost three. He's y'all's, and he's become mine too. His well-being is most important to me. Not just because you trust him with me. It's because he's my nephew. My only nephew. I'll be locked up for fuckin' up Colene or anyone else before anyone hurts him on my watch. Hell, I'll box with you about him." She smiled, hoping to lighten the mood again.

"I know, sis. Thank you, man." He reached across the table for her hand, which she happily placed in his.

"No thanks needed. You've had me since Mom and Dad brought me home from the hospital, and I'ma always have you." She squeezed his hand, grateful he finally relaxed.

Chapter 3

Lemere sat at the end of the long mahogany table in the boardroom of his record label with Thomas to the right of him and a few other executives and producers filling the other seats, leaving only the one at the head of the table for the label's vice president. Vice Records had been Lemere's label going on two years, and over the time span, he'd learned a lot and had become one of their biggest-selling artists. Hence one of the reasons he sat at the end of the table, displaying his importance to the company. Not only that, but he always wanted to be able to look everyone in the eye so they could make no mistake how serious he was when discussing his future.

Each meeting, he walked in with the mentality that they needed him just as much as he needed them, for right now anyway. So, with that in mind, he always voiced his disapproval, wants, and needs, and he never exited a meeting without a verbal and written compromise. The time he spent hustling in the streets taught him about slick fast-talkers, so getting anything past him when it came to business was difficult for the other side. Even if he didn't have the same credentials as the other people in the room, he knew enough to avoid getting played. "You can't outhustle a true hustler," was always his motto, and a true hustler he was.

"My fault for being late, everyone," David, the vice president, said as he swaggered into the room. He was dressed all in gray. His suit contained specks of black and white—not a lot, but enough to make the suit pop. He wore leather shoes with a gray pattern. David looked every bit of power and rightfully so. Also a handsome man, he stood at least six feet tall, with a mocha complexion, sprinkles of gray in his low-cut fade, and a perfectly lined goatee. He was what women would call an old Zaddy, although he was slightly younger than 55. David started as an artist just as Lemere had, working his way up the corporate ladder, landing himself in a seat Lemere hoped to one day sit in. Well, not literally. Lemere wanted to create his own seat at his own table. For him, that would be worth a lot more than to have it given to him.

Nevertheless, he admired David and his grind, making him one of the few people Lemere fucked with at the label. He didn't think they were friends. He knew his and David's relationship would sever immediately if he were to ever jump ship. Still, David was one of the very few people he had a lot of respect for.

"It's cool," Lemere spoke, nodding his head at him to say, "What's up?"

"All right, let's get this meeting going. We're here to talk about the release of the sophomore album and heading into the studio to work on the third?" David asked, looking at the notebook in front of him.

"Yeah, although I got a few things that need to be adjusted with my sophomore album," Lemere voiced, looking at David, whose head was still down, reviewing the notes. Lemere kept his eyes on him as he waited for his head to lift and acknowledge what he'd just said.

"What do you have in mind?" David asked, finally raising his head, his eyes meeting Lemere's.

"I want to release another single before the drop. The last single is not doing as good as the one before that, so I need to reignite the buzz surrounding the album. I want to drop the song with me and Danni, or 'Lifestyle,' two songs y'all wanted to hold off on, but they need to be bonus tracks on Aye-2."

"Sounds like you thought that through," David spoke with a smirk. He always appreciated that Lemere knew what he wanted. One thing he knew for sure was that Lemere thought things through whenever it came to his artistry and his pockets.

"You know I did. This is chess and not checkers. Those singles need to drop ASAP. I got a few interviews and shit to promote the album. In addition, I want something new to drop so that I make the songs another topic of discussion."

David nodded slowly as he rubbed his chin hair and pondered the request Lemere was making. He made valid points. The last single didn't do the numbers they wanted, although the numbers weren't bad. Still, they had a program, a formula they followed, and giving Lemere what he wanted would not make A plus B equal C in their system of things. He'd also have his work cut out for him if he went along with this single and bonus track idea.

"You thinkin' real long, Dave," Lemere spoke, slightly agitated. His idea wasn't one that needed to be dwelled on. In his mind, it was a simple yes or okay, because without a doubt, he knew what he was talking about.

"Chess not checkers, remember?" David chuckled.

"Exactly, so you should know my motives protect the strongest pieces on the board."

Chuckling, David nodded again, completely sold this time. "All right, you got it. However, you already know if—"

"Say less. I got this. I performed 'Lifestyle' in the club the other night, and the crowd went crazy. So crazy, I performed it twice." He smiled slyly.

"Yo, y'all do what you need to get the radio spins for the new single he chooses," David spoke to his employees, who were already taking notes and strategizing in their minds.

"All right, so album three will be worked on during free time between tour dates, after the tour, or what?" David asked, placing his attention back on Lemere.

"All of the above. You know my best work comes in spurts. If I'm feeling it, I record. If not, I don't. I always meet my deadline."

"All right, looks like you got this all under control. I'll see you in six weeks. The album will have dropped, and you'll have completed more than a few shows."

"Cool," Lemere agreed.

David stood, and so did Lemere as he met him halfway. Once they closed the space, the two shook hands and embraced in a brotherly hug.

"You came in here dressed like Nino Brown like I was gon' be intimidated or some shit?" David asked, laughing as he quickly scanned Lemere's attire. He was dressed all in black: black jeans, black long-sleeve crew tee, black shoes, a simple gold L chain, gold Audemars watch, and black-lined Cartier clear lenses.

"Nah, not at all. I got places to be when I leave here. I wasn't even thinking about that nigga when I got dressed," he laughed. "Now that you mention

it, 'Money talks, and bullshit runs a marathon,'"
he quoted, giving his best Nino Brown impression. "Yeah, I'm definitely needed if they ever do
a remake." He spoke cockily with his arm bent,
checking his watch.

"Yeah, all right." David chuckled, slapping five
with Lemere once more before he exited. Shortly
after him, everyone else left, leaving only Lemere
and Thomas.

"That went well," Thomas spoke once Lemere sat
back down.

"Yeah, thanks to me. What is it you do again?"
Lemere asked sarcastically.

"Not today, Lemere. We need to discuss these
interviews and side show dates." Thomas sat with
pen in hand and planner open, ready to jot and
adjust what was deemed necessary.

"I'm still doing everything as listed on both our
calendars, so what else do we need to discuss?"

"Your interview with *Extraordinaire Magazine*.
You need to push it back. Stephanie wants that
date, and since the other magazine isn't that big—"

"I ain't changing shit," Lemere cut him off. He'd
been secretly looking forward to the interview
since he met her. It wasn't because of the questions she was going to ask, but because he'd be
in her presence again. It would give him another
opportunity to shoot his shot, and he had no intention of missing this time around.

"Why not, man? That magazine don't have nothin' on this one I'm trying to get you to do first. Plus, you're on the top ten list of rappers for them. What these other people offering you?"

"As my manager, you should know what I'm being offered. Besides that, though, I don't give a fuck what you talking about. You only trying to change the date to appease the broad. I already told you about using me and my brand to do that shit. Fuck they top ten if that's the case, especially when I'm more of a top five nigga anyway. Keep the date I got with them already or drop the whole thing. It don't move me either way," Lemere said, standing. He knew the interview was important and necessary for the promotion of his album, but he refused to be moved for them when no one other than Thomas would benefit. Not only that, but he wasn't trying to wait any longer than he had to.

"All right." Thomas bowed out gracefully, knowing he wouldn't be able to sway Lemere.

"All done?" Shakil asked as Lemere stepped out of the room.

"Yeah. Is the car downstairs?"

"It is."

"Cool, my moms was expecting me an hour ago."

Lemere continued out of the building with Shakil watching his back. It had been two months since the last time he hugged his mother, and he was excited to be in the presence of his favorite girl. Thankfully, he'd be able to do so within the next forty-five minutes or so.

However, that would be too much like right. What was supposed to be a forty-five-minute drive turned into an hour due to the hectic Indiana traffic. When he finally pulled through the gate, and Lemere looked up at the 2,500-square-foot, five-bedroom, three-and-a-half-bath home he'd purchased for his mother, he was still in awe. He was proud of what he'd been able to do for her after all the stress he caused trying to transition from the streets to the rap game. The home wasn't as big as his L.A. home, though it was about five upgrades from the small two-bedroom home he grew up in, dead smack in the heart of the hood.

Lafayette was a block he'd rep 'til the death of him, but it was also a lifestyle he'd die first before going back to. The hustling put food on the table. Nevertheless, watching his back, dodging bullets, and even shooting some of his own, were all things that kept his mother on edge when he walked out the door. And his head was on swivel with a pistol on his hip when he walked out. Mere put in more work than he'd have liked in order to send a message that he'd do whatever necessary to make it home at night. There were times like now coming up to his mother's place that reminded him of how far he'd come and that his past life wasn't so far in his past. Lemere's walk into fame had only taken place two and a half years ago. And he knew, to real niggas, retribution had no expiration date. There was still a nigga out there who couldn't care less about his new start.

He was still Lemere who toted and busted his gun. That idea wasn't too far-fetched, because if it came down to it, he'd jump right off the porch again, reverting right to the toting and busting gun holder if he had to. That was why he kept men like Shakil and a couple of goons from the old neighborhood around, to keep him guarded and show niggas how ugly things could get if he had to deal with them.

Shaking off thoughts of his past, he exited the car, keys in hand, and let himself inside. Immediately the aroma of good home cooking filled his nostrils, causing his stomach to growl. He didn't know he was hungry until that moment.

"Mama," he yelled through the house, mimicking Chris Tucker when he played Smokey in *Friday* and laughing as he walked toward the back of the home. The shutting of a door sounded behind him, making him stop and look back. When he saw it was only Shakil, he turned back around, chuckling at Shakil's comment on how ready he was to tear up some food.

"Boy, why are you yelling my name?" She playfully hit him with the oven mitt she had in her hand.

"'Cause it's our little tradition and you like when I do it." He smiled brightly, showing all thirty-two pearly whites as he pulled her into his arms, slightly lifting her feet from the floor as he spun her around. She giggled loudly as she did when he greeted her this way.

"Boy, put me down," she ordered, still giggly.

"Hey, Ms. Leandria," Shakil greeted her, walking into the kitchen just as Lemere put his mother back on her feet.

"Hey, Shakil baby," Leandria greeted him with a smile, causing Shakil to blush. His caramel cheeks flushed with red.

"Ma, what I tell you 'bout callin' this nigga 'baby'? You know he got a crush on you," Lemere spoke, cutting his eyes at his mother before looking at Shakil with a furrowed brow.

"Man, go 'head with that," Shakil drawled.

"I think it's cute that he has a crush on me. However, since he's not much older than you, that's all it'll ever be. I like my men seasoned and with more than a speckle of gray on his head and face. I want a Zaddy. It's what your cousin said are the type of men that fall into the category I like." Leandria hiked up her shoulders in a cutesy way and smirked over her shoulders, ignoring the bewildered expressions on their faces.

"Man, I'm cussing Shantia's ass out. She and her brother don't have any kind of sense. She

ain't supposed to be teaching you that sh . . . stuff."
Lemere sucked his teeth, taking a seat at the table
with a scowl on his face.

"You swear I'm old. I'm younger than Stella was
when she got her groove back. Difference with
me is I never lost mine. Ain't that right, Shakil?"
She winked at him, and Lemere slapped his hand
on the table, making both his mother and Shakil
laugh.

Shakil nodded, still smiling. He couldn't deny
that Leandria looked good. Damn good for her age,
which intrigued him, because he preferred older
women. To him, Leandria resembled the actress
Regina King. She was a bit more youthful, but
similar nonetheless.

"Y'all play too much. Shakil, don't let my mama
be the reason you end up jobless, then come up
missing."

"Ms. Leandria, what you cook?" Shakil asked,
purposely ignoring Lemere's threat because he
knew Lemere was in his feelings. He also knew even
if Lemere fired him, his coming up missing was not
likely. He knew Lemere had his time in the streets.
Still he was skilled in so many areas that being
taken out was the least of his worries. Not only
that, but this was the usual friendly banter among
them all. The only time he and Lemere would ever
fall out would be if he acted on the crush he had on
Leandria—a line he would never cross.

"Fried chicken, dirty rice, Southern-style cab-
bage, peach cobbler for dessert, and home-baked
rolls," she replied.

"That sounds good. We haven't had a home-
cooked meal in months," Shakil told her.

"Ma, who all did you tell I was coming home?"
Lemere questioned curiously because the meal
she had run down sounded like too much food for
just a few people. And as she removed the large
catering-style trays from the oven, it looked like
enough to feed a small congregation.

"Just the usual, boy. They know not to tell anyone you're home either."

"Good. I just want to relax with you and my son
before getting back to my spot in Cali and having
to work—tour and studio. I have a lot of dates
coming where I'ma constantly be on the go," he
informed her.

He wasn't trying to come off like a jerk, but
having too many family members around when
all he wanted to do was relax would always be an
epic fail. Not only that, but everybody always had a
need or a request. Being home when everyone was
around never felt like being home. Some days he
only wanted to be Lemere from Lafayette and not
Lemere the superstar.

His busy schedule wasn't anything new, but he
always found it important to let his mom know
when his days and nights would run together,
leaving him damn near impossible to reach.

"Well, you'll be able to relax. Your aunt and cousins are coming to eat and see you, and then they're heading out. Your son was supposed to be here an hour ago. I'm sure his mother is purposely taking her time so she can disturb you," she chuckled.

"I'll be in the basement as soon as the doorbell rings," he said, laughing yet honest as hell.

"Okay, you two help me set the table," Leandria ordered, and both men sprang to their feet, doing as they were told. It took all of ten minutes to get everything in order.

"Ma, I'm about to go freshen up. I'll be right back," Lemere spoke up, kissing her cheek, then heading up the stairs to his bedroom. Removing the keys from his pocket, he unlocked the door only he and his mother had access to. Though she didn't have many visitors, she had enough to find it necessary to have this room locked when he wasn't there.

Though this wasn't the home he grew up in, the layout of his bedroom mirrored the one he had as a teenager, minus the king-sized bed and master bathroom. The black and blue color scheme was the same. Posters and photos he cherished decorated the wall. Trophies from his days playing little league through high school sports lined the wall shelf. His most prized possession, a photo of him and his father when he was a baby, took up half the wall space near his walk-in closet. His closet was full of clothes and sneakers, as well as a safe containing a hundred grand in cash in case of an emergency—the second reason no one outside of his mother had access to his room. Removing the Gucci sneakers on his feet, he pulled on a pair of Gucci house shoes to feel more relaxed, then removed all his jewelry minus the gold chain, placing all other items into his custom jewelry box before heading back downstairs.

"Daddy."

The sounds of little feet and a high-pitched voice coming his way had Lemere smiling so hard his cheeks hurt. His own excitement had him making quick, long strides to meet his son halfway. With his arms outstretched, Lemere bent down enough to scoop his son into his arms, hugging him tightly and kissing his cheek.

"Ugh, Daddy. Don't kiss," LJ spoke, wiping his cheek.

"LJ, I can kiss my own son on the cheek," he said, tickling him as he placed him back on his feet.

"When you get back in town?" Kiana, his baby mother, asked with attitude, stepping into the dining room.

Involuntarily, Lemere's eyes lustfully scanned her body before landing on her face and shifting to a scowl of disgust. Kiana was undoubtedly a beautiful girl with a nice body, but her attitude and the way she dressed made her ugly to him. What used to turn him on about her was now irrelevant because she somehow seemed to remove all of those characteristics from her identity.

"Quit starin'. This don't belong to you anymore." She smirked.

"Trust me, I don't want it. I'm tryin' to figure out why you lookin' like a nightwalker with my son." Seeing the shift in her face, he turned his attention back toward his son. "LJ, go help Grandma," he told him.

"I have a date. And I look good, so I can dress how I want. Just 'cause you used to those botched-body bitches, don't try to play me." She placed her hands on her hips, looking like she dared him to say she was wrong.

"All right, you should head out so that you're not late," he spoke, emotionless.

"So, do you have a girlfriend now?" she asked, ignoring his dismissal of her.

"Bye, Kiana."

"Well, if you do, don't be having nobody around my son." She clicked her tongue and rolled her neck.

Turning on his heels, Lemere left her standing there, disappointed that he'd loved her once upon a time. His mother told him that Kiana would become a bigger headache than he wanted, but he was in love and ignored the signs. Oh, how he wished he had listened. Well, if he had, his son wouldn't be here, and he wouldn't trade him for anything in the world.

As soon as he stepped back into the kitchen, he took a seat next to his son and listened to him tell him about everything, from school, to video games, to a little girl who liked him, down to all the trips he was trying to go on. Lemere sat there listening, taking it all in, promising himself to find ways to spend more time with LJ. He was growing so fast and looked taller each time he saw him. The money he made to provide for him was good, but lost time he could never get back. Unfortunately, his reason outside of work for staying away was Kiana. He loathed dealing with her so much at times. It kept him from his son. It was wrong. He knew it and would have to change that sooner rather than later.

Chapter 4

"Okay, Tyler Maksym, you need to hurry up. Neither of us can be late today!" Amree yelled toward the top of the stairs of her home. She stood at the bottom of the wooden steps of her three-bedroom, two-bath townhome, looking at the time on her MK watch. They still had a good twenty minutes to spare before leaving. However, she was trying to teach him about punctuality.

"I coming, Auntie," he yelled back.

"Then why aren't you here?" she asked prematurely, just as he came into view at the top of the stairs with a sullen look on his face.

"What's wrong, Ty?" Her tone softened. Seeing him look like he'd lost his best friend shifted her mood immediately.

"It's 'bring a toy to school' day, and I can't find my Black Panther toy." His little nose scrunched, and his lip poked out in a pout as he made his way to her.

"You're so handsome. You know that?" Amree smiled, taking her hand and rubbing it atop his curly mane.

"Yes, but I'm sad, Auntie," he informed her in a whiny tone.

Chuckling, she knew that was an innocent way for him to say that he couldn't care less about her compliment.

"Well, would taking a different toy make you happy? You have so many toys, nephew. I'm sure you can find another."

"No, I want Black Panther because he's my favorite."

"Okay." She chuckled again before taking him by the hand, leading the way to the smoke gray leather sectional in her living room.

"There he is." Tyler smiled so big it lit up the already-bright room.

She couldn't help staring at him in amazement, and she had been looking at him with the same amount of love since the day he was born. Tyler was everything to her, and she hated that, eventually, he'd probably be leaving to live with his father whenever he returned home. It was something she tried not to think about often and instead chose to enjoy his being there now.

"Remember we put him here with your backpack last night so we wouldn't forget it?" Amree asked.

"Oh yeah," Tyler said, still smiling and throwing his head back slightly, releasing the cutest little chuckle.

"Okay, can we go now?"

"Yes, Auntie."

Shaking her head, Amree watched in awe as he put the toy inside his backpack, zipped it, and put his arms in the straps.

"Okay, I ready," he spoke, so sure of himself. It was too cute to correct at the moment.

"All right, let's grab our lunches and we can leave," she spoke, heading toward her kitchen, which happened to be her favorite part of her home, minus her master bedroom. It was an open kitchen with the sink and counter space in the center. All appliances were stainless steel, playing off the light gray paint.

Tyler pressed a button on the fridge, and the door opened slowly. He removed his personalized lunch pail and stepped aside for Amree to grab hers before pressing the button again, closing the door. They entered the garage through the door toward the rear of the kitchen, where they got inside her Tesla before she opened the garage door and backed out. The drive to Tyler's school was rather quick, being that his private school was only a few blocks from the gated community they lived in.

She pulled up to the designated drop-off spot and helped Tyler out of the car. Amree always made sure to walk him to the door of his classroom, although there were many kids he could've walked inside with and two adults on schoolyard duty in front as well. Still, she made sure he got to the classroom and in his seat before she left for her peace of mind. There were too many women and children being preyed upon, and she always did her best to be sure that neither she nor Tyler became one on the list. She even purchased him a watch for kids with GPS and SOS features.

"Have a good day," she told him as she watched him walk to his seat. As soon as she turned to head back to her car, she came face-to-face with Kyle, father of a little girl in Tyler's class.

"What's up, Ms. Haylin?" he greeted her, broadcasting his straight teeth. They weren't yellow, but they weren't pearly white either.

"Hey, Kyle." She smiled back.

"Still waiting for you to take me up on the offer to take you out," Kyle spoke, getting straight to the point.

"I gave you an answer, remember?" she questioned with a smirk on her face.

"Yeah, I ain't buyin' that one though, so again, when can I take you out?" he asked, smiling wide.

She stared into his eyes with a smile of her own. Amree shook her head, chuckling low at his persistence. "How about you give me a little more time to think about it?"

"I can do that. *If* you promise not to take another two weeks to give me an answer." He smiled again. His smile alone was enough to force her guard down. However, she was a very stubborn woman, so the weights weren't heavy enough to move her . . . completely.

"It hasn't been that long," she protested.

"I'm pretty sure it has." He grinned, rubbing his chin as if he were contemplating the positivity in his answer.

"Well, I'll give you an answer before two weeks from now, even if it's on the thirteenth day," she laughed.

"Ahh, so it's like that?" He placed his hand over his heart like she'd just wounded him.

"I was only joking, but I do need to go."

"Okay, Ms. Haylin, I won't hold you. Guess I'll see you around."

Amree produced a tight-lipped smile before she nodded and rushed off. Kyle was indeed handsome, and she would be lying if she said she didn't find him attractive or couldn't see them making a cute couple. In fact, he was fine as hell, reminding her of the actor Terrence J with a little less swag. She wanted a man who gave her chills and made her clit jump, and besides his face, nothing else about him did that for her. As charming as he was, she didn't get those butterflies she wanted to feel when with a potential bae.

"Maybe that's my problem," she mumbled as she started her car. Amree was fully aware she had a type. Also she was aware that who she considered to be her type were men who didn't aspire to be husbands. They'd do everything right but aspire to fully commit to her. Granted, she wasn't looking to be married anytime soon. She had a lot going on, goals to accomplish, and a nephew to raise until further notice. Her relationship goal was to have a man who at least saw marriage as even an aspiration of their relationship. Kyle seemed like he'd be the type to want that. He had a career and was raising his daughter by himself. She was almost sure he was a good catch. However, for her, he was missing that bad-boy quality she loved so much. That look that told her he'd have her climbing walls and singing Summer Walker's "I'll Kill You" with conviction.

And for that, she found it difficult to take him up on his offer for a date.

"I was always told looks can be deceiving. Maybe I'll agree on day thirteen," she said to herself, releasing a chuckle. One thing Maksym taught her about men, on top of the other million things he schooled her about when it came to the male species, was that a man will approach a woman based on how he sees her. He'll come at a ho like she's a ho and a lady like she's a lady. His approach doesn't mean he's a good dude, nor does it mean he's a bad one. It only means he knows how to approach a situation to get what he wants. As her brother's gems crossed her mind, she hit the call option on her steering wheel and scrolled on the huge dashboard screen of her Tesla to Erynn's number and hit call.

The phone rang twice before, "Hey, trick," came blaring through her speakers.

"Hi to you too. It's too early for name-calling, don't you think?" Amree asked her.

"Not when I'm two hours ahead. It's eight thirty there and ten thirty here. My petty started over an hour ago," she teased.

"Whatever. Apparently, you got some penis last night, because you're a little too chirpy this morning," Amree teased knowingly.

"You don't know my life," Erynn said, laughing.

"Yeah, so who was it?" Amree asked. She had called to get advice on what she should do about Kyle, but obviously Erynn had more exciting things going on.

"Girl, nobody special. I had an itch, needed it scratched because I couldn't reach it myself, and then I sent him on his way before the sun rose this morning," Erynn said in a tone that said she was completely unbothered and unimpressed. Amree knew better.

"I can't believe you backtracked to Hyndrex. Yuck." She knew who Erynn was speaking about without her having to mention his name. Hyndrex was Erynn's crutch, and she couldn't stand it or him.

Although the words seemed harsh, there wasn't an ounce of disgust in Amree's tone. And from the depth of their friendship, Erynn knew she was more teasing than judging.

"I said the same thing when I put him out this morning." She laughed. "No worries. He served his purpose and is back on the blocked list." She meant every word, hoping that Amree believed her.

The last thing she wanted was to be in a relationship with Hyndrex.

"Bruh, I swear you're such a nigga sometimes," Amree chuckled.

"Yeah, maybe. And I ain't stressed off one either though. I'm done getting in my feelings and giving my heart only to not have the act reciprocated."

"No, you're only waiting for my brother," she teased.

"So, you called me on your way to work. What dilemma you got now?" Erynn asked, blatantly changing the subject.

"You not slick by passing by my question, and you don't know my life," she said, rolling her eyes.

"Okay, now that the dramatics are over, what's up?"

"Kyle asked me out again. I want to say no, except I don't want to look like an asshole. Not only that, but I keep thinking, what if I say yes, and the date is shitty, and I have to keep seeing him when I drop Tyler at school?" The conflict was evident in Amree's tone.

"First of all, quit sounding like it's the biggest dilemma in your life. There's nothing wrong with him, except he's softer around the edges than the dudes you are used to, and he's a parent at Ty's school, right?"

"Right," she grumbled.

"Then take yo' ass on the date. Try something new. Ya never know. He may be yo' Russell Wilson."

"Bad comparison, 'cause that man is nerdy too," Amree chuckled.

"A nerd loving the fuck out of his woman. Tell me you don't want that life."

"I do, with someone with a little more thug appeal." Blowing out an exasperated breath, she admitted, "You're right, let me stop acting like this. I'm going to accept his date."

"Good. So tomorrow tell him he can take you out this weekend."

"Nah, I have two weeks to give him an answer. I need a few days to wrap my mind around this and build my courage up."

"I never pegged you to be this superficial or a sucka. You've changed."

"Erynn, don't do that," she whined.

"Girl, I'm joking. I get it. Give dude a chance, though."

"I am. What else do you have planned today?"

"I'm showing a house at one and a commercial building at three. Then tomorrow it's back to the nine-to-five."

"You are for real my she-ro. A Realtor and medical transcriber? You are really securing the bag, friend."

"Girl, look who's talking. You are soon to be one of the world's top-sought journalists. This interview with Lemere is about to put you on the map," Erynn said excitedly.

"Thanks, best friend. I sure hope so. I haven't heard from his camp yet, so who's to say if it'll even happen?" Her excitement switched to solemnness quickly.

"You gave him your office number, right?"

"Yes, also my emails, which go directly to my phone, and I haven't heard a peep."

"How close are you to your job?" Erynn asked.

"I'm pulling into the parking lot now. Why?"

"Because all hope isn't gone until you check your office phone's voicemail," Erynn chuckled, prompting an eye roll from Amree.

"Girl, you know so much," Amree said in an undeniable sarcastic tone.

"Duh, now have a good day at work, and call me with the deets later. Love you."

"I will. Love you too," Amree said before ending the call. She took her purse and Fendi laptop satchel from the passenger seat of her car before exiting and then entered the brick building.

"Hey, everyone," she greeted her coworkers. There were only five people in attendance including herself.

"Hey, you look cute," Jade, the coeditor of the magazine, complimented her.

"Thank you," she spoke back, continuing toward her office. Today she dressed in a teal pantsuit with a black short-sleeve bodysuit underneath. Her hair was pulled into a ponytail, flowing down the middle of her back, orange tips swaying carelessly as she walked. As soon as she stepped into her office, the red blinking light on her office phone caught her attention, and she could've sworn she felt her heart skip a beat.

Slowly, nervously, Amree made her way to her chair, placing both her purse and satchel on her desk rather than removing her needed contents and placing them neatly on her desk as she'd normally do. Taking a seat in her chair, she sat back, staring at the blinking light, as a ton of what-ifs flowed through her mind. Taking a deep breath, she lifted her dominant hand, her right, extending it to press the button on her phone to reveal the awaiting messages.

"Hey, Amree, can you step out? We're about to have a quick meeting," Ashley, the editor-in-chief, asked, poking her head through the door.

"Sure," Amree said with a tight-lipped smile. She was annoyed to be interrupted but would never let her boss know it. Pushing back the rolling chair, she stood, straightening her clothes, and headed back to the front.

"Okay. This meeting is just like the others to get updates and to hand out assignments. Taylor, let's start with you," Ashley spoke, leading the meeting as she always did.

"I'm working on the 'Music Matters' article and then the video interviews with the new YouTube sensations," Taylor rattled off. Johnathan, the photographer, went over a few photoshoots he had lined up, and then everyone's attention was turned to Amree.

"So, Amree, how was the event?" Ashley asked.

"It went well. I'm supposed to be interviewing Lemere, the rapper. I'm waiting for his team to send me a date," she spoke confidently, although her stomach felt as if there were butterflies inside flying blindly. She had only met Lemere at the event. Her nervousness and introverted manner kept her from boldly going up to people asking for interviews. She'd hoped her journalist badge was enough to get people to spark up a conversation with her that would lead to an interview, and it somewhat happened with Lemere. She had also turned down his advances to get to know her personally. For a guy like him, that could be a turn-off and a shot to his ego. What better way to get back at her than to play her by not doing the interview?

"Wow, that's amazing."

"That's a good look for us."

"Good job, Amree."

The applause from her coworkers echoed in the room, and Amree could feel her face heating. "Thanks, everyone," she said shyly.

"Okay, so let me know once they've gotten back to you about the interview. In the meantime, I want you to put another event on your calendar. Taylor will accompany you this time so you two can cover more ground. There will be a Grammy party in Los Angeles, and I was able to get two press passes," Ashley informed them.

"Ooh, that's exciting," Taylor cheered giddily.

"Yes, let me know the dates, and I'll be ready." Amree nodded.

"All right, I'll be updating the office calendar. Any other questions, you all know how to reach me," Ashley said, and with that, the meeting was adjourned.

Feeling a bit better, Amree headed back to her office way more relaxed than she had been, knowing she'd at least get another opportunity to interview someone big if Lemere did flake. Sitting back at her desk, she hit the voicemail button on her phone without hesitation.

"You have four new messages and five saved messages," the recorder alerted her before the messages began to play. The first, an automatic recording from Tyler's school, informed her of a food drive they were having. She noted the date on her desk calendar, making a mental note to add it to her phone so she and Tyler could go shopping for canned goods. Giving back, and instilling that in her nephew, was something she was big on. They were blessed financially, and for that reason alone, she saw fit to give back.

Message number two was another automated message, this one offering deals on internet services. "Nope, got that covered," she said as she deleted it.

"Hello, this is Thomas, manager of Lemere, the rapper. We want to confirm the one-on-one inter-

view in Los Angeles on April fifth. To confirm the
date, please call 765-555-0100 as soon as possible.
He's a busy man."

Amree rushed to copy the phone number down,
while also rolling her eyes at Thomas's last comment before saving the message. She looked at
the dates on her calendar and saw the requested
date was two weeks away, and fortunately, she
had nothing going on that week. She would need
to find a sitter for Tyler and doubted that would
be too difficult. Taking a deep breath, she picked
up her phone and dialed the number Thomas
left her, hoping he didn't answer her call with
an attitude, because she would have no problem
giving attitude right back.

"Hello," the caller answered smoothly, yet a bit
of confusion was evident in his tone. And she was
sure that was due to the unfamiliarity of her phone
number.

"Um, yeah. Hi, this is Amree Haylin, journalist
from *Extraordinaire Magazine*. I'm returning the
phone call to confirm the interview with Lemere,"
she spoke, trying to sound as professional as possible, even though her whole body nervously shook.

"Oh, what's up? So that date works for you?" he
asked.

"Um, it does. Do you mind me asking who I'm
speaking with?" The person didn't sound like
Thomas, the guy who left the voicemail, and though
the person she was speaking with sounded like . . .

well, she doubted it was him. She just wanted to be sure and have a name to reference just in case.

"You speaking with Lemere," he chuckled.

"Oh. Oh, hi, thanks for meeting with me," she stammered out, getting pissed with herself for having lost her professionalism even slightly. Amree was far from that girl who fanned out or groupied out over celebrities. She prided herself on being unapologetically herself twenty-four seven. There was just something about Lemere.

"No problem, beautiful. So, I'll be seeing you then?" he confirmed.

"Yes, I'll be in L.A. to meet with you, but you didn't say where."

"What number is this you're calling from? It's not the one my manager called."

"It's my business line."

"All right, well, when you get to L.A., I'm going to send a car to pick you up and bring you to me. I know we got NDAs and shit, but stuff happens, and things unintentionally get out. To avoid all that, I'll have someone come get you. Just drop me the spot you'll be staying at, and I'll handle the rest."

"Uh, well, is it too much to ask what proximity of L.A. so I can make sure I'm booked close by?" She really wasn't feeling his stipulations, as much as this interview meant for her career, but she had to suck it up. Besides, she doubted he'd pull anything crazy. He had way more to lose than she.

As she held her breath waiting for his answer, she frowned at the sound of him chuckling. Apparently, she was funny.

"Beverly Hills," he said, still a hint of humor in his tone.

"Okay, thank you. I'll see you then."

"Looking forward to it," he said coolly.

"Thanks. Okay, have a good day."

"You too."

She waited silently wondering why she didn't just end the call. Well, she slightly knew why—she didn't want to be rude by hanging up first.

"Still there?" she heard his voice.

"Uh, yes, sorry. I was gonna hang up. I got, um . . ."

"It's cool," he tittered. "G'on and hang up. I wouldn't feel right being the first ending the call. I don't hang up in women's faces."

She felt the corners of her mouth widen and her cheeks heighten as she unintentionally smiled . . . hard. "All right. Have a good day." This time, she didn't hesitate to end the call and place her phone on the desk.

"OMG," she exclaimed with both hands over her mouth, muffling her scream as she stomped her feet lightly in excitement. She knew if anyone were to walk into her office and saw how crazy she looked at the moment, not only would her sanity be questioned, but also her ability to do her job. However, she couldn't contain her excitement and budding crush on Lemere.

Chapter 5

"Your cheap-ass company paid for this?" Erynn asked slightly above a whisper as she covered Tyler's ears.

"Now, you know they weren't paying for all of this. Especially when I'm the only one who's supposed to be here," Amree verified with a chuckle.

"Girl, please, how can they dictate who comes with you on your trip?" Erynn rolled her eyes.

"Um, because this isn't a personal trip, Erynn. You do know why we're out here, right?"

"Duh. However, I wouldn't have come if a trip to Disneyland weren't in the cards," she reminded her.

"Yes, you would have. I needed a babysitter, and neither you nor my brother wanted me to leave Tyler with anyone else, so here you are."

"I could've watched him at your house or even mine. I'm only here for Mickey, a'ight, ho?"

"Whatever, and keep covering his ears when you're talking reckless."

"This baby is asleep. The first time was just a courtesy. Now, which room is mine?" Erynn grinned as she looked from left to right. There were two doors to choose from, and though she didn't care which she got, she had to ask.

"You know how I am. Take the left, and I'll take the right," Amree told her. She had this weird thing about sides. Everything she started was on the right. She felt that if she went right, things wouldn't go left, and so far, she had been correct. She needed tomorrow to go that way as well for the interview with Lemere. Especially since the extravagant room they were staying in was courtesy of him.

"Cool. Now, after I put my things away and get settled, you meet me right back in this living room so that we can discuss this interview and this hotel. I know your money ain't short, but it ain't long enough for all this," she spoke, waving her left hand in the air to emphasize the expensiveness of the room. "I wanna know who paid for this hotel. I got a feeling who it was, but I wanna hear you say it," Erynn spoke over her shoulder as she walked into the room she'd be sleeping in. She knew exactly what she was doing by walking off as she spoke, because Amree wouldn't yell after her, fearful of waking Tyler. Rolling her eyes toward the ceiling, Amree carried Tyler to the bedroom they'd be sleeping in.

As soon as she opened the door, her eyes widened in surprise. The room was like a mini suite in itself. After placing Tyler on the small sofa and removing his clothes, wiping him down, putting on his pajamas, and placing him in the king-sized bed, she finally took a moment to look around the rest of the room. Attached was a master bathroom with a Jacuzzi tub and a separate shower. She knew once Erynn saw the room, she'd be saying how she hated that Amree always chose right. She'd be joking, of course, as they never operated from a jealous place. But it would be hard to deny how dope her room was. After taking a quick shower and putting on her nightclothes, she headed right for the living room.

"Took you long enough," Erynn said as soon as she stepped foot into the living room.

"You know I had to change Tyler's clothes. No way was I putting him into a bed with his outside clothes still on, and since I knew you were taking a shower, I decided to take one too. I knew I had time." Amree laughed as she took the wineglass Erynn handed to her.

"You swear you know my life," Erynn spoke in a tone that mimicked singing.

"I do. Anyhoo, my interview is in the afternoon at two. I want to make sure I'm well rested before. So g'on and ask me all the little questions you're burning to know the answers to."

"Don't rush me. I'm still trying to process how beautiful and rich this mothafuckin' room is. Like, we have stayed in nice places, but this shit right here? Might as well be a damn apartment in the sky."

"It is nice," Amree agreed as she looked around. She knew when she originally looked the hotel up, it would be top-of-the-line. Yet, what she saw online was nothing compared to seeing it all up close.

They sat on the tan sofa, looking out the large glass window that overlooked the city. The night lights glowed in the evening, providing the most beautiful view.

"My room has a bathroom connected, and it's huge. What about yours?"

"It's cool." She shrugged.

"You ain't shit," Erynn teased as they both fell into a fit of laughter. She knew that Amree's non-chalant response was admission that her room was all that, better than hers, and she hadn't even seen it yet. And it was.

"I'll check it out tomorrow. So, did Lemere get this room for you, and why?"

"He did, but I honestly only found out about us having this suite tonight," she said honestly.

"Elaborate. As smart as I am, sometimes I'm slow."

"Sometimes?" Amree mumbled sarcastically.

Rolling her eyes, Erynn then focused back on Amree, waiting for her to explain how she ended up in the Beverly Hills Four Seasons two-bedroom Beverly Suite.

"He called yesterday to make sure I was still coming. Asked me what hotel I booked and under what name. You know I was skeptical at first, but I went ahead and told him. He said okay and he'd have my transportation ready. That was it." She shrugged.

"And did he ask if you were coming alone? Because, look, he had to know that this was way too much room for one person."

"He didn't. Maybe he just assumed that I wasn't."

"Hmm," Erynn said, then placed her index finger and thumb on her chin as if she was in deep thought.

"What?" Amree quizzed, knowing Erynn's skeptical look only meant she was plotting some bullshit.

"You did say when y'all met he tried to holler at you, right?"

"Yes, and I shut that down, so that's no longer relevant." Amree's brow furrowed as she looked at Erynn as if she'd just said the dumbest thing ever.

"This room says otherwise. He could've let you keep the regular-sized room with the two queen beds for our little seven hundred eighty a night instead of this room that's gonna run him about fourteen thousand dollars by the time we check out."

"This room is expensive, but it's not going to cost him that much," she said nervously.

"It is. You know my nosy ass researched the price of this room."

"Why would he do that?" Her question was more for herself than Erynn. She had only spoken to him twice. He was also aware her company was supposed to be responsible for the cost of the trip, even though she footed the bill herself. Well, intended to.

"Why do you think, Amree?"

"Erynn, I'm not in the mood to do the sarcastic back-and-forth with you. I'm not sure why he would spend so much. It doesn't matter, because I can assure you we're checking out of here once I get back from my interview."

"Like hell we are. He got this room for us—you—to enjoy, and it ain't like he can't afford it. Besides, this room is a decoy," Erynn spoke as if she'd solved the final clue on *Jeopardy!*

"A decoy?"

"Yes, he paid for this high-ass room to gain some brownie points 'cause he likes you."

"You mean a ploy?"

"Yeah, that. Shit, don't talk to me like I'm dumb. I have a degree too. It just isn't in English."

Releasing a sarcastic chuckle, Amree rolled her eyes before attempting to set Erynn straight. "All right. Regardless of whether or not it was to be nice or to get close to me, he wasted his money," she spoke in an unchanging tone as she watched Erynn's demeanor change. She could see from the pout Erynn's lips had formed into that she was disappointed.

"Ugh, you can be too damn reserved sometimes. Gosh."

"I'm not even going to respond to that. I'll meet you here in the morning so we can have breakfast." Placing the wineglass to her lips, she downed the last bit of it.

"Wait. I wasn't even done talking," Erynn protested.

"I am," Amree said, standing from the sofa. She knew the rest of their conversation would be Erynn trying to convince her to see what was up with Lemere, and to take him up on his offer if he asked her out again. And as nice as that all sounded, she wouldn't do it. Couldn't do it.

"Watch how I treat you when I go back home, and you call me."

"You'll answer and give me whatever advice I need. Good night, bestie."

Erynn looked at her and rolled her eyes before standing and stalking over to the bedroom door.

"Good night. I love you too," Erynn said before walking into the room and slamming the door shut. Shaking her head, Amree laughed before getting in the bed with Tyler.

A million and one thoughts roamed her mind, and the main one she couldn't let go of was the one that constantly asked what it would be like to be Lemere Webster's girl. Or even how it would be to have sex with him. Everything she probably shouldn't have been thinking about the two of them she was thinking, enhancing the minor crush she already had.

Amree sat in the back of the black Town Car with her eyes closed and her hands in her lap, holding her cell phone tightly as her head rested on the headrest. Her left leg shook violently as she willed herself to calm down. Luckily, she sat behind the passenger's seat, because the driver would've probably felt the vibrations from her shaking even with the decent amount of space separating the back area from the front. It wasn't until her phone vibrated in her hand, slightly making her jump as her eyes popped open, that the shaking halted.

Erynn: It'll be fine. But also make sure to shoot me your location when you get to your destination. If his ass didn't have so much to lose, I probably wouldn't even have let you leave. He trying to be on some top-secret shit, not giving you the location beforehand.

Amree smiled as she read Erynn's text. The feeling was mutual. It irritated her a bit that Lemere was being so secretive about where she'd be meeting him for the interview. However, she came all this way to do a job, and that was what she was going to do.

"We're here, ma'am," the driver announced as the car came to a complete stop.

Amree looked out the window and smiled at the beautiful buildings surrounding her. The drive hadn't taken long, and from what she could tell, they were still in Beverly Hills.

"That was fast," she said as the driver opened the door for her.

When she stepped out, she noticed the streets were busy, and Lemere was nowhere in sight.

"Um, where do I go?" she asked the driver.

"Right this way." He pointed toward a door, which she assumed to be the back of the establishment, as it was large, gray, and aluminum like most alleyway doors she'd seen in movies.

She waited as the man knocked three times before a guy dressed in a waiter's uniform opened the door.

"You're the journalist, right?" he asked, making eye contact with Amree.

"I am."

"All right, right this way," he said as he pushed the door farther open for her to enter.

As she followed him, she took a moment to message her location to Erynn.

Erynn: Girl, you straight? MapQuest says it's about a fifteen-minute walk from where you are to the hotel.

Amree: I knew we got here quick. I didn't think it was that close though. Yo' ass moves fast. Lol.

Erynn: You know I wasn't about to play when it came to knowing where you were.

"Mr. Webster is right through this door," the waiter spoke.

"Okay, thank you," she said as she quickly responded to Erynn's text.

Amree: I do. That's why I love you so much. But I gotta go.

Amree placed her phone in her black YSL clutch and slowly entered through the door the waiter had taken her to.

As soon as she entered, her eyes scanned the dim room. It wasn't dark enough to seem intimate, yet it was low enough to establish privacy. She was interested in the setting before her, and a slight smile graced her face. The establishment was nice. Real posh like, and she loved it. His effort to woo her didn't go unnoticed as she took in the burgundy and gray decor and candles burning in the center of the large, round table, where Lemere sat with a sexy grin as his eyes bored into her.

"What's up?" The smoothness of his tone hit her right in the chest as her heart skipped a beat. She could hear the pounding of her heart through her ears as she stood almost like a statue and watched him slowly rise from his seat and smoothly make his way over to her.

"H . . . hey," she stammered while trying to pull herself together. She had to snap out of the lustful trance he'd quickly put her in.

"You look beautiful. As always."

"Thanks, I guess," she chuckled.

"Why do you guess?" he asked with a raised brow.

"Because it's like you're implying that I always look beautiful as if you always see me."

"Well, you've looked beautiful both times I've seen you. Today and the first time. Is that better?" With his head slightly tilted to the side, he looked her in the eyes, smirking. Whether he knew it or not, that smirk had quickly become her favorite expression of his to make. It was sexy, domineering, and more confident than a mothafucka, and she enjoyed it—way more than she should.

"Thank you. You look nice as well." Nice was the subtle and professional way to put it. Lemere was the finest man she'd seen in a long time. In fact, at that moment, he was in the top five of the sexiest men alive, holding a deserved position at number two. The number one spot went to Tupac. Although he was no longer among the living, he'd yet to be knocked out of that position, in her opinion anyway.

She could tell by the crisp box line across his forehead and down his sideburns that he was rocking a fresh haircut. His waves, from what she could tell, had to be a mixture of genetics and wearing a wave cap up until she was due to arrive. Though the room was dim, she could still see how moisturized his brown complexion was. His full lips looked smooth and slightly wet, indicating that some form of lip moisturizer had been used.

"You ready to sit down?" he asked, interrupting her thoughts, interrupting her exploration of his features.

Though she knew he couldn't, she couldn't help feeling like he had read her mind. The confident and sexy look on his face was one of a man who knew he was looking at a woman who was very close to risking it all for him.

Pull yourself together, Amree. Silently she scolded herself before nodding her answer and following him over to the table. She smiled at his pulling the chair out for her to be seated.

"Thank you." She smoothed down her midnight blue short-sleeve, knee-length bodycon dress before sitting with her clutch in her lap.

"I wasn't sure what kind of food you like, so I didn't order. That's the menu right there. We can order, and then you can get all in my business." He chuckled as he nodded toward the tan paper with black italicized writing on it.

"Okay." She picked up the menu, immediately recognizing the restaurant's name, Mastro's Steakhouse. She read an article about famous eateries, and this one happened to be mentioned as top-tier.

"What kind of food do you like?" he asked, removing her attention from the menu.

"I love seafood. Well, crab, shrimp, and salmon. I also love pasta." She smiled.

"Guess I picked the right spot, 'cause they have all that here."

"I see." She mulled over the menu for a few seconds more before the waiter came and took their order. She tried to order the cheapest thing on the menu, but with everything being high as hell, she decided to order what she knew she would eat. Besides, she could cover her own meal without issue if it came to that.

"Do you mind being recorded? I promise it won't end up in blogs or anything. It's just easier if I ask the question and have your response recorded for transcribing the article later," she asked, getting right to business. They hadn't set a time frame for how long the interview would take. Because of that, she assumed they had ample time. Still, she didn't want to drag out the day with small talk. And having Tyler and Erynn sitting in the room all day waiting for her was something she didn't want to do either.

"I've done interviews before. That's cool," he chuckled, keeping his eyes on her as she removed a small tape recorder from her clutch and placed it in the center of the table. "Besides, that's best, 'cause if you miswrite my words, I'm going to assume you can't hear well, can't spell, or just don't care."

Had she had a drink in her mouth, she would've spat it out as she burst into laughter from his comment. "I can assure you, none of the above describes me. Whatever you say today will be written verbatim," she assured him, still unintentionally smiling.

"I'm holding you to that."

Nodding, she silently let him know she wasn't worried. Removing the smile from her face, she looked down at the table, quietly gathering herself, and as soon as her head rose, she was ready.

"Before we start, is there anything I shouldn't ask or topics you want to stay away from?" She hoped he didn't restrict her to mediocre questions.

"Nah. You can ask me whatever you like."

She wasn't sure if there was some sort of underlying message in his reply, as it sounded like he was suggesting intimacy, or daring her. She, however, was going to frame her mindset around the latter. "So, my first question is probably the easiest one. What made you decide to rap? Is this what you always wanted?"

"Straight to business, huh?" He smirked, revealing a small dimple she hadn't at first noticed. Had it always been there? It had to be. Regardless, the look he gave her made her clit thump and her mouth water. Despite those feelings, she hid the uncomfortable yet arousing feeling well, as she stared back at him as if she wondered why he'd expect anything less.

"Nah. So, to keep it a hunnid, I didn't always want to rap. Honestly, at one point in my life, my only goal was to survive. I thought my time in the streets was really going to be enough to put my mama in a bigger house. Yeah, I was hustling backward than a mothafucka back then." He paused, releasing a sarcastic chuckle as a faraway look told her he was thinking of his next move. His pause, whether for dramatic effect or not, had her waiting anxiously for what he was planning to say next.

"I can't tell you what I wanted to do before rap. What I can tell you is how I got started. The shit just fell in my lap. An OG from around my neighborhood made me ride with him to the studio. I had been getting into a lot of bullshit, and he didn't want me hanging in the hood that day. He told my ass to go in the house when he rolled up on me while I was posted up with my crew. I nodded and told him all right, but I guess he knew better, 'cause he switched from telling me to go in the house to get in the car." He paused again. Chuckled, again. Left her in short suspense, again.

"He was right to put me in the car, 'cause although I was heading in the house . . . once his car cut the block, I was stepping out again. Anyway, we got to the studio. Him and a few cats got in the booth. The rhymes were a'ight. I wasn't impressed though, and it showed on my face. I was asked if I could do better, and bein' the type of li'l nigga I was, I said yeah, scared as shit. Still, I figured what they were doin' wasn't so hard. Shit, the worst that could happen was me sounding just as bad as them."

"Were you as bad as them?" Amree asked, curious to know the answer.

"Hell nah. I did better, like I said I could. The crazy part is I felt I was trash, and they saluted me. From that point forward, OG kept me in the studio."

"That's awesome. You just tried something and it worked out. Now you're one of the biggest artists out there right now."

"I know, man. Shit's crazy."

"Now that you've hit this level of success, what's next?"

"I like to move in silence, so my next move is usually revealed after I've moved. I will let it be known that I have more music on the way."

Chuckling, she looked him right in the eyes. "I can respect that answer." And she could. Many people's endeavors failed, not because they didn't try or because they didn't work for it, but because of who they told. One negative thought can alter one's entire course toward a goal. She knew this, and for that reason, she wouldn't push him for an answer. No, she wouldn't be the one to manifest negativity his way. It could be a reader of the article. So to avoid it all, his answer would suffice.

"Can I ask you a question now? Off the record, though?" He smiled, looking at her while nodding his head toward the tape recorder.

"Um, sure." Although she was hesitant, she figured his question would be work related, so she agreed. Right as she reached across the table to pause the recorder, the waiter came with their entrées.

"What would you like to drink, ma'am?" the waiter asked as he filled her glass with water, topping it off with a lemon slice and strawberry.

"A mimosa will be just fine," she told him politely.

"Coming right up," he said before taking Lemere's drink order and walking off.

"You ready for my question? I want an honest answer, too."

"I wouldn't answer any other way. Well, besides no answer if I feel one isn't warranted."

Lemere looked at her and smirked at her comment as he was fully aware of the front she was trying to put up. "What's an ideal date for you?" he asked. His question surely wasn't work related, and though she should have shot him down immediately, she decided to humor him by answering.

"I'm simple. I'm an introvert, so more laid-back intimate settings are my thing. An ideal date could be chilling in the house or visiting the zoo."

She shrugged while he nodded, looking as though he'd ingested everything she said. Reaching back to the center of the table, she pressed the record button, letting him know the interview was back on.

"That's what's up." He nodded silently, giving her the okay to resume her questions.

"So, you've been attached to multiple women. Any of them close to making you go from bachelor to honest man?"

"None of the ones the media has attached to me. I'm single."

"That answer might make a few women upset."

"Can't be mad at the truth."

"So, your sophomore album is due to drop soon. What do you want listeners to know about it?"

"I put my all into it, just like I did my first album. This album is about my growth as an artist and a man. I got real personal with this album, so even questions you don't ask today will probably be answered on this album."

"Last question. Who is your favorite rapper?"

"The man. Tupac. I mean, I like the living rap beast, Jay, E-40, Wayne, Kendrick, and Cole. However, Pac and everything he was about, and his fearlessness, is unmatched. The person right after him for me though is X in his prime. Shit, even now dude a beast. So, those are my favorites."

"Inspired by greats. I can see that. You have songs on your first album that reflect inspiration from them, especially Pac."

"You calling me a copycat?" he tittered, looking at her as if she'd offended him.

"No, not at all."

"I'm fucking with you." His smile seemed to ease the distress she felt thinking she'd offended him. "That was my plan, though, to sound similar to him on my track 'The World Against Me.' Pac's 'Me Against the World' was my inspiration behind it. Only a few people got that, so it's dope that you really know yo' shit."

"Thank you."

"Any further questions?"

"No, I think we covered everything." She extended her arm across the table to stop the recording.

"Now we eat." He nodded toward her plate, and instead of replying, she lifted her fork, placing her pasta in her mouth. Silently, they ate, his eyes occasionally studying her.

"Why'd you shoot me down when I tried to holla at you?" he asked, breaking the silence between them. Though she was happy he spoke, eliminating the slight awkwardness she felt, his question was the last thing she expected.

"I was at work," was the easiest reply without sounding rude. How could she tell him nicely that, though he was fine, she wouldn't be duped into becoming one of the many groupies he bedded and tossed to the side?

"So was I, and yet I still made it a priority to try to get to know you. What? You think a nigga ugly or something?"

"No, I don't, and you seem like a great guy, but you're not for me." She shrugged, hoping that he would leave well enough alone. Luckily, she'd already gotten the answers to her questions for the interview, because had she not, she was sure he'd probably be offended and not want to continue.

"You said I'm not for you, not that I'm not your type, so there's hope." He smiled, showing his dimple, making her heart thud. Making her clit jump. Lemere was handsome, no doubt about it, and he knew it as well. As tempted as she was, she still couldn't give in. Wouldn't.

Shrugging, she looked up from her plate, allowing her eyes to meet his. "Sure, if you say so."

"I do, even though I'm slightly offended."

"I offended you? How?" With a furrowed brow, she looked at him as if he'd grown another head.

No way could he be offended when she should have been feeling a way because of the lack of professionalism he was showing.

"Because you're fighting off getting to know me, yet you claim I'm not the nigga for you when I feel I'm *that* nigga for you. The only one for you." Though his smile widened, his tone told her there was no joking behind it. He meant exactly what he said and believed it, too.

"Well, you're not," she stated firmly, yet internally she was unsure. How could she be sure when she didn't know anything about him other than what the media put out and the questions he answered for her?

"Why?" he asked, almost in a panic, praying she wasn't in a relationship. As beautiful and driven as she was, he would honestly be surprised if she weren't.

"Can you be with one woman and one woman only?" Placing her fork on the plate, she looked back at him, making sure to make eye contact. In her heart of hearts, she knew he'd say no. She expected him to say no. She hoped he'd answer no so she had an easy way out and could shut down the rest of his questioning.

"Can you be the kind of woman your man needs, as long as he loves and respects you?"

His eyes never left hers. He was deflecting. She knew it and found it funny that he thought he was getting one over on her. Of course she could be that woman, but since she wouldn't be it for him, he didn't need to know her answer.

Laughing, she shook her head before asking, "How about we focus back on the business we came here for?"

"You got that for now." He went back to eating, still stealing glances of her occasionally.

She was proud of herself, proud of how she kept her composure and remained professional. Lemere had taken the hint, only asking work-related questions, when he still had a desire to get to know her personally.

"So, how you feel about sitting with me again after my album drops?"

Amree smiled, happy he asked her. Her mind was already made up that she'd be listening to and reviewing the album. But to actually be able to share a dialogue with him after it dropped was even better. She'd be able to get more clarification on certain lyrics. Her follow-up article would be amazing. "Sure."

"Okay," he accepted with a smile, glad to know he'd be seeing her again. "I enjoyed the interview, even though you made me feel like the ugly kid."

"So did I, and of course, that was not my intention."

"What you got planned for the rest of your time in L.A.?"

"Oh, I meant to thank you for the extravagant room. I'll be checking out tomorrow."

"So, then you're free tonight?"

Laughing, she shook her head. "You have a lot of perseverance. I'm not free tonight."

"I had to try again for the road." He shrugged. "Your car is outside. The driver will take you back to the hotel. And I booked the room for you for a few extra days. You don't have to leave so soon."

"Yes, I do. I have plans." She smiled as she stood, letting him know she was ready to go.

"All right," he agreed almost too easily for her. However, it was necessary. She followed him closely as he led her to the same back door that she entered through. When he opened the door, the driver was there waiting.

"Will I get to read the article before you release it?"

"I can arrange that. I'll send it to your manager. Well, I need an email to send it to."

"I'll make sure you have it. Enjoy the rest of your day," he said, doing the driver's job and opening the door for her.

"You too." She smiled, getting inside the car. He hesitated, shutting the door. The expression on his face told her he wanted to say more. Instead, he painfully shut the door and watched the driver pull off.

That man is something else, she thought, smiling to herself.

Chapter 6

"Good morning, handsome."

A delicate voice graced Lemere's earlobe, effort-lessly sending a shock wave from his ear to his dick, causing an instant erection. The teasing chuckle that fell from her lips caused his eyes to flutter open and look at the woman to his left. She was gorgeous with the complexion of light brown sugar, a slender body yet thick in all the right places, ass and hips, and a pair of CC-cup breasts that sat perkily. Her lips were full, and as her tongue slowly swiped across them, he remembered how amaz-ing they felt wrapped around his shaft only hours ago. Looking her in the eyes, he nodded toward his midsection, letting her know it was time for her to handle what was underneath the tent he uninten-tionally created.

"I'll handle that, daddy."

Lemere turned to his right, allowing a small smile to grace his lips as he looked at the honey-complexioned, curly-haired woman. Although she wasn't as stacked as the brown sugar woman to his left, she had features to be proud of, like her enticing gray eyes. At first, he thought she had on contacts. He even accused her of wearing some, only to be proved wrong. His eyes followed as she slowly eased down his chest before taking her hands with short, manicured nails and easing his manhood from the basketball shorts that had it restricted.

"Sss," Lemere hissed from the sensational contact of her wet tongue and warm breath sliding down his shaft.

"You know I can't let her have all the fun, right?" pretty Brown Sugar whispered in his ear, right before she eased her way down, boldly lifting her homegirl's head. He wasn't sure of each woman's name, so he named them based on their complexions: Brown Sugar and Honey.

"We're sharing," was all Lemere heard her say before the sensation of two tongues gliding in opposite directions could be felt. Throwing his head back, shutting his eyes tightly, he enjoyed the feeling they were giving him. At that moment, he was happy he hadn't turned down their advances a few hours ago, because he strongly considered it. He hadn't been in the mood to deal with groupies and hadn't felt like having the company of a woman other than the one he quietly desired and couldn't have. In all honesty, it was the blow to his ego that granted the women access to his hotel bed. Two weren't always better than one. In this case, though, he wanted double the assurance, even though it would probably take ten women to equate to that one.

"Shit." His train of thought was interrupted by the need to voice the pleasure he felt. He wasn't sure which woman had ahold of him currently, but she was sucking his dick as if she were trying to take his skin off and ingest his last drop of cum.

Soft giggles took the place of the slurping sounds, prompting his eyes to open as he sat up on his elbows, right in the nick of time.

"You must want to get kicked the fuck up out of here." The seriousness in his tone suspended honey girl's ass in midair.

"No, daddy, what's wrong?" The shocked expression she thought he hadn't caught swiftly shifted to one of innocence.

"You know I'm not fucking neither one of y'all raw. And I don't want no condom you came in here with."

"I know, I wasn't trying—"

"Yeah, you was." He called her out as he moved from the bed, not bothering to excuse himself. He took quick strides toward the hotel safe, put in his combination, and removed a condom that he placed on himself after shutting the safe's door. Slowly he walked back over to the bed, looking at each woman, sizing them up. As a form of punishment, he was going to start with Brown Sugar since Honey tried to play him, thinking she was about to hit him with the okey-doke and pin a baby on him. She would be getting the dick hard and second if he didn't nut from putting it on her homegirl first.

"Bend over," he said as he slapped Brown Sugar's ass. Without hesitation, she bent over and tooted up.

Just as fast as her ass hit the air, his dick slid inside of her, pausing him on impact. She didn't squeeze him as tight as he'd like. However, her warmth enveloped him, and for a moment, he wanted to savor the feeling.

"Yes, daddy," she squealed as he slowly stroked her with force. Slowly he'd ease out, then thrust into her. Hitting her with strokes, he had to eventually keep her from running from him. He was taking his frustrations out on her with no remorse. Though it seemed to be bringing her immense pleasure, for Lemere, he was trying to take his mind off someone else.

"I . . . I'm cumming." Her satisfied cries brought him back to what he was doing. Oddly his body had been moving while his mind was somewhere else.

"Good," he chuckled, hearing Honey's relief that she was possibly getting a turn. He had something for her, though.

"Ay, get in front of her and open wide," he said to Honey.

"I wanted to feel you inside me, though."

"You not about to do it?"

Instead of answering, she crawled over to the head of the bed, then lay on her back, spreading her legs open as wide as they would go. As soon as Brown Sugar's tongue touched her, she was shivering. Within seconds, she was moaning so loud that he almost wanted to pull out of her friend and slide into her. She was supposed to enjoy the head, just not that damned much. Watching the show they were putting on, he continued to pound into her before he felt the head of his dick finally begin to swell. Without holding back, he pumped harder and faster, releasing into the condom, then collapsing on her back, his weight causing her to fall face-first into Honey's vagina.

"Don't fall asleep. I want my turn," Honey spoke up as soon as he rolled onto his back.

"I'm not, and y'all about to dip. I got somewhere to be." He half told the truth. There was something on his agenda for the day, only what he had to do was hours from now. They served their purpose, slightly. Momentarily. And it was time to go.

The sucking of teeth could be heard almost like a mini orchestra as he stood from the bed to properly dispose of the condom. When he returned, both women were still lying on the bed naked, legs open, hoping to entice him into another round. Turning his back to them, he went back into the safe and removed a stack of money, ten grand to be exact, and tossed it on the bed.

"I enjoyed kicking it with y'all," he spoke up, interrupting the silence.

"When will I see you again?" Brown Sugar asked, getting up from the bed. She took the hint and refused to be thrown out of the room. Besides, it was better to play it cool and have him contact her again than to lose connection with him altogether.

"I'll be back in town in a few months. I have your number."

She nodded and continued to get ready without a care in the world. However, her friend was another story. The sour expression plastered on her face would have made Lemere think she was born that way if he hadn't seen her smile.

"Lord, please don't let this broad be a problem," he prayed, briefly shutting his eyes.

Though it seemed like it was taking a while, within ten minutes, the women were dressed, ten stacks richer, and out of his room. Walking over to the room phone, he called down to room service, requesting his bedding be changed and informing

housekeeping that it was fine to let themselves
in. After the call, he made sure every important
possession he had was locked away in the safe
before heading to the shower.

Apprehension, nervousness, and regret were all
the emotions flowing through Amree as she sat inside her car, staring at the restaurant she was due
to walk inside in less than five minutes. In fact, the
person waiting for her stood in front, looking at his
watch in what she assumed was disappointment
at the thought that she was standing him up. If he
was contemplating her not arriving, he would've
been right to assume that she wasn't coming, even
though she was there.

Staring.

Contemplating.

"What am I doing here?" she mumbled as she
threw her head back on the headrest of her car.
She stared at him, trying to figure out why she
was so afraid to get out of the car and meet with
him, especially when he stood there looking good
enough to eat. He was fine as hell, all six feet of
him. He was dressed in black slacks, black loafers,
and a cool gray dress shirt. He was looking better
than she'd ever seen him, and that was saying a lot,
because he always looked good. She couldn't deny
his handsomeness even if she wanted to. Still, she
was holding back.

"Two minutes," she breathed out, looking at the time on her dash. She removed her phone from her center console, opened her text messages, and went right to Erynn's thread.

Amree: Erynnnnn!

The exaggerated message was enough to get her apprehension through to her best friend.

Erynn: Girl, take your ass inside that restaurant.

Amree: Ugh, okay.

Erynn: Have fun and let me know how it goes.

Rolling her eyes, she removed the keys from the ignition, placed her phone inside her Chanel bag, and exited her car. Her heels clicked against the concrete as she made her way to him, heart racing, palms slightly perspiring. There was even a slight feel of moisture above her brows. She was so nervous.

He didn't see her coming. His head was down, and he was presumably still checking the time. The closer she got to him, the more she could make out his doubt and disappointment from how his shoulders slumped and how he furrowed his brow.

"Waiting for me?" she asked politely, tapping his shoulder.

When his head lifted, his eyes meeting hers, the genuine smile that spread widely across his lips instantly tugged at her heartstrings, resulting in a wide, genuine smile of her own.

"You showed up."

"I told you I would."

"That you did. A woman of her word. You look beautiful as always."

His eyes roamed from the shiny black heels on her feet to her slightly exposed calves, up to the black knee-length pencil skirt and red button-down blouse that looked amazing against her complexion.

"Thank you. You look handsome."

"Handsome." He bit his bottom lip, nodding his approval.

"Yes, handsome." She chuckled, a little surprised at herself that she admitted it out loud.

"Thank you. Shall we?" He extended his elbow for her to take, and surprisingly, she did without hesitation as he led them inside the Ruth's Chris restaurant.

"Reservation for Kyle Walker," he spoke to the hostess as soon as they made it to the front. She mulled over the reservations list a few seconds longer than Amree thought was appropriate before acknowledging them again.

"Right this way." Without further acknowledgment, she started walking. Amree took a deep breath in hopes of calming her nerves. She was trying to keep herself at ease, as this date was already a leap out of her comfort zone. Then to have to deal with a bitch of a hostess . . . she refused to do so. As long as their waiter or waitress didn't provide any attitude, she would get through their date without cussing someone out.

"Your waitress will be right with you," she spoke sourly with her back to them as she walked off, not caring if they heard her or if they desired to reply.

"Somebody pissed in her Cheerios," Kyle teased as he pulled out Amree's chair like the gentleman he was.

"Apparently. She's lucky I know how to act in public, because I wanted to correct her funky attitude when we first walked in."

"I didn't take you for the type," he admitted, taking the seat across from her.

"The type?" she quizzed, not in an offended way, only curious to see what he thought of her. Well, what he thought outside of her looks.

"Please don't take it the wrong way. I only meant that I . . . Damn, there's no way to say it without sounding like an asshole." He shook his head, covering his mouth with his right hand as if he was trying to suppress a laugh.

"Wow, I didn't take you for the type," she laughed.

"Huh?" His lifted brows displayed his confusion.

"The cussing type. This is the first time I've heard you use profanity."

"Nice way to break the ice. I'm still not going to speak on what I meant because it won't sound good no matter how I word it. Not because I'm trying to be disrespectful either. I would hope you know without a doubt I'd never cross that line. And believe it or not, I use profanity, but not a lot. I try not to anyway, especially around my daughter. Around her, I become the softest man on earth. Shit becomes Shane around her," he said, then laughed.

"Aw, Shane." Amree laughed, having to say it out loud to understand how it would sound as a substitute.

"It sounds way worse when you say it." He placed his head down, slapping his forehead in embarrassment.

"How so?"

"'Cause you've brought to light how ridiculous I sound every time I say it. I gotta find something else to use now."

"It's not that bad, honestly. I switch up curse words around my nephew too."

"Kids will change everything about you, man," he admitted without a hint of regret in his tone.

"So true. I kind of got thrown into parenthood with my nephew, and I wouldn't change it for anything in the world."

"Same way I feel about fatherhood. The plan was never to raise my daughter alone, but God had other plans. We do all right, though."

"You're doing better than all right. Every time I see your daughter, her hair is combed, her clothes are put together nicely, and she conducts herself like a little princess. Honestly, I assumed you had a wife, girlfriend, or constant woman around, as well as you keep her together. A man doing that well on his own was the last thing I expected."

"Trust me, it wasn't always like this, and I've dated, just nothing too serious since losing her mother."

"Sorry about the wait. Are you two ready to order?" The slightly tense moment came to an abrupt end due to the interruption of the waitress, which both of them were thankful for. After looking over the menu quickly, they placed their orders, then fell silent.

"So, enough about the past. Tell me something about you besides being an amazing aunt to your nephew. Who is Ms. Haylin, well, Amree?" He smiled.

"Thank you for the compliment. You're full of them tonight, huh?"

"Being honest about my observations is easy."

"Well, outside of taking care of Tyler and working, there isn't much to tell. I'm doing what I love, I'm usually surrounded by good people, so I mean . . . I'm simple." Her reply was very vague. She knew it. However, she didn't feel comfortable divulging detailed information when she still hadn't felt that spark between the two of them.

"I'm sure there's more to you than that. Hopefully time allows me to know more."

Amree looked at him, wondering what she was going to say. How would she reply to his optimism with her truth in a way that wouldn't hurt his feelings? It wasn't possible.

The sound of glass shattering took Kyle's eyes off Amree and hers from their downward position toward the noise. A waiter had dropped a tray of empty dishes, and she was grateful for the distraction.

"A five-star restaurant does not mean less clumsy," Kyle stated, shaking his head.

"But it should. I hope he doesn't get fired over one mistake."

"Nah, the look on his face says he done messed up a couple of times." Kyle began to laugh. He balled his fist and held it to his mouth to muffle the sound, but he found the whole thing hilarious.

"It's not polite to laugh at someone's pain." Although the statement was true, Amree was not scolding him. She was attempting to keep the mood light.

"I'm not laughing at his pain. It was his expression. He is over this job."

She looked at Kyle, then chuckled. He was right. Everything about how the waiter looked when he got up said he was done. She hadn't expected Kyle to laugh, and seeing this lighthearted side of him felt good.

"Is it okay to place this here?" their waitress asked as she approached them.

"Sure." Once her plate was placed in front of her, she bowed her head, said grace, and began cutting into her salmon.

Kyle wasn't crazy. He noticed immediately how his statement shifted her mood. But the incident with the clumsy waiter seemed to turn things around, so he decided not to bring the topic back up. Though he was dejected by her shift as well as her quiet rejection, he was going to enjoy the now.

"Can I ask you something?" he asked, getting her to remove her attention from her plate.

"Yes."

"How long have you been single?"

The way her eyes bulged let him know his question caught her off guard, but then she retreated the shocked expression by taking a sip of the red wine. He watched as her shoulders relaxed.

"It's been almost two years." Saying the time period out loud unexpectedly made her stomach turn. She knew it had been a while. The number of times she had to change batteries in her vibrator was proof of that. Still, there was something about speaking the words, acknowledging the time to someone else, that made her feel shame, though in her heart she knew there was nothing to be ashamed of. The last thing she would do was settle only to change a relationship title. She'd stay

single another two years if that was what it took for
the right man to come along.

"That's prime time. The more time one takes to
rediscover and learn, the better they are when a
second, maybe even a third, chance at love comes."

"I've heard that saying before. Not in those exact
words. Close enough though."

They spent the rest of the evening eating and
making small talk. She surprised him, talking
sports and her favorite basketball and football
teams, which they had in common. When the
waiter came back to offer dessert, she politely
declined, honestly stuffed from their main course
and the glass of wine she consumed.

After paying the bill, he walked her to her car. "I
wasn't a horrible date, was I?" he asked with a sly
smile.

"Absolutely not. I have to be honest with you,
though."

"This was a one and done kind of thing," he
chuckled.

"Not for the reason you think. You're an amazing
guy, and I had fun. It's just our kids are at the same
school, in the same class, and I'm not trying to
confuse my nephew, nor do I want you and me to
end up being less than cordial."

"I'd never let that happen, but I get it. I'ma be
single for a minute since the girl I want turned me
down. Hopefully when she realizes how great of a
catch I am, it's not too late," he chuckled.

"Trust me, I don't doubt you're a catch." She smiled up at him from the comfort of her driver's seat.

Nodding, he bent down, placing the softest kiss on her cheek. "Let me know you've made it home safely?" he asked, standing back upright.

"I will," she promised as he closed her door, and she drove off.

The date had gone better than expected. Still, he wasn't who she wanted.

Chapter 7

Sweat dripped from Lemere's face as he looked into the crowd of people. Removing the black hand towel resting on his right shoulder, he wiped his face dry. Then he placed the towel back onto his shoulder before picking up the water bottle sitting on the stool near the DJ booth. The crowd was singing along loud as hell to one of his old mixtape joints. The mixtape, *Not Yo' Average Hood Nigga,* was the second tape he put out, and almost four years later, the people were still rocking with it tough, especially the title track. As he bobbed his head, he realized the crowd hadn't missed one verse, not one word, and it felt good.

Damn good.

The smile on his face as he slowly turned his back to the crowd showed it. As soon as he made eye contact with his DJ, the music stopped. The lights went out, causing the room to become pitch-black. The once-loud, rap-reciting throng of people seemed to have gone quiet in sections. The right side of the room quieted down first, then the middle, with the left to follow, in that exact order, from the front of the room to the back, floor and balcony seats included. The room was quiet enough to hear a pin drop, which was saying a lot, given the massive amount of people in the room. There were over 50,000 people in attendance, and they all came to see him. Lemere's chest swelled. He knew he influenced people, yet there was something about the moment he was currently in. The power he held at that moment fed his ego. He tapped the mic twice with his left hand. The sound echoed through the room, causing murmurs throughout the crowd, before the bright stage light shined on him. Only him. Highlighting his importance. Taking his right hand, Lemere lifted the mic to his lips.

Ain't no love in the hood, you gotta learn to sin
I made it out, though. Down south without dough
You ain't bussin moves, little nigga, what you out fo?
You had it hard, huh? Me too
I took four stacks and turned it to a three-two

By the time he got to the fifth bar, the crowd had joined in.

"Rap my shit," he yelled through the microphone before turning it to face the throng of fans. The diamond-encrusted L chain swung wildly around his neck as he bobbed excitedly right as the beat dropped, microphone-clad hand still extended. This made all the late nights and early morning sacrifices worth it for him. A kid who never thought about being a rapper had over 50,000 people rapping words he wrote. Words he wrote, telling stories of the life he lived before and after the fame.

If a real nigga fall off, he gone regroup
Wit' no handouts, yeah, that's what we do

With the crowd's participation, he rapped the last bar before raising his hand and stopping the beat.

"Yo, Mississippi, thank y'all for the love you showed me tonight. When 'King Me' hits, I need all y'all in here to hit the store and download my shit. And most importantly, keep it one hunnid with a nigga. Tweet, blog, FB, all that shit. Let me know what you thought. I put my all in the words I spit, hoping they resonate and change somebody's life. I'm a rapper, but I'm still Mere from Lafayette, but if I can make it, anybody who dedicated damn sure can. Until next time, do you, be you, and stack yo' mothafuckin' paper." Dropping the mic, he stared into the crowd once more before nodding and smiling approvingly. He kissed his index and middle fingers before extending them in the air and walking off stage.

"You killed that shit, young'un," Shakil said with a proud grin on his face, being the first to greet him.

"Thanks," he told him before giving him a pound. The two of them, with a small group of others, walked toward the dressing room designated for him. As soon as the door opened, a cloud of smoke hit their faces. Stepping into the room, Mere's eyes wandered for anything he disliked. Whenever he stepped off stage, he liked to puff his blunt and wind down before he dipped off. Today would be no different. Walking over to the burgundy sofa, he took a seat, putting his feet up on the brown coffee table in front of him.

"Here you go, Lemere," said his assistant, who was also his cousin, handing his phone to him.

"Damn, thanks. I ain't even see you walk in here," he told her, taking his phone and placing it on his lap.

"That's 'cause I was behind that curtain setting the food up. What would you like?"

"I ain't too hungry. Just put me some fruit on a plate with a chilled water. I'll grab something to eat when we head out."

"Okay," she agreed.

"Ay, Millie, where Mason at?" he asked, stopping her right as one of his boys handed him a blunt.

Her rolling her eyes at the mention of their cousin's name let Mere know he wasn't going to be too fond of whatever she was about to tell him about Mason.

"He went groupie shopping. Swears you wanted to be bothered with some hoes when you got off stage." She shrugged, then walked off. Usually, he did want to be bothered. Another way he wound down after a show was watching half-dressed women dance and strut in front of him, and even a few would get to leave with him. Tonight, however, was different, as far as womanly entertainment was concerned. His mind was other places, on other things, on one particular person. Since he woke up, his mood felt off. Something was missing, which was the reason he made it clear: no hoes in his dressing room.

"Here you go." Millie came back, extending the plate of fresh fruit to him.

"Ay, I thought I told you I ain't want no hoes in here," he said to her.

Taking the seat next to him, she leaned closer to her cousin so their conversation remained private. "So, you know I'm going to keep it two more than ninety-eight with you," she said to him, shifting her body to face him and leaning a bit closer for added privacy.

"I wouldn't have it no other way, cousin," Lemere expressed, looking her directly in the eyes.

"Good. So you can't get mad at me when I tell you this."

"What, man?" He could sense she was about to be on some bullshit. He could see it in her failed attempt to not crack a smile. The forcefulness in her trying to keep the corners of her mouth from spreading into a grin showed through the slight quivering of her mouth, giving her away.

"So, I told Mason you didn't want anyone back here but the people who rode with you. I reiterated it to him twice, but he was adamant that it was what you wanted, so I let it go. Now, we both know I probably . . . well, I could've stopped him. Truthfully, I like seeing you cuss his blockhead ass out. So, I'm letting him dig his own grave." She shrugged before releasing the laugh she had been struggling to hold in.

"You ain't shit, Mills," he chuckled. He couldn't be mad at her, though he probably should have been. Dealing with Mason was a job in itself, and if it weren't for his aunt and him being blood, he wouldn't even deal with him. One thing he always was big on was family, and he'd rather bring Mason around to annoy the hell out of him than release him to the streets and let him die in them. However, he knew he'd have to give him something more productive to do.

"Man, Mason be needing to get cussed out. I mean, I hurt his feelings when I do it. But you be breaking his heart. Not in a bad way. It's just my scolding gets him right for a few hours, a whole day at most. Yours, though, he be on his best behavior for at least a week." She laughed again.

"That's yo' cousin, mayne."

"Our cousin. I swear Auntie dropped him on his head." She shook her head with a sullen look on her face.

"She definitely did," he agreed.

"Look, I'll handle Mason and whatever hoes he comes in here with if you do one thing for me."

"You know I'm the one who pays you, right?" His brows rose in question, emphasizing the desire to receive the correct answer.

"I know that." She rolled her eyes. "This isn't an employee-to-employer request. It's cousin to cousin."

"Coo', what's up?" His tone and stoic expression gave the impression that he had no emotion toward her request when, in actuality, he was anxious to know. Lemere prided himself on being able to provide for his immediate family. Millie was included in that group, so whatever she wanted he hoped he could provide, unless she was on some other shit. His right mind told him she was, but still he had to be sure.

"Tell me what's going on with you. You've never not wanted to be surrounded by women. So, which is it? You either got the clap, got somebody pregnant, or you're in love. Well, maybe not love, but you for sure feeling someone," she spoke with emotion, never losing eye contact with him as she hiked up her right shoulder before tucking a loose strand of hair behind her ear. It was a gesture she'd always do when trying to feign innocence, when she was fully aware she'd just said some off-the-wall shit.

Staring at her, Lemere pulled his bottom lip into his mouth as a tactic to not say the first thing that came to his mind as it was undeniably going to be disrespectful. The "in love or feeling someone" comment wasn't so bad. However, the clap and pregnancy comments . . . hell nah.

"Man, if you don't take yo' 'almost looking like La'Myia Goode' ass somewhere." He laughed as his words caused her to react by pushing him in his chest. He knew the words would get to her because she did favor the actress, not that she was insulted by it. The woman was gorgeous. Millie cared more to be remembered and looked at as none other than herself, though. Comparisons to her basically said she needed to interview more to make *her* name larger.

"That's what yo' ass get. I damn sure don't got no clap or a woman pregnant. I should fire yo' ass for saying some off-the-wall shit like that. I expect that from Mason, not you. Damn, cuz."

"So, then you're feeling someone? Who is she?" She smiled brightly, bouncing on the sofa anxiously, and excited for Lemere to be feeling someone. It said a lot.

"What up, y'all? Mere, these ladies wanted to meet you." Mason came in the room loud as hell with a large grin on his face and with a row of at least ten women behind him.

Lemere took a deep breath before putting his head down and covering his face with his hands. He truly wasn't in the mood.

"We're finishing our conversation right after I handle this," Millie spoke as she removed herself from the sofa.

"Mason, they gotta go. You can go with them if you want, 'cause this is not happening." She motioned her hand between the women and the room.

"Man, g'on, Mills. You don't run nothin'."

"You wanna try me?" With her hands on her hips and body weight shifted to the right side, she dared her cousin to give her a reason to further embarrass him and the group of women he was with. Sucking his teeth, Mason turned around, facing the women.

"My fault, ladies. Y'all gotta go."

"But I thought you said you ran shit for Lemere. This girl gets to stay and we can't? She not even a seven," one girl spoke up, clearly hating. Millie looked her up and down, releasing an arrogant chuckle. The girl was cute, but her entire body was fake. Even with the decency in her appearance, she wasn't the one who should be giving out ratings.

Mason was good for dealing with and dishing out bullshit. But one thing he'd never be cool with was someone disrespecting his loved ones. He'd go to war with anyone behind his blood—especially Millie and Lemere, given the bond they had and how they looked out for him.

"Fuck outta here, since a nigga can't dismiss y'all the nice way," Mason spoke, looking at the woman who had the most mouth, yet speaking to the entire group of women. There were eye rolls and sucking teeth as Shakil intervened and escorted them out the door.

"Man, Mills wasn't lying about the hoes, huh?" Mason asked as he plopped down on the sofa next to Lemere.

"Since when you know Mills to relay a message for play?" Lemere replied as he mugged his cousin.

"I don't know. I thought she was hatin'." He frowned.

"Well, she wasn't." He wasn't in the mood to go back and forth with Mason, nor did he feel the need to offer a further explanation. "Yo, I'm ready to roll out," Mere said, standing.

"We're going to finish our conversation, cousin," Millie spoke up, smiling.

"Maybe." He winked at her. "Mason, stay with Mills and make sure she gets back to the hotel. Y'all call me as soon as y'all make it."

"All right," Mason said dejectedly as the men slapped five.

"I'm leaving Tyson with y'all, too. Ty, take care of my people," he spoke to the other security guard.

"I got 'em, boss."

"Cool, let's roll." He turned his attention to Shakil, who was already posted at the door and ready. The walk to the waiting car took no time as long legs carried him.

"You want to stop anywhere before we get to the room?" Shakil asked once he was seated comfortably in the passenger seat.

"Yeah, whatever's near the hotel," he said as he removed his phone from his pocket.

Lemere held his phone in his hand, looking at it as if all he had to do was press a button for a bomb to go off. He couldn't understand why he was having such a huge battle between the little people on his shoulder, urging him to do something as simple as sending a text. Fear wasn't an emotion Lemere was familiar with, yet here he was, scared as shit.

"Fuck it," he spat, opening the messages option on his phone.

"You don't want to stop for food anymore?" Shakil asked, turning in his seat to face Lemere.

"Yeah. I'm on some otha shit. I wasn't talking to y'all." Shaking his head, Lemere silently scolded himself for not being able to hold in his emotions. That alone should have told him that what he was getting ready to do shouldn't be done. However, his desires prompted him to throw caution to the wind and send the text.

To My Future: How about letting me take you on a date? I'll fly you out to me or come to you. You tell me what's good. Just don't hurt a nigga feelings by telling me no.

He sent it and waited for what he hoped would be a yes.

Uncontrollable giggles left Amree's lips as she was gently tossed face-first on to the bed. Teasingly, she lifted her ass in the air, wiggling it for added enticement. Thoughts of him telling her he wanted her face-down and ass up when he finally got ahold of her came to mind, causing her to blush while her ass wiggled. She'd initially acted offended when he expressed the desire to see her that way. Keyword: "acted." The truth was, his assertiveness, his honesty of all he wanted to do to and with her body, turned her on.

The unexpected slap on her ass pushed a loud yelp from her lips, catching her slightly off guard, though she should've been prepared for him to reach out and touch her cheeks. The gesture of putting her ass in the air was merely an open invitation for the hand-to-ass connection, and still the act surprised her, but only momentarily, as laughter fell from her lips again. While laughing, she rolled onto her back, making eye contact with him as soon as she did. The goofy yet sexy smile on his face sent chills up her spine as her heart raced from nervousness, and her clit jumped in anticipation.

"You're gorgeous as fuck, you know that?" he complimented her.

Shit, so are you, *she thought, deciding not to voice it for fear of emasculating him and ruining the moment.*

Yet had she voiced it, she would be telling the truth. He stood before her, looking like an entrée and dessert—the kind of dessert that was so mouthwatering one had to taste it even if they were full. Even if one bite would result in stomach pains. And even with him standing before her in all his handsome and edible glory with lust-filled eyes, she wouldn't compliment him, yet she couldn't stop herself from saying something stupid.

"Thanks, but you don't have to do that," she told him.

"Do what?" he asked as his once-sexy expression twisted into a small scowl. It wasn't a scowl displaying irritation, but one of pure confusion.

"Compliment me. Sweet-talk me. You're already about to get some, so you don't have to lay it on thick." She removed her eyes from his handsome face as she spoke, feeling as dumb as she probably sounded.

"Man," he chuckled, "I'ma compliment you 'cause you deserve it. Don't have nothing to do with whether you giving me some pussy."

"Oh, okay." Now she really felt dumb, hoping she hadn't just fucked everything up.

"Nah. Get up," he spoke in a serious tone, taking a step back from the foot of the bed.

"Excuse me?" Shock was etched in her tone.

"I'm 'bout to take you home. Since you think a nigga only wants to fuck, I'm about to prove you wrong by dropping you off at your crib."

"Are you serious?" she asked, almost in a panic. She couldn't believe he was not trying to do her.

"I am. Sex ain't the only thing I'm after, so dropping you off is how I prove it."

"Lemere," she screeched. Irritation was etched on her face.

What the hell am I doing? Hell, what is he doing denying me? Damn, I must look crazy, she thought as he stared at her. He did his best to hold his composure, but once she poked her bottom lip out, pouting like a brat, it was hard to do. He fell into a fit of laughter that was so contagious she joined him, laughing as well, even though the joke was at her expense.

"If I give myself to you after the first date, you promise to call me?" The laughter had ceased, and his question through her for a complete loop. She wasn't expecting that at all.

"I . . . I mean, yeah. Shouldn't I be asking you that question?"

"Nah, 'cause you the only one of us who only has sex on the brain."

"Can we not talk anymore?" They were doing entirely too much talking. All the talking would, at some point, ruin the mood, and she couldn't chance that. She wouldn't risk any further her opportunity to see and feel her fantasies come to fruition. She'd thought about this moment since the night she met him in person and so many more times after interviewing him. To have the opportunity now and miss out on it would be like having the winning numbers to the lottery and tossing the ticket.

On purpose.

She surely wasn't foolish enough to do that, so she was holding on to this moment with Lemere with the same passion.

She stared up at him with hopeful eyes while he smirked at her and bit his bottom lip before taking slow steps toward her. The moisture that had been very present between her legs had lessened from the constant back-and-forth, yet it came flooding back right then. That simple look on his face was enough to get her juices flowing. Hell, if she was being honest, she was wetter now than she was when he tossed her on the bed.

"You ready for me?" He leaned into her, placing a hand on each side of her, forcing the mattress to go down some.

Since she had already said they'd done too much talking, she leaned into him, pressing her lips to his, hoping he took that as her answer. His deepening their kiss was proof that he got the point.

"Mmm," she moaned into his mouth.

"Auntie!"

What the fuck? Amree's brow furrowed as she slowly pulled away from Lemere's lips. Her eyes darted around the room because she just knew she heard Tyler's voice extremely too close to her.

"Auntie," he yelled again as she looked up at Lemere in shock, confused as to how he wasn't hearing her nephew call her. Or how he seemed to be unbothered at all, except for the lust lingering in his eyes as he leaned back into her for a kiss. Before his lips could touch hers, she felt her body shake wildly.

"Auntie, wake up." Tyler's voice seemed to possess the magic words as her eyes popped open. It took a second to focus on his face full of bewilderment.

"What's wrong, Auntie's baby?" she questioned as concern filled her entire being.

"You were making noises like you were hurting." The innocence and worry in his tone kept her from laughing yet didn't halt the embarrassment she felt.

The dream felt so real. Lemere being so close to her felt so real. Since he'd texted her two days ago, he'd been on her mind heavy. She read the message and didn't reply. She wanted to say yes. Since she knew agreeing to go on a date with him was unprofessional, she opted to not reply. In her mind, not responding was far better than saying no. Not actually saying no would leave the door open for the future. At least, that was what she hoped. At some point, she was sure he'd get tired of her rejecting him.

"I'm okay. Auntie was just having a bad dream," she fibbed.

"Well, no monsters can hurt you, so don't be scared, Auntie." He smiled before embracing her with the biggest hug his little arms could muster, then kissed her on the cheek before going back to his video game. She couldn't believe she'd fallen asleep while she was supposed to be working, while Tyler sat a few inches away from her playing on his Nintendo.

She looked at her nephew, whose attention was back on the game, so intently as if he didn't just ruin what would have possibly been the first time Lemere penetrated her. The fantasies she was having about him always stopped before penetration of any kind could take place. She frowned slightly behind Tyler's back, a bit frustrated at his ability to cockblock without remorse.

Shaking her head, she exhaled out of minor frustration. Tyler's waking her up was a small part of the issue she had. The major issues were lusting after a man who clearly wanted her, and her refusing, for moral purposes, to stop blocking his shot.

"Tyler Maksym, are you hungry?" She removed Lemere from her mind as her eyes scanned the time displayed on her laptop next to her. She had napped longer than she thought, putting her behind on their dining routine. Dinner should've been done or at least underway.

"Yes," he spoke, not taking his eyes off the game.

"Okay." She stood, heading toward the kitchen. Before she made it all the way, she realized all the food she had in the home was frozen. Turning around, she was glad to see that Tyler was still clothed. Her nephew hated clothes, and any chance he got to rid himself of them, he did. Tyler preferred to walk around in his basketball shorts and nothing more. She wasn't mad at him about it either. It was something that ran in the family. Neither she nor Maksym cared for clothes either.

"Go get your shoes, Ty. We're going out to eat."

"Yay. Can we have Chuck E. Cheese pizza?" The glow on his face would always be enough to make her avoid telling him no.

"Sure," she agreed, though chasing him around and listening to a loud group of kids was the last thing she wanted to do on a Saturday.

"Thank you."

"No running."

"Sorry." He slowed his pace to start walking as fast as his little legs would allow.

The ringing of her cell halted Amree's strut toward her bedroom to get herself together to leave. "Hey, bestie," she spoke as soon as the call connected.

"Someone's in a good mood," Erynn teased. "You must've accepted Lemere's date."

"Not at all. I told you I wasn't going to."

"Girl, why? You need to tell that man he can take you out and fuck you good right after. That's what yo' ass needs. Shit, you don't want to go with the good boy from Tyler's school, and now you got the bad boy and you dodging him too. You gon' have to choose a nigga to struggle with, because they don't come as medium rare as you think. May as well take your chances with the rich one," she laughed.

"I cannot stand you. It doesn't matter what you say. I am not texting him."

"Yes, you are. So g'on and tell him that you will go out with him. But if you nervous, tell him it has to be on your terms, and once he accepts, make sure you give him a location where you're most comfortable."

"Ugh." Amree groaned into the phone, full of frustration. She couldn't believe she was going to accept this man's date after all the resisting she was doing. She wanted to agree when he asked. She only needed the push that only Erynn could give to do so. Stubbornness was what allowed her to hold out as long as she had.

"If he asks why it took you two days to reply, say your phone was broke."

"I'm not gonna lie. Maybe if he knows how hesitant I am, he'll make sure to be on his best behavior."

"If you think so. Okay, so what are you waiting for? Text him."

"We're still speaking. I will message him when we get off."

"Oh, no you won't. Text that man now."

Rolling her eyes, Amree removed her phone from her face, went right to the messages, and hit reply to respond to Lemere. Taking a deep breath, she began typing.

To Lemere: Sure, we can go out only if I can choose the location.

She placed the phone back to her ear. "I sent it."

"Good. Now we wait."

"No, now I have to finish getting ready to take Tyler to Chuck E. Cheese. I fell asleep before cooking dinner or taking something out to cook. Now we're about to eat out, and you know he had to choose his favorite place."

"Maksym needs to franchise one of those for my boy when he gets home, because y'all are there every other week it seems like."

"Tell me about it. Oh, shit."

"What?" Panic was etched in Erynn's voice.

"He texted me back."

"Well, dang, that was faster than I expected. What he say?" Giddiness was Erynn's entire mood.

"Hold on." She removed the phone, putting it on speaker before opening the text message. "He said, 'Whatever and wherever you want.'"

"Oh, shit. That's right, Lemere, give my friend what she wants," she spoke in an overly excited horrible singing voice. "Okay, so tell the man what you want." Erynn's tone changed quickly, getting serious.

Taking a deep breath to calm her nerves, she tried thinking of what to say. She was not expecting him to agree, let alone reply, willing to do things on her terms to be with little ol' her. Since he did, she had to tell him something. She'd come too far to punk out now.

"I did," she spoke, hitting **send**. Amree hoped her reply didn't sound too thirsty. If it did, it was too late to take it back.

Chapter 8

Amree paced the walkway nervously as she watched people go in and out of the glass doors. For a Friday afternoon, there wasn't a lot of traffic. Although she probably shouldn't have expected much anyway, given the small town she lived in. Each time she saw a pair of people walking, her heart skipped a beat. Her guest was supposed to be traveling solo, which was hard for her to believe, given his status. So even with all the assurance he tried providing her of his individual travel plans, she still was looking for him to have someone with him. A bodyguard, to be exact.

Looking at her watch, she realized his flight landed fifteen minutes ago, and she had been pacing for the last eight. The airport wasn't big at all, but like anyone traveling from out of town, she knew, getting to the exit wasn't so simple. She removed her phone from her back pocket to see if he'd reached out, and he hadn't. Not seeing a missed call or text was not only disappointing, it was mind-boggling. If he'd made it and knew she would be waiting, why not reach out to simply say, "Just landed"? Blowing out an exasperated breath, she put her cell back into the pocket of the black Adidas workout pants she wore.

I should've known he would play me, she thought as she looked through the airport doors that opened due to more people exiting.

"Five more minutes," she mumbled, feeling like a dumbass for deciding to wait that long. The action was underlying desperate. Taking a seat on the bench next to the doors, she forced herself to relax as she glanced at her watch again.

"Amree?" The sound of her name accompanied by an uncertain tone caused her to look up.

"H . . . hey," she spoke nervously. His presence and unsureness caught her off guard, but only momentarily, as recognition set in.

Standing, she slowly walked into him, initiating a quick hug. Usually, she wasn't so forward. However, he'd come all this way for her, and shaking his hand for a greeting surely wouldn't suffice. The short time in his arms felt good, a feeling she wished to savor a little longer.

"How was your flight?" she asked as she slowly pulled away.

"It was coo'. No one recognized me," he chuckled.

"That's because not many people travel in and out of this airport. I mean, someone will surely recognize you depending on the area. You did do good with the incognito thing, though," she told him, referring to his all-black attire. He was dressed in black Nike sweats and a hoodie, a black face mask covering his mouth and nose. Had it not been for his mesmerizing eyes, the diamond-encrusted L chain around his neck, and expensive luggage, she wouldn't have recognized him either. Slowly he removed the mask, lowering it to sit underneath his chin, and he smiled at her. As if an electric current rushed through her body, his smile had awakened all of her senses. Especially the one below the small pudge in her stomach she vowed to get rid of.

"Well, I guess we can get out of here." She smiled back, letting it linger shortly before removing her attention from his handsome face. She was already nervous and anxious about him being there, and this being their first date. Then to have him arousing parts of her body from a simple smile, she had to start walking to regain some composure, or either the weekend they were spending together would be too long or she'd go against her code and be too easy.

"Right behind you," he spoke confidently.

Lemere followed a few steps behind Amree through the lot where he assumed her car was parked. He followed her readily. Though they didn't know each other, everything about Amree read comfort for him. The sway of her hips and the way her cheeks moved in her pants were enticing. A sight for his eyes, for sure. Though he doubted she would have sex with him this time around, he couldn't help wishing to feel and caress her. Besides, after coming all this way, he for damn sure deserved it. Lemere had never gone through these sorts of hoops for a woman, and he hoped she knew that she was getting a part of him he hadn't given to another woman, his baby mother included.

"This you?" he asked rhetorically, impressed with her car. He had a feeling she was doing all right financially, but the Tesla she was driving proved it. It also proved to him she could be the one. Most women he dated outside of the industry were not driving $50,000 cars.

"Yes, this is my car," she replied sweetly as they got inside.

"I had to Google the best hotels in the area since you didn't want to tell me which one was closest to your home," he chuckled. "So, I'd like to stop by the Hilton on . . ." He paused, pulling out his phone to get the address.

"I have a spare room. I didn't tell you about hotels because I figured you could stay in the room at my place, unless you're not comfortable with that," she babbled, halting whatever address he was going to give her. The day he asked for hotels, she spoke around his question. At the time, she felt

a bit rejected and insulted that he hadn't asked to
stay with her once he agreed to make the trip.

She was also conflicted, because she knew a hotel was exactly where he needed to be staying even
though she wanted him closer to her. Of course,
when she discussed her conflict with Erynn, she
chewed her out, urging her to not be a punk and
slightly guilting her into making her guest room as
comfortable as possible for Lemere. Even after deciding her guest room would be perfect for Lemere,
she was too chicken to tell him before now. Her
main concern was placing the idea in his head that
she wanted this date so she could be easy and offer
her ass in the confines of her home.

"I mean, long as you not on some *Misery*-type
stuff, I can rock with your spot," he agreed, happy
he wasn't going to a hotel. Her offering up her
home—well, the guest room—let him know she
was at least somewhat aware of the efforts he was
making for her.

"Man, I forgot all about that movie," she laughed.
"And of course not. I figured since you went out of
your way for a date with me, the least I could do
was ensure your comfort. You're a celebrity, in
case you forgot, and you came all this way alone. I
can at least assure you that you won't be bothered
by fans or paparazzi at my place. And I'm hospi-
table, undoubtedly better than any hotel workers."

He nodded as he got comfortable in his seat as she pulled off. Lemere watched the road as Amree drove, with music softly playing in the background. So far, only one song played, and it was an old L.T.D. song, a song his mother played consistently when he was growing up. Her choice in music taught him a little more about her. She had an old soul, a trait he could rock with.

Lemere could see Amree lived in a small city. There were lots of fast-food places, a college, and a movie theater, yet everything seemed so close together. Compared to Los Angeles and his hometown Lafayette, it was extremely small. When they finally pulled up to a gated community, he found himself impressed again. The neighborhood looked pricey. A few kids were playing outside as they drove through. She made two right turns before turning into the driveway of a nice-sized gray and white painted home. She pressed the button on her visor, and the garage door opened. He could tell this garage could fit two cars with room to spare. He again was impressed, this time keeping his feelings of admiration to himself. She was glad Lemere noticed, because she did not want him to assume his money was what attracted her.

It was her car and her nice home. Her home she'd purchased outright with money her grandparents left to her and Maksym when they passed. The car was a gift from Maksym's money before he had to go away. Everything else came from her working. She still had money left from both, but it had been a while since she had to touch any of it, as her job helped her maintain a nice lifestyle. She didn't need him for anything.

"We're here," she told him as she shut off the engine, and the garage door shut behind them. Exiting first, she walked around to the door leading into her home. After grabbing his bag from the back seat, Lemere followed.

"Um, I'll give you a quick tour as I show you to your room. While you're here, feel free to make yourself right at home. The kitchen and living room television are not off-limits," she nervously chuckled. She was trying her best to seem as if this all weren't foreign to her. It was, though. It had been a while since she entertained a man. In her home especially. The date with Kyle was cool, but Lemere's presence confirmed she had been missing the umph she was looking for. All he'd done was smile at her, and she was ready to ride him 'til the sun came up on Sunday, when he was due to depart.

"Thank you."

"I have food. I don't know what you like or don't like, so there's a high chance that one of your favorites isn't here. But this is the kitchen." She did a small twirl showing off her immaculate kitchen.

"I'm not real picky, so don't trip. You do a lot of cooking in here?"

"Actually, I do." She smiled proudly before walking into the living room. "This is my living room." She twirled again, smiling at the nod of approval from Lemere. His approval wasn't a big deal to her because she knew that to have done this all by herself, from her car to her home, was nothing average, and the accomplishment alone was admirable. Her furniture was nice, and the sixty-inch television on the wall cost a pretty penny as well, and a few photos were hanging on the wall that he planned to check out later.

"Right this way." She led the way up the stairs. Lemere counted four doors. The first she opened was her bedroom. She didn't walk all the way in, only opened the door wide and allowed him to peek inside. He held in his chuckle as he followed her to the next door.

"This is another general restroom. Oh, shoot, I didn't show you the bathroom downstairs. Anyway, this is one bathroom, and right here is the guest bedroom you'll be sleeping in." She opened the door, and the two of them stepped inside.

"That's the closet, and through that door is the bathroom." She watched as he looked around the room. This room was close in size to the bedroom he had at his mother's home, so he'd surely be comfortable.

"Thank you. This is dope."

"You're welcome. Well, I'm sure you're tired, so I'll give you a few to yourself, and when you're ready, we can eat."

"Cool." Lemere watched as she exited the room. Removing his phone, he texted Shakil, letting him know he made the trip and everything was going smoothly. He sent him his location out of habit and precaution before letting him know he'd be in touch. He then placed his phone on the nightstand and began emptying his luggage. He hung the few outfits he brought and left his lounge clothes and underwear in his bag. As excited as he was to spend time with Amree, he was also exhausted. He'd barely had a full three hours' sleep each night that whole week. Not only that, but he did a show Thursday night only to catch the flight he took to be with her today. To say he was drained would be an understatement. He wasn't sure what she had planned for the two of them, and asking was out of the question as he didn't want to come off as overbearing.

Picking his phone back up, he scrolled to her number.

To My Future: What time should I be ready?

He sent the text, shaking his head slightly at the name he had her saved as. He believed in speaking the things he wanted into existence, and until she could be his present, his future would have to do.

My Future: Honestly, take all the time you need. I know you're coming off of a long flight and crazy schedule. If you need to rest, do so. Can I grab you anything?

Damn, this girl tryin' to really make me fall for her. He thought her reply was so considerate it turned him on.

To My Future: Thank you. I am tired. My resting won't take up the whole day, though. And water, that's it. Thank you.

My Future: No problem. And if you go to the back of the closet, there's a small refrigerator. It has water and other drinks. Next to it is a small cabinet of snacks. Help yourself. Towels are in . . .

Lemere read the message, a bit confused that she didn't finish the sentence. When he heard light taps on the door he understood why.

"Come in."

"I felt silly texting with you from the next room. Oh, and here's your water." Amree extended her right hand, giving him the bottled water. There were waters in the closet, but he asked her for one, so from her it would come. "The towels are in the closet in the bathroom with a ton of other toiletries."

"Thank you."

"You're welcome. I know you only asked for water. Are you sure I can't get you anything else?"

"A hug. That's it. Is that asking too much, Ms. Amree?"

She stared at him, and he almost wanted to smack himself for being so forward. *I scared her,* he assumed as she continued to look dumbfounded.

It wasn't his question that had her stuck. It was him. The hoodie he wore was off, and the white T-shirt exposed his frame. Lemere was perfectly built in her eyes. Not too big, not too small, and cut the fuck up. His sweats were hanging loosely, showing a hint of his V-shape. Yet it was the print below that kept her eyes focused and mouth watering.

"My bad," he spoke, pulling her from her trance.

"No. I mean, yes, you can have a hug." Quickly, she made her way to the other side of the room, directly into his arms.

"We seem to fit well like this," Lemere whispered, holding her.

She agreed. She wouldn't voice her agreement, however.

A few moments longer, she stayed in his embrace. Then she forced them apart because if she didn't, her lips would be on his, and they would end up doing much more than kissing after that.

"I'll either be in my room or downstairs. So, after you rest, you can come find me."

"All right," he hesitantly agreed. Amree walked out of the room this time, and Lemere couldn't determine if he felt empty because her entire presence was gone, or because she was no longer in his arms.

"Shit," Lemere cussed as he slowly wiped the slobber from his mouth. The loud vibrating of his phone against the wooden nightstand jolted him from his sleep—an apparent deep sleep, given the drool that escaped the corners of his open mouth. He wondered if he had been snoring, too. He extended his left arm to grab his phone, not out of curiosity of who was calling, but more to stop the nagging ringing. With his head still on the pillow, he forced one eye open to see who was calling. Seeing his son's photo on the screen, he answered without hesitation.

"Hey, son," he grumbled into the phone.

"I knew you weren't shit. How you answer your son's call all dry and shit?" The sound of Kiana's voice on the other end of the phone instantly irritated him. He purchased and faithfully paid his son's phone bill so he wouldn't have to speak with his baby mother unless it was absolutely necessary. Given her tone, he was sure she was on some bullshit.

"Is my junior good?" he questioned, wanting to get to the point of her phone call.

"No. He is not," she stated matter-of-factly. Her response got his full attention as he slowly sat up in the bed.

"What's wrong?" he asked as calmly as possible, doing his best not to panic.

"His daddy ain't shit. How you get a break from tour and not see your child?"

Lemere shut his eyes out of habit to calm his nerves. He had to take a moment to avoid cussing Kiana out. He thought about replying to her nonsense by politely putting her in her place, reiterating once more that she should mind her business. Instead, he chose to end the call. His mother would reach out to him if Junior needed him.

Now that he was fully awake, it took him another moment to remember where he was.

"Fuck. How long was I asleep?" he mumbled. The room was pitch-black, and the home was eerily quiet. Looking at his phone, he saw that the time read 3:00 a.m.

"What the fuck?" he spoke angrily, completely disappointed with himself. He knew he'd set his alarm before he lay down. Obviously, he slept through it. Though he knew he was exhausted, he didn't think his body would need as much rest as it took.

"I fucked up. How I'ma make this shit up to her?" he mumbled.

Removing the covers from himself, he headed for the bathroom and relieved his bladder. After washing his hands, he eased his way to the bedroom door, not surprised to find the hall dark. Taking a few steps back, he grabbed his phone, using the flashlight to guide him. Her bedroom door was shut, and as tempted as he was to open it just to see her sleeping, he chose not to. Instead, he made his way to the kitchen as quietly as possible, where he found a note with his name sitting on the countertop.

Your food is covered and in the fridge. I didn't want to wake you. Hopefully, you feel rested. I'm not upset nor disappointed that you chose to sleep on our first date. Lol. I'm flattered that you found my home comfortable enough to fully relax. I'm an early riser, so I'll see you in the morning. Good night.

"Damn, man." Lemere was conflicted. He felt like an ass and stupid at the same time. The level of consideration and understanding she was showing him was something only his mother and Millie showed him. No other woman cared enough to be thoughtful like this. Here she was doing it, and he was fucking up the plans she had for them.

"I don't know how, but a nigga definitely gonna make this up to her," he promised as he opened the fridge and removed his food. His stomach was growling as he put his meal in the microwave. While he waited, he looked through the refrigerator, pantry, and cabinets, pleased with the wide selection of food. The beeping of the microwave halted his snooping, so he grabbed his plate and sat at the island to eat, contemplating how he'd make day one up to Amree. As he ate, thoughts of what he could do to make up falling asleep on Amree seemed to be nonexistent, then as if a light-bulb had been turned on, the perfect idea came to mind. Patting the pockets of his pajama pants, Lemere removed his phone. He smiled, knowing his cousin would be up with the time difference.

"I thought I was on vacation," Millie said as soon as the call connected.

"Nah, I'm on vacation. You still gotta work, hence the reason for my call."

"Of course. You need something? You must want the soonest flight up out of there," she spoke, unenthused.

"Nah, man, why would you assume that?" His face scrunched.

"Uh, maybe because you're supposed to be chilling with this girl, and yet you're calling me. So . . ."

"Get the fuck shit out your head, Mills, so you can get serious and do what I'm about to ask you to do."

"Well, excuse me. I knew you were feeling her, but dang. When do I get to meet her?"

"Millie," Lemere chastised her.

"Okay, okay, what do you need me to do?"

"I need you to call Dave & Buster's in this little-ass town. I'm surprised they have one. Find out what it'll cost me to rent out the whole place for like two hours. My budget is ten stacks, though if they not fucking with that or less, then see if you can find a discreet security company to tail us."

"Oookay, I'll get back to you. Let me see what I can do."

"Thanks, Millie."

"No thanks needed. It's what you pay me to do," she said, then ended the call, not giving Lemere a chance to clap back.

Setting his phone beside his plate, Lemere smiled as he stuck his fork into the scalloped potatoes. Millie wasn't one to take no for an answer, so he was sure she would be able to honor his request, and he hoped Amree would appreciate his effort and enjoy it.

"Hey." She spoke hesitantly, seeing him preoccupied.

Mere looked up quickly, being caught off guard and damn near knocking over his plate. Luckily, he was almost done eating, so had it dropped, there wouldn't have been a big mess to clean.

"What's up? Did I make too much noise and wake you up?" he asked as his eyes went from the bashful expression on her face to her exposed legs. Not allowing his eyes to linger too long, he slowly eased them up her body back to her face. The burgundy camisole and shorts pajama set Amree had on had him adjusting in his seat.

"No." She smiled at him. "Just came down to grab a water."

"You're about to go back to bed?" His tone was hopeful. He knew it was late. Yet, he still hoped she would bless him with a bit more of her time.

Giving a slight shrug for her answer, Amree walked over to the fridge to grab the water she came for.

"I'm not sleepy anymore. It'll probably take me a little bit to fall back asleep," she spoke, turning toward him. Her eyes landed on the empty plate, pulling a small smile from her. "Either you were starving or the food was good."

"Both. Did you cook everything?"

"I did."

"Damn, now I really feel bad," he pushed out.

"It's fine. Did you read my note?" She moved closer to him, standing at the corner of the island.

"I did, and I appreciate you not goin' off on me. I feel bad regardless, though. I'ma make it up to you before I dip, that's my word."

"Okay," she easily agreed.

Lemere's falling asleep had been disappointing. However, she didn't allow the feeling to linger. She knew he came to her directly off the road. She expected him to be tired. She wouldn't have blamed him if he told her he'd be out for the count on night one.

"Is that okay because you don't believe me? Or because you not trippin'?" he asked as he stood with plate in hand, walking over to the trash to scrape off the remnants of food before heading back to the sink, fully prepared to clean it.

"You don't have to wash that," Amree spoke up, stopping him before he was able to add dish soap to the rag.

"Nah, it's the least I could do. Plus, my mama would have a fit."

"Your mother isn't here," she chuckled.

"I know. That's how much she has me in check."

"She raised you right. Still, my guest doesn't wash dishes."

"What about repeat guests?"

"Possibly." She did a slight shoulder lift. Removing the plate from his hand and taking over, it took no time to clean the plate, dry it, and place it back into her cabinet.

"Sleepy yet?" he asked as the two of them stood in the kitchen, wondering what was next.

"Uh, not really."

"Good, come chill with me." Though he was asking, it came out as more of a demand. And as he took her by the hand, she realized he was giving her no choice. "All right, how you work this TV?" he asked as they made it into her living room. Snickering, Amree walked over, turning on the lamp before grabbing the remote and handing it to Lemere. "Cool, you got a blanket or something?"

"I do." Slowly, she made her way to the hall closet and grabbed a fleece blanket, surprised at how easily she submitted to his requests. Slowly she made her way to Lemere, who patted for her to take a seat next to him. She tried putting some distance between them, but he wasn't having it, pulling her into him so that her back was against his chest.

"It's been a minute since I've watched TV. Recommend something good. No sappy or 'I hate men' typa shit."

"I like action and scary movies. I mean, I watch the others, though."

"My type of woman. All right, pick something then." He handed the remote to her.

She went directly to Netflix and chose *Deuces*. Though the two wanted to ask each other a bunch of questions, watching the movie and being comfortable next to one another felt better than speaking. All they needed to do was be in the moment, enjoying it until they fell asleep.

Chapter 9

"I didn't take you to be so damn competitive," Lemere laughed as he and Amree stepped inside her home. They had just returned from Dave & Buster's, and he had to admit he hadn't had that much fun since he was a kid. Millie had come through for him like he knew she would. Though it cost him ten stacks and some free advertising, Lemere was able to enjoy a fully staffed Dave & Buster's for him and Amree alone.

"I tried to warn you when we got there that I was competitive," she chuckled before continuing. "Did I scare you?" She looked over her shoulder at him. She knew she was going hard at the games they played. She was a very competitive person and couldn't help it. Playing video, arcade, and interactive games were a few of the things that brought out the competitive spirit in her. She also knew some men, mainly insecure ones, who didn't like their women so gung ho with beating them. And she had been trying her best to beat Lemere. With little success.

"Hell nah, that shit was sexy. You gave a nigga a run for his money, too. I was trying to take it easy on you, and you turned around and made me have to work." He provided a sexy smirk before placing the bag of prizes he got with all the tickets they racked up by her front door.

"Yeah, what happened to allowing your date to win? Isn't that how it's supposed to work?" she asked sarcastically.

"You held yo' own and won a couple of games. I don't believe in letting no one win, not even my mama. We all gotta put in our own work for the results we want to see," he spoke honestly.

"I won't argue with that. My brother would tell me something similar when I'd cry about him beating me in mostly everything. I mean, he did let me win at some stuff. Not everything, though, for the same reason you gave and to make me tough."

"Your brother sounds like a smart dude," Lemere complimented him.

"Yeah, he is." She smiled yet turned away from his gaze. Maksym was one of the smartest men she knew, and she loved him like she could never love anyone. He was her brother, father, and best friend molded into one person. Still, his current situation weighed heavily on her, and it would continue to do so until he was home. Lemere noticed the slight change in Amree's demeanor and realized her brother was a soft subject for her. They hadn't done the "get to know you" conversation, given he had fallen asleep on her. Then, they spent the last few hours at Dave & Buster's, enjoying freedom: Amree, free from her day-to-day routines, and Lemere, free from his celebrity status, even though that was what got them in the door.

Now that they were back at her home, there was no better time than the present to dig a bit deeper into each other's lives. Taking Amree by the hand, Lemere gently pulled her into him before plopping down onto her sofa, making sure she landed in his lap, where he held her.

"Tell me something about you."

"Like what?" she giggled, feeling good in his arms.

"When I asked you about dating when you interviewed me, did you mean what you said about me not being your type?"

Amree felt her chest tighten. She wasn't expecting him to go back to that day. She had meant what she said at the time because she didn't know him. She didn't really know him now either. Yet the feelings he gave her since she'd picked him up from the airport told her she had been wrong, and he *was* her type.

"I meant it." She sucked in air, then turned slightly to look him in the eyes. "I'm guilty of judging a book by its cover, and I was wrong," she spoke honestly.

"So, I'm your type now?"

"I mean, you have a couple of qualities I like."
She smiled.

"Only a couple?" he questioned with a raised
brow.

"That I can be sure of? Yes. I still don't know
much about you."

"Let's change that. What do you want to know?"
he asked.

"Okay." She smiled big, sitting up a bit to face
him. The look on her face told Lemere she was
ready to ask him a million and one questions.
Enough questions to where he probably wouldn't
get a word in, so he quickly redirected.

"Nah, let me know a bit more about you first.
Who are all these people in the photos around your
house?" he asked as he nodded his head toward
the wall near her stairs that was lined with photos.

Smiling, Amree slowly sat all the way up, not
really wanting to leave his lap, even though it was
necessary for her to explain the photos to him.
Placing a comforting kiss on her cheek, Lemere
slowly removed his hands from around Amree's
waist, allowing her the release she needed to stand.

"So, this is a photo of my brother and me. He's
older. We took this photo right before he got
sentenced and had to turn himself in." She then
moved over to a photo to the left of that one. Had
she allowed herself to linger on that memory any

longer, her mood would've changed and not for the better.

"This is my best friend, Erynn. We've been friends since grade school. She's the sister I always wanted but my parents never had. And this . . ." Amree moved over to Tyler's photo with the largest smile on her face. It was the widest Lemere had seen her smile since he'd been with her, and her smile had been wide when she finally beat him in a game of Skee-Ball. He paid attention to how much joy she seemed to have flowing through her as she prepared to tell him who the little boy was. Lemere allowed the idea of her having a son and how he would feel about it linger in his mind briefly before concluding that he didn't care. Hell, he had a son who came with a crazy-ass mama, and if she was willing to put up with that, he could do the same.

"This is my nephew, Tyler. I call him Tyler Maksym. He's my brother's son, whom I'm raising until he comes home." She smiled before walking back over to Lemere and taking a seat. He didn't miss how she only found it important to explain those three people, when she had a few more photos of people who weren't her brother, nephew, or best friend on that same wall. He wanted to ask why she didn't find them important enough to tell him about, especially when he was trying to get to know her, but he decided against it. She would tell him in due time.

"That's dope you're taking care of your nephew for your brother. How old is he?"

"Four. I've had him for almost two years. I'll more than likely be crushed when my brother comes home and takes him from me." Amree spoke sadly, almost as if she'd be giving her nephew back to her brother tomorrow. Her feelings toward her nephew gave him something else to admire about her. Instead of having her elaborate further, he decided to change the subject somewhat.

"My son isn't much older than him. He's the best thing that happened to me, even though I can't stand his mama," he chuckled, and Amree did the same.

"It's unfortunate that two-parent homes aren't normalized much anymore. Coparenting seems to be the thing to do, and I'm assuming even that's difficult. I know for my brother it's going to be if it comes to that. I noticed how your face lit up when you said your son is the best thing to happen to you. That's admirable."

"I mean, I wanted to raise my son in a two-parent home. For a minute I did. It just didn't work out. It's best he sees both his parents happy rather than together and miserable."

"True. I take it you're the only one genuinely happy though. If you weren't, you and your son's mother would get along."

Lemere looked at Amree and pondered what she'd said. Some of what she observed was correct while some of it wasn't. Kiana could be as happy as she wanted to be. She chose to allow their separation to make her bitter, and that wasn't on him. He refused to take complete responsibility for Kiana acting the way she had been since them splitting, hell, since before their split.

"I mean, I can't say you're a hundred percent correct. You're also not a hundred percent wrong. I do want her happy. Her being happy means my son is happy. He's with her the majority of the time, so I want her to be the happiest person in the world. Only she can do that for herself, though."

"That's true. So, is this your subtle way of telling me you deal with baby mama drama?" She knew Lemere was telling her he dealt with the unfortunate typical bullshit that came from a woman who couldn't fully let go. She hoped by the time they became serious, *if* they became serious, the situation would be different. She was an easy person to get along with and loved kids. Those two qualities should win anyone over.

Amree, you're thinking way too deep into this, she thought as she looked at him.

"I mean, with Kiana you never know. I ain't one of them niggas who let his baby mama or anybody else dictate how I move and who I move with. If you rockin', I'm rolling, and we'll be good regardless."

We. That simple word caused the corners of her mouth to spread. She wasn't sure if it was a Freudian slip or if he saw the two of them eventually being more.

"Okay," she replied simply.

"Why are you single, Amree?" he asked, stopping her from getting into her head too much, which was exactly what was going to happen if they allowed silence to dwell too long.

"I was in a relationship about a year before I took custody of my nephew. It lasted about six months after Tyler came to stay with me. I guess he couldn't deal with how I had to change or adjust to having a toddler living with me. My nephew required a lot of my attention because he didn't understand why he wouldn't have his dad around like he always had. His living with me wasn't an issue, because I've been helping my brother with him since the day he was left by his mother. Still, having me twenty-four seven and not his father was an adjustment. I also wasn't sure how to handle raising my nephew and tending to his needs while being in a relationship. It was hard keeping him happy when my main focus was my nephew. Things were good with us until they weren't. There was never a choice to make between him and Tyler. My ex knew that, so he ended things."

"That nigga broke up with you?" Lemere asked as if he was appalled by the truth. Honestly, he *was* appalled. The dude she used to deal with had to be dumb. He was glad dude practically threw him an interception. Had her ex not broken up with her, she and Lemere more than likely wouldn't have crossed paths, nor would he be with her right now, so he was grateful.

"He did. It was a big blow to my ego. Thankfully, my brother and my best friend helped me put things in perspective, and I was able to move past the hurt. I don't regret taking my nephew and putting him first during a time when he needed me the most. I'd do that in a heartbeat over and over again. Anyone who couldn't understand that didn't deserve me."

"So, why haven't you dated anyone since him?"

"Did I say I haven't dated?" She smirked.

"You didn't have to. I know you haven't."

"I have been on dates, thank you very much. No one has stuck, though. I mean, I'm looking for a certain feeling, and if I don't get that, then I feel it's best not to waste my time or—"

"You find that feeling with me?" Lemere halted her from speaking. He felt something with her. Since the day he met her, he felt something. Now to know that she was chasing a feeling in order to move forward with the guy she decided to date, he needed to make sure he wasn't wasting his time. His gut told him he wasn't. There was definitely a spark between the two of them. Only Amree could give him the assurance he wanted.

"I mean, there's something there," she giggled. It was more than something. She wouldn't lay it all on the line just yet. Her brother had gamed her up pretty well on the male of the species. Not only that, but she refused to give a man like Lemere that much leverage. If he knew she saw he had some staying power, there was no telling how or if he would take advantage of that information.

Chuckling, Lemere only nodded. Unbeknownst to her, she'd given him the assurance he needed. "What else is there to know about you?"

"I told you everything. You know who's important to me and what I do for a living, and there's not much else to tell."

"There's more to tell. I'll let you live with saying there's not. Eventually, we'll get there. I want to know everything there is to know about you. The corny stuff like your favorite color, who raised you, your childhood secrets and embarrassing moments, how many kids you want, what type of wedding you'd like to have. I'm trying to know all that." He smirked.

"Are you willing to tell me all about you?"

"I am. What you want to know?"

"Why are *you* single?"

"Because I haven't met the right one. Well, I thought I hadn't until this journalist chick piqued my interest at an industry party," he chuckled. "Nah, shit, it's hard to date when you're in my position. Most women treat me like a piece of meat. Apparently, it's better for a woman to say I fucked her than I love her."

"Is that really what you think?"

"Shit, that's what I know. It worked for a while, so it doesn't bother me. It was enough until now." His eyes bored into hers, and the intensity of his stare shot through her, making every fiber of her being feel the message he was conveying. She was his "until now."

"Why now?" There was a form of innocence in her question. She still wasn't sure what was happening between them.

"I need to spell it out for you?" He cocked his head to the side, giving her a look that insinuated he knew she was playing clueless.

"Yup." She smirked.

"You, man. I don't know what it is about you, but I'm feeling you. I also know you ain't like everybody else, so a nigga gotta step his game up with you. The note you left me last night let me know you more respect that I'm Lemere the rapper but care for Lemere Webster. That spoke volumes, because only a few people recognize I was human before I became a rapper," he spoke honestly. Although his status was what brought them together, he knew it would take much more than that to keep Amree around.

"Why wouldn't I, though? I understood that you were on the road working, then made your way to me without issue. I asked and you agreed." Amree's voice lowered slightly at the realization of her words. Lemere had done exactly that. She was aware of what he'd done to visit her. Hell, it was the awareness of his actions, sacrifice, and time that had her trying to be overly accommodating. There was something, however, about speaking it as well as acknowledging this awareness to him that made her attraction toward him grow.

"I'm sure you know a lot of people not built like that. Especially people around me. That's one of the reasons I'm trying to have making my way to you without issue something like a habit if you'll let me."

Amree looked Lemere in the eyes, trying to find a hint of a joke or bullshit behind his words, to no avail. Her mind ran rampant as to how he could even suggest such a thing when they still didn't know each other. It felt good. It was also scary. To think of them moving so fast . . . though the thought of moving any slower was mild torture. Lemere held eye contact with her as a smile slowly crept across his face.

"How can you be so sure?" she finally spoke, doubt etched in her tone.

Instead of replying with words, Lemere decided to do what he'd been dying to do since the day he met her. Slightly tightening the hold he had around her waist, he pulled Amree into him a bit more before allowing his lips to meet hers. Lemere felt her hesitancy yet refused to let it deter him. Thankfully, his passion overpowered her hesitation, compelling her to allow her body to receive and reciprocate the feeling he was giving.

It was at that moment she understood how he could be so sure as she could've sworn their entire future flashed before her eyes. As his lips held hers captive and his tongue intertwined with hers, Amree saw their kids—a boy and a girl—their wedding on the beach, and Lemere thanking her for keeping him grounded as he accepted his fifth Grammy. She saw and felt more with him at this moment than she had with the ex she spent over a year with, and she welcomed it.

Lemere felt her relaxing in his arms. Her body seemingly melting against his gave him the courage to make his next move. Easing his hand from around her waist, he slowly slid it to her front, allowing the tips of his fingers to press the space right below her abdomen. He wanted her aware of his traveling hands, hoping she didn't stop him once he met his desired destination, and as he stopped right above her clitoris, he waited to see if she'd stop him. The moan that escaped her lips beneath the kiss they hadn't parted from provided him with what he hoped was an okay to access, because that was exactly what he did. Moving her shorts to the side, Lemere took his middle and index fingers and pressed down on Amree's clit.

"Sss," she moaned, pulling her head back enough to breathe out without disconnecting her lips from his.

"You want me to stop?" he asked as he began making his way into her pants. Her moisture was leaking through the fabric. However, it wasn't enough. Lemere wanted direct access to her slippery folds.

"I, uh . . ." Amree took her hands, grabbing Lemere by the wrist. "It's not that I . . . I mean, I—"

"It's cool," he spoke, relaxing his hand as he leaned in, pecking her lips.

"Lemere," she spoke with guilt etched in her tone. She could feel his manhood hard as hell beneath her. Hell, she could feel her own puddle between her legs. Not going all the way was torturing them both. She wanted to. Desired to. Still, she couldn't.

"I gotta get that." The sound of her phone allowed her the needed distraction as she stood from his lap, making her way to the coffee table, where her phone lay inside her purse.

"It's cool. I got a couple of calls to make as well. I'ma go shower, too. Don't trip, Amree, for real." The disappointment he masked in his tone couldn't be hidden in his eyes.

She saw it clear as day. Instead of making things more awkward, she pulled a tight smile from her lips, nodded, and watched him walk away as she accepted a call she could have let go to voicemail.

Frustrated, Lemere tossed and turned on the bed in Amree's guest room. He had hit and kicked the mattress at least three times because he was so flustered, a feeling he was not used to when it involved him being pleased. His dick was still hard even after the cold shower he exited about ten minutes ago. He had tried everything from taking a shot to puffing his blunt and uncomfortably lying as still as possible with his eyes closed in hopes of falling asleep. Not one of his attempts worked as his physical need and desire for Amree lingered heavily on his mind.

"Shit," he grumbled, sitting up, placing his back against the headboard, retrieving his cell from the nightstand. He knew falling asleep with his manhood still at attention was not going to happen. Scrolling through his contacts, he paused at the name of the one woman he could tolerate and knew would do anything he asked.

To BB: Send me a photo. Better yet, a video.

He didn't go into specifics of what the video should entail. There was no need. She knew her place in his life. She knew that anytime he contacted her, it was to fulfill one duty, nothing more.

Lemere made himself comfortable as he lowered his boxers just enough to free his manhood.
He looked around the room for some form of lu-
bricant, knowing BB, aka Big Booty, would send
him what he needed to get himself right. She always did.

Fuck it, he thought as his phone chimed. There
wasn't anything in sight that he could use, so he'd
have to find another alternative. Opening the
message, his eyes were greeted with BB's juicy
honey-colored thighs spread-eagled as her hand
slowly moved south, stopping at her clit. The
visual was amazing, yet it wasn't what he wanted.
She damn sure wasn't who he wanted. As he stared
at the video of BB pleasing herself and moaning
sexily, he finally felt his manhood deflating.

"What in the entire fuck?" He groaned, looking
down at his dick as if it had personally shamed
him. In a way, it had. The slow drip that had
been coming from his tip dried up, and he was
no longer standing at attention, more like leaning. Grumbling, he exited from the message and
powered his phone off before placing it back on
the nightstand. Aggressively, he pulled his boxers
back up before lying on his back with his hands
clasped behind his head. This was all new to him,
not getting pussy when he wanted it and because
he wanted it. Then not feeling the need to dismiss
a woman because she wasn't trying to get with the

program. Lemere wanted Amree to be a part of his life so much that he was willing to fall asleep with blue balls to avoid making her uncomfortable or feel disrespected.

"This shit crazy," he acknowledged again through a mumble, shutting his eyes. He knew sleep wouldn't come easy. However, it would come eventually, which was all that mattered.

"Lemere?" The softness of his name being called, along with a light tap on the bedroom door, caught him off guard yet excited him. He was sure she wasn't coming in the room to sit on his dick. Still her presence was wanted.

"Yeah, come in." The door opened, and the only sound to be heard clearly was their heavy breathing, proof that they both were nervous.

"I, uh . . . Can we talk?" she asked as she shut the door behind her and made her way closer to the bed.

"What's up?"

Without saying anything more, she walked around the bed, opened the bathroom door, and turned on the light. She used it so the room was lit enough for them to see one another but not too bright to take over. Lemere watched her closely, trying to read her as she took a seat on the bed. She sat Indian style with her hands in her lap as she looked back at him. She'd finally worked up the courage to come into the room to face him,

only to have her nerves about to break her down
again. There was no question in her mind that
she wanted Lemere. She wanted him bad, which
was what scared her. In so little time, she had
grown comfortable with him being only a few feet
away from her. In so little time, she had realized
how his kisses awakened parts of her that hadn't
been awakened in a long time, including areas of
her femininity she didn't know existed until him.
Taking a deep breath, she decided now was the
time to lay it out there. She wanted him. She just
didn't want to be treated like every other woman
who wanted him. She feared giving herself to him
would result in him losing interest and respect—
two things she doubted she could handle.

"I like you," she admitted softly.

"I like you too."

"This is all new to me. It's been a while since
I've felt any sort of connection to someone. I also
am having a hard time believing you see me in
a different light from other women. Your status
doesn't bother me in a way that excites me. It
bothers me in a way that makes me afraid I'll
become just another chick to you. If that makes
sense," she forced out.

There, I said it, she thought as she looked at him,
waiting for a response. His reply would determine
a lot of things. However, her mind was already
made up that they would be having sex. The inti-

macy was for her, not him, so she would have to deal with whatever consequences came due to her actions.

"If I looked at you the way I looked at these other women, you would know it, Amree. You are different. I feel something with you that I ain't felt with no one in a long time, real shit. This isn't a one-time thing for me. You can trust that I didn't take a flight straight off tour for some pussy, then to throw you away like yesterday's trash. I wouldn't put this kind of effort into knowing or being around you for it to be like that. I'm trying to get to know you and have you around as long as you'll allow me to. That's all I want from you, for now."

He winked, then bit his bottom lip, producing a smirk that had her throwing caution to the wind. There was nothing else to talk about. Her mind was made up, and he said everything she wanted to hear. What happened later on she would deal with when the time came.

Amree switched from Indian style to her knees, leaning into him for a kiss she initiated. As soon as their lips touched, the sparks that had been flying all over the two of them became full-blown fireworks, igniting more passion between them. So much so that Lemere found himself slightly frightened and pulling away from her. He needed to be sure she was ready for him because neither he nor his dick could deal with being rejected again.

"You sure about this?" he asked, cupping her face as his forehead rested on hers.

"I am. I want you, even if it's only for tonight."

"I'ma show you better than I can tell you that this is not a one-night thing."

Taking her by the back of the head, Lemere allowed his lips to do the rest of the communicating for them.

"Ahh," Amree moaned against his mouth as she used her hands to rub up and down his exposed chest. Every part of her body tingled as he slowly alternated their bodies, pushing her onto her back, as he maneuvered between her legs.

"Do you have protection?" Amree asked, pulling from their kiss.

"I do. I want to taste you first. Is that all right?"

Lemere smirked as she nodded with wide eyes. He could tell she was nervous even though she wanted him as badly as he wanted her. Making her feel good enough to fully relax was now his priority as he slowly slid down her body, removing the small shorts she had on. He sniffed her, enjoying the smell of her essence, and appreciating the little light from the bathroom, which allowed him to see her perfectly plumped, hairless pussy lips. It had been a while since Lemere not only ate pussy but also craved the taste. Yet here he was, practically salivating over Amree.

He extended his tongue to its full potential before taking it and licking Amree from the bottom of her pussy to the top of her clit. He performed that act twice before taking her entire clit into his mouth and sucking it. He used the perfect amount of pressure from what he could tell by the way her ass lifted from the bed.

"Shh, shit shit shit," Amree moaned, placing her hands on top of Lemere's head. She alternated between pulling it deeper into her, then attempting to push it away from her. "Mere," she moaned again. The sound of his name leaving her lips encouraged him to lick and suck harder.

"I'm . . . I'm cumming," she screamed as her body began to shake. Still, Lemere didn't release his grip, enjoying the taste of her nectar spilling from her.

"Oh, my God," she breathed out as her body fully relaxed into the mattress.

Lemere lifted from between her legs, smiling at the relaxed grin on her face.

"You trying to tap out on me?" he questioned, looking down at her.

"Not at all. But if you don't make another move soon, I may fall asleep on you—deep sleep," she spoke with her eyes closed, and he chuckled.

Lemere removed himself from the bed, quickly making his way to his suitcase to remove the Magnum condoms. He wasted no time dropping his boxers and covering himself with it. As soon as his manhood was covered, he made his way back to the bed, inserting himself inside her. It wasn't an easy task. Amree's pussy gripped him from start to finish. If he hadn't known any better, he would've assumed she was a virgin, given the tedious task of inserting himself. Once he was fully submerged inside her, he knew she was foolish to think what they were creating would end tonight. There could be no one after her. And he for damn sure didn't want anyone experiencing her after him.

Chapter 10

Clothed in her most comfy attire—a fuzzy cream-colored shorts and crop tank set from her favorite online boutique—Amree danced like a madwoman as she wiped the counters of her kitchen. Her favorite oldies playlist blared through the Bluetooth speakers connected to her cell. Her hips swayed from side to side as her hands followed suit as she sang along with Aretha Franklin's "Day Dreaming" loud and off-key without a care in the world. The lyrics were hitting her core just right, especially the second verse.

I wanna be what he wants when he wants it
And whenever he needs it

She sang along with a smile plastered on her face as Lemere came to mind. She wasn't sure who Aretha wrote the song for, but she was feeling the words as if she'd penned the classic herself. What she thought would be the end of something two weeks ago after she gave herself to him before he left turned out to be the complete opposite. Since the day he left, they hadn't lost contact. Lemere hadn't missed a beat with showing her that he was trying to build something beyond that night. Calls and texts throughout the day, no matter the length, had been done so much between the two that going one day without would feel like something was missing. Lemere would call whenever he got a moment of free time.

Their conversations flowed easily, making it sometimes difficult to end their call and falling asleep on the phone at times due to neither wanting to hang up. When Lemere couldn't call, he would text, sometimes turning a simple "have an amazing day" text into full-blown conversations. He was attentive to her, even being extremely busy. She couldn't deny it if she wanted to. He was growing on her and being even more honest. She missed his physical presence.

Tossing the rag she'd been wiping the counter with in the trash, she made her way to her phone and switched to the version of "Day Dreaming" by Mary J. Blige. She was in a mood—a happy-go-lucky, high school crush kind of mood, daydreaming about a future like a mothafucka. Placing her phone back onto the counter, she took a step back, placing both hands on her hips, admiring her handiwork. She never kept a messy kitchen. However, a spotless one was always the goal.

Just as Amree opened her mouth to hit the semi-high note with Mary, mouth agape, the music stopped, interrupted by the loud iPhone ringtone. Slowly, she stepped back toward her phone, immediately smiling at the caller FaceTiming her. Resting her elbows on the counter, she held her phone with both hands as she used her right thumb to answer the call.

"Hi," she greeted him, all thirty-two straight teeth showing. Her heart rate sped up slightly as she looked at Lemere, who was looking as handsome as always.

"What's up, beautiful?" He smiled back at her, making her blush as she casually pulled a stray strand of hair from her face.

"Nothing much. Doing a few chores around the house. I thought you were going to be in the studio all day," she said, recalling their earlier conversation when he asked her to listen for his call although it may be extremely late. Like Amree, Lemere had gotten comfortable with their day-to-day interaction. He had to speak with her when he woke and before he closed his eyes at night, even if most times she was groggy.

"That's where I am right now." Before she could say anything, Lemere turned his camera, giving her a quick view of his surroundings. He wasn't sure why he felt the need to prove his whereabouts to Amree, but he did. Well, he had an inkling of an idea as to why. He was still trying to win her over, prove to her that she could bet on him and win.

"Nice," she complimented him when Lemere's face came back into view. "So, to what do I owe this pleasure?" She removed her elbows from the counter and started toward the living room, where she sat on her sofa, tucking her feet underneath her butt.

"Shit. The pleasure is all mine. My eyes getting blessed big time right now." He smirked, causing a jolt of electricity to shoot through her.

"Thanks, even though I'm extremely comfortable right now. Nothing glamorous going on over here," she chuckled.

"Let me see how unglamorous you claiming to be."

With a smile and a roll of the eyes, she turned the camera, taking her phone and slowly rolling it up her exposed thighs to her top, the bun on top of her head, and back to her face. When she looked back into the camera, Lemere was biting down on the knuckle of his index finger, giving her a look so lustful she wished she could jump through the phone to fulfill their yearnings for the other.

"Yeah, you were right. You not glamorous at all. More like flawless than a mothafucka."

The expression on his face told her he was everything other than joking. He was serious, and his feeling that way about her so openly provided an intoxicating feeling she didn't want to get rid of.

"So, how are things at the studio going?" she asked, wanting to stop the intense stare he was giving her.

Chuckling with a slight nod, Lemere decided to humor her with an answer knowing she was folding under his gaze.

"It's cool. I laid down one track so far. We're taking a quick break, though."

"Oh, how many more songs do you have to record?"

"Just a couple. That's not why I called you, though."

"Okay." She removed her feet from underneath her butt, sitting straight up. She wasn't sure what he was about to say, but her gut told her it was serious.

Lemere noticed how Amree's demeanor changed. It took some willpower not to laugh at her seriousness and fear. Her shift also let him know that he still had work to put in when it came to her, so he hoped what he was about to say erased some of her doubts.

"Amree, I miss you. Is it too much if I ask you to come see me?"

"You want me to come see you?" Shock poured from her tone. She wasn't expecting a question, so a question for an answer was all she could provide at the moment.

"Yeah, because I miss you. I would come back to you. However, I remember a conversation between the two of us where you said the next date was up to me. So, I've made plans that I hope you'll humor me and show up for. Not only that, but I'm going to reiterate that I miss you." He spoke those last three words with feeling, wanting her to understand that his desire to see her was because her physical presence was needed.

"I miss you too, Mere," she admitted.

"So, that means you coming to see me?"

"I'd like to. I, uh . . ."

"Don't overthink it. All you have to say is yes. I'll handle the rest." Lemere looked at her, hopeful, noticing how her shoulders relaxed along with the tightness of her cheeks.

"When would you like me to visit?"

"As soon as I get back into town. Next week on Thursday. I want our flights to land around the same time."

"Shit," she mumbled, knowing that date wouldn't work.

Lemere instantly noticed her become tense again. "What?" he asked, trying to brace himself for a letdown.

"Can I let you know later? It's not a no. It's a—"

"Yeah, you can tell me later," he cut her off, irritated.

"Mere, I'm not trying to be difficult. I didn't expect a date so soon."

"To be honest with you, it would be sooner if possible, Amree. A nigga missing you. I understand your plight, though. So, it's cool. I'm going to call you back."

"All right." Amree produced a tight smile before ending the call. She knew he didn't like hanging up with her first, so each time their call was to end, she did the honor of ending the call.

Tossing her phone to the other end of the sofa, she pushed out a frustrated breath as her head fell back. Being with Lemere was something she undoubtedly wanted. The issue was her being ready to do so on his terms at *his* place. Having him at her home was one thing. It was simple: her playing field, an area she could control. Going to his house would expose her to a life she was still trying to figure out if she was ready for. Being behind the scenes talking to him and him visiting her was less scary, less public.

"He's not even yours, Amree," she scolded herself, shaking her head as her phone ringing again captured her attention.

Without checking the caller, she answered quickly.

"Damn, the only time you answer that quickly is when something is bothering you or you have something to tell me. So, which one is it?" Erynn spoke knowingly.

"Thank you," she mouthed, looking toward the heavens. God always knew when she needed her best friend. "Erynn," she whined.

Chuckling, Erynn blew her breath into the phone in exaggeration. "Girl, don't 'Erynn' me. Spill the beans."

"So, Mere wants me to fly to L.A. in a few days basically, to see him."

"Hmm, Mere, eh? I knew you two were getting close. Have to be since it's 'Mere' and not 'Lemere,'" she teased.

"Erynn, focus. I can't go visit him. One, I have to work, and two, Tyler's home. I'm damn sure not taking him with me."

"You can miss a couple of days from work and ask your aunt, or I'll pay the nanny for you. That man is sending for you, so you must go."

"Why did I even think I'd get some sensible advice from you? I just hoped today would be at least the first time," she pouted.

"No, you hoped I'd lie to you and pacify your fear, which I'll never do. Go see that man."

"Erynn, do you realize what my going to see him will represent? Or worse, the situation it'll put me in?"

"Girl. What situation? The opportunity for you to get dicked down again? Him asking represents his wanting to see and be with you. Otherwise, he wouldn't have asked. Amree, do I have to fly out there just to make you fly to him? I'm not against dragging your ass to the airport."

Amree knew Erynn's heart was in the right place, and usually, she'd jump to take her advice. However, this time was different. Not only was she afraid, but she was aware that being seen out in public with Lemere would have the internet buzzing. If she was going to trend for any reason, she wanted it to be because of the work she put in as a journalist, not because of crowd speculation that she was fucking a celebrity. Even if she was.

"Erynn, I'm being serious. You and I both know I'm not like the women he usually deals with. I'm not a celebrity, gold digger, clout chaser, or a person who likes her privacy invaded." Blowing out her breath in frustration to gather the rest of her thoughts, she continued, "He wants me to meet him at the airport and leave there with him. That's extremely public. I like him. We all know that. I'm not sure if I want to be put out there only for nothing to come from him and me."

Erynn listened to Amree, already knowing what she disclosed was pretty much the issue holding her back. What bothered her about it all wasn't Amree becoming a bit famous because of her association with Lemere. Amree could handle that and herself. There was zero doubt about that. What bothered Erynn was that Amree was avoiding something that could potentially be good because she was scared of falling for a guy only to lose him again.

"Amree, I get everything you're concerned about. I also am aware that you're making this all bigger than it has to be. Have you taken the time to think that man wants you because you're not like everyone he's been with before? You're golden, friend. Stop overthinking and live in the moment."

"Ugh, I still—"

"Hold that thought. Your brother is calling," Erynn interrupted her as her line clicked with Private Caller showing up on her caller ID. Without waiting for Amree to reply, she accepted the call. Amree waited patiently for Erynn to come back on the line as thoughts of what she said flooded her mind. Erynn was right, as she usually was.

"Hey, I'm back."

"He's still on the other line?"

"Yes, so I'll call you back."

"Uhh, I'm the one who has his child, and I'm his sister, yet he's calling you first." Amree fake pouted.

"Don't go there. Look, you should go and enjoy yourself. It's not like he proposed. We both know he's a big deal, so it's only right you have your guard up and guard your heart."

"How can I guard my heart when he's seeping his way in, which is what frightens me?" she finally admitted out loud.

"That's fine, friend, if he is showing you that he feels the same. Think on it, and whatever you choose, I'll have your back. We'll talk about it when I call back. Your brother is going to kill me having him wait so long," she chuckled.

"Okay, bye." She ended the call, knowing she had a lot to think about.

"So, what's this I hear about you dating some new nigga?" Maksym asked as soon as the call connected.

"Well, hello to you too, big brother," she snickered, taking a mental note to cuss Erynn out for putting her business in the street. She would cut her some slack though, since she obviously hadn't told Maksym Lemere's name. Had she told him, Maksym wouldn't have called him, "some new nigga."

"What's up? Now, who is this dude, Am-E?"

"He's just a guy, Maksym. We've been talking for a little bit, nothing serious, which is why I don't understand why Erynn even opened her big mouth," she groaned.

"Because she knows I'll be out soon, and anything withheld she'll have to pay for later on a king-sized mattress."

"Ugh, TMI. I don't need that in my head. Plus, the two of y'all keep saying you're just friends. That don't sound like no friendly shit to me."

"So, why you talking to a dude you're afraid to go kick it with? If you scared to spend time with dude, then you may as well cut the talking y'all doing, too."

Amree took a deep breath while she rolled her eyes. It wasn't that she didn't care to hear what her brother had to say. It was the fact of it being repetitive. He said these same words to her with each guy she dealt with. Maksym's theory was straightforward: if his sister was getting to know a guy yet didn't think enough of him to spend time on him, then she needed to stop trying to get to know him. Trusting a person's vibe was number one. The only reason not to be in the presence of someone you were trying to get to know or grow with was because the vibe was off.

"It's not that. I'm going to go. Erynn exaggerated as she usually does."

"I mean, she is good for exaggerating," he chuckled. "When were you going to tell me you had a little boyfriend, though?"

"You do know that I'm grown. If I'm messing with anyone, it'll be a man, not a boy."

"That's right. I know I taught you better than to let a nigga ho you."

"Absolutely. I'm still getting to know this man, Maksym. I am feeling him. I am also going to visit him, so are you cool with Tyler staying with Auntie or here with the nanny? I—"

"Sis, you're his guardian. I trust your judgment. If there's anybody you love more than me, it's my junior, so do what you gotta do. Hell, I'm glad you met somebody. For a second, I thought my baby sis was switching to the opposite side of straight," he laughed.

"You are really trying your hand at this comedian lifestyle, huh? Can I ask you something?" She became serious.

"Anything. What's up?"

"Are you worried about me, like, messing with someone?" She wasn't sure why she asked. She already knew his answer. The question was more for herself. Amree knew she could handle a relationship and whatever came with it. It had been so long since she gave herself to someone. Then raising Tyler had become her number one priority. She wasn't sure if she cared to make a relationship work, even if it was one she wanted.

"I'm going to always worry, Am-E. Hell, I worry about you with things as simple as you and Ty driving to the store. When it comes to you dating, I know without a doubt you'll be good. I gave you game that puts you at more of an advantage than Steve Harvey did with his *Think Like a Man* book. You know signs to look for, and you know what's acceptable as well as what isn't. You're not a game-goofy female. People mistake your calm and cool demeanor for that to be who you are, when in actuality you're a beast, little sis. You're the realest nigga on my team, so I know you're good. Any dude gon' be lucky to have you. I understand, though, because you are a woman, for the right or wrong man you'll lose sight of some of the lessons I taught you as well as yourself. The best part of all that though is you'll bounce back. You'll be fine, sis. Live a little. Shit, a lot. Don't hold back for no reason. If I know anything, I know you know how to handle yourself in any situation."

"Thank you, Maksym." Amree wiped the lone tear that fell from her eye. She needed this conversation with her brother. Every conversation she had with him she needed. In only a few minutes, Maksym helped bring so much into perspective for her. She'd been pussyfooting around with Lemere. She was giving him parts of her, leaving out a lot. It was time to present to him the Amree Maksym described.

"You're welcome, sis. Let me talk to my son now, big baby."

"Tyler." she yelled, calling him from his spot on the living room floor. She had long ago finished cleaning. She had showered, bathed Tyler, and placed their dinner on the table.

"Yes, Auntie," Tyler spoke energetically, rushing into the dining area.

"Your dad is on the phone." She smiled as she extended her cell to him.

"Hi, Daddy." He took the phone, smiling wide, taking a seat at the table. Amree swooned, proud of how well her nephew was able to hold a conversation with his father.

"I want to stay home with the nanny. Auntie doesn't have good toys or games at her house. And she treats me like a baby," Tyler spoke adamantly while Amree shook her head. Maksym wasn't slick at all. She wondered what Erynn offered him to get him so gung ho on getting her to go out on a date with a guy whose identity he still wasn't privy to.

"Okay, Daddy, I love you too. Auntie said we will be back to see you soon. I'm happy. Okay. Bye." Tyler passed the phone back to Amree, barely paying attention to whether the phone was placed in her hand before he put his head down and began eating his food. She made spaghetti, his favorite, so he wasn't trying to waste any more time.

"Do not be putting him in grown folks' business," she teasingly chastised him once the phone was to her ear.

"Let me know how it goes. I love you."

"Love you too," was all she got out before the line went dead.

"So, you don't like going to Auntie's, huh?" she chuckled, eyes on Tyler as he devoured his food.

"Not really, 'cause I'm a big boy and she treats me like a baby," he admitted after he finished chewing.

"Well, I'll get the nanny to stay with you while I go out of town for a couple of days."

"Okay," he easily agreed with a slight shrug.

Chuckling, Amree went back to eating her dinner. After she and Tyler were done, she allowed him to play for a couple of hours before tucking him into bed at 10:00 p.m. She wasn't sure when Lemere planned to call, yet she would try to stay awake as long as possible because she was looking forward to telling him she would be on whatever plane he booked for her come Thursday.

With her lamp on and back against her headboard, laptop on her lap, Amree looked through her list of things needing to be done for the week, including writing a short article on the event she and Taylor attended about streaming. Given the event wasn't big, nor were there many interviews conducted, she'd only have to write up a general post, making it sound good. Besides that, she had a parent meeting with Ty's teacher and an interview with a YouTuber, Lady Banks, who'd been making herself known. She'd have to find a way to squeeze all of these things in by Wednesday night so she wouldn't have anything to do on Thursday other than get to and be with Lemere.

The vibrations of her cell against her nightstand pulled her from her thoughts. Seeing his name across the screen pulled a mile-wide smile to her face. She hadn't doubted him calling as he said he would, although she allowed the thought of him not calling to enter her mind. His disappointment when their call ended earlier was evident, and she knew a call back wasn't really deserved. Lemere had yet to tell her he would call and not do so. He used his actions to show he was interested, so she was going to do the same.

"Hey," she answered.

"I figured you'd be asleep." He sounded like he was relieved she was awake.

"No, I was going over work stuff and didn't want to miss your call because I have something to tell you." She allowed her words to penetrate his ears for a few seconds, which felt like minutes. "Lemere?" she called to him, making sure he hadn't blanked out on her.

"I'm still here, waiting for you to say what you gotta say, even though I hope it's not about to take away the little bit of hope I had when dialing your number." An uneasy chuckle released from his lips.

"I don't think so. I wanted to talk about what you asked me earlier."

"What I asked you earlier?" he repeated.

"Yes, I'd like you to ask me again." She laughed this time partially from nervousness, and partially from truly being amused with how she was approaching this conversation.

"Amree, will you come to visit me on Thursday? Because I miss you and want to see you."

"Yes, Lemere, I will come to see you. After you've booked my flight, give me the information, and I'll be there."

"Already booked. I'll forward the info to you when we get off the phone. You don't know how happy I am to not have purchased this first-class flight for nothing."

"Wow, you knew I was going to agree to visit?" she spoke as if she was shocked.

"Not at all. A nigga kept hope alive, though. I refuse to put in the universe anything less than what I want," he spoke honestly.

"And what if I said I wasn't coming? What would that have meant for us?"

"Not sure. I'd probably make my way to you."

"Are you serious?" She wasn't expecting that to be his response. She expected him to say that tonight would've been the last time they spoke.

"Yes, I'm dead-ass serious."

She could hear it in his tone that he was.

"Why are you trying to make me fall for you?" she mumbled while shaking her head.

"What you say?" he questioned.

"Uh, nothing. Well, I have to be honest with you."

"Wouldn't have it any other way."

"I wasn't going to agree to visit, initially. It's not because I didn't want to. It's because I'm afraid of all the attention I'll get being seen with you in public. I'm a low-key kind of girl. I don't like extra attention, drama, or none of the stuff I'm sure is going to come from these bloggers when people start digging, trying to figure out who the girl is with you."

"I get it. I have people to handle that. I want you with me. You'll be good regardless, and I wouldn't put you out there for blogs to do the bullshit they do. I know what asking you to come see me and kick it with me in my world entails. So please understand, once again, I'm asking you to step into this part of my world because I want you here Thursday and beyond. Trust that I got you. Can you do that?"

"I can try," she spoke honestly. She also knew better than to say yes. Trust was earned, though she could admit he was doing okay so far.

"That's better than nothing."

Chapter 11

"How was your flight?" Lemere asked as soon as he and Amree were comfortably seated in the back of a Sprinter.

"Uh, it was fine," she said as she looked ahead at the men sitting up front. There were five, six if she counted the driver. Although she didn't feel completely comfortable being the only female in the presence of so many men, the possessiveness Lemere displayed with the grip he had on her hand and keeping her at his side made her feel a bit more secure.

"Ay, Lemere, let's stop and get some food. A nigga hungry," one guy turned toward them and spoke. Amree wasn't sure of his name, given that Lemere had only introduced her to two of the men: his cousin, Mason, and his bodyguard, Shakil. They were two names she was already familiar with from previous conversations.

"You want to get something to eat?" Lemere ignored the guy, turning his attention to Amree.

"No, I'm okay," she spoke timidly, watching as Lemere nodded before turning back toward the front.

"Nah, man, jump in yo' shit when we get to my spot and go get something to eat." Chuckles erupting on the Sprinter caused Amree to shrink in her seat. She hadn't expected him to talk to the dude like that. Not only that, but Lemere's energy was different. He was soft and patient with her. With them around, he seemed more tense and arrogant.

"This nigga." Dude sucked his teeth yet left well enough alone.

Please don't let this whole weekend go this way, she prayed silently with her eyes closed and head resting against the seat.

"You good?" Lemere's hand on her thigh regained her attention as her eyes popped open.

"I'm fine." She forced a smile.

"Coo'. We'll be at my spot shortly," he told her.

"All right," she replied smoothly as she removed her phone from her tote.

To Erynn: I'm about two seconds away from regretting this trip.

"You pressing those buttons almost as fast as you were the night I met you, and you wasn't feeling too great that night. You sure you good?" Lemere's voice caught her off guard, causing her to practically drop her phone.

"I text fast sometimes. I'm good, though," she said with a smile on her face. This time she was being genuine because she felt good that he noticed her. He'd noticed her movements and aura that night as well as the facade she obviously was currently putting up.

"I believe you now since the smile reached your eyes," he chuckled, taking her by the hand and kissing it, and she relaxed.

Her cell vibrating on her lap regained her attention.

From Erynn: OMG why? What happened? The paps? Or are you exaggerating?

Amree read the message, rolling her eyes because Erynn could never be *not* extra.

To Erynn: Surprisingly, no paps. It's all these extra niggas with him. I'm the only female. Not that I can't handle it. It's just extra.

She felt less irritated than she had been seconds ago. She still could have done without his entourage.

From Erynn: Yeah, he trippin'. If he wanna bring friends and shit, you can bring a friend too. I can be on a flight tonight.

Amree laughed, causing everyone to look at her.

"My bad." She shook her head, placing her attention back to her phone.

To Erynn: Chill. You not slick. I'll be fine. Lol.

From Erynn: You always wanna have all the fun. JK. I'm so proud you've come this far. Enjoy your new man. Call me if you need me. I'm only a flight away.

"We're here," Lemere announced as she placed her phone back into her tote. Lemere told her they would be to his home soon. Still, she didn't expect it to be as quick as he mentioned. They had been driving for a bit, and she just assumed they would have farther to go. Because of how the Sprinter was parked, and all the heads in front of her, she couldn't see anything other than what the back window beside her presented: a tall black iron gate, with a symbol she didn't recognize. Yet she hoped it didn't mean he was a part of anything ungodly.

"'Bout time. A nigga hungry as fuck," the guy from earlier spoke again.

"Right, so you can hop in yo' shit and g'on 'bout your business," Shakil spoke up, clearly irritated to an almost-amusing level. However, she held in her laugh.

"Hurry up and get off my shit," Lemere chimed in. His quick command made the men start scattering like roaches when the light comes on—all but Mason and Shakil.

"Yo, Amree, that's what people call you all the time? Or you got a nickname or somethin'?" Mason turned to her and asked while he stood to grab his bag.

"I do. It's only reserved for my big brother, though."

"Damn, like that? Where yo' brother at?"

"Do you know how you sound right now?" Lemere asked seriously with his face contorted.

"I get pussy on top of pussy, and pussy is all I want. Don't try to play me," Mason shot back, clearly offended.

"You the one asked the question. Shit, and you knew what I was insinuating without me having to say the exact words." Lemere chuckled.

Though Amree hadn't been too comfortable with all the men around, Mason and Lemere going back and forth was pure comedy. She didn't see herself becoming too tired of having them to laugh at.

"He's in prison," Amree spoke up, hoping to stop the men from bickering. Yes, they were funny, but right now she wanted off the Sprinter.

"Ah, so you not some bougie female."

"Where her brother is don't have shit to do with her being bougie or not, you know that, right?" Shakil chimed in.

"Duh, big mothafucka. I'm just saying, though," Mason shot back.

"Do us all a favor and don't say nothing else." Lemere extended his hand to Amree, stepping in front of her, motioning toward Shakil and Mason to exit the Sprinter.

When she stepped off, the sight before her paused her in her tracks. She was sure Lemere was living like the famous rich man he was. To see how his money was being put to use in the flesh was a whole other ball game. His home—no, mansion—was massive. It was like four of her townhouses put together. His paint job on his place, however, didn't surprise her. It was white with black trim, typical of a dude who could be taken out of the hood but the hood couldn't be taken out of him.

"Ay, Lemere, I got y'all bags," Shakil spoke, removing the luggage from the back.

"You can grab mine. Give me hers, though. Shit, don't feel right, you carrying her luggage when I know her underwear is in there," he said seriously, reaching for Amree's bag. His comment followed by Shakil's and Mason's laughter pulled her from her daydream.

"This nigga really feeling you," Mason said, walking past her with a smirk.

"Come on." Lemere ignored his cousin, pulling Amree along with his left hand holding her luggage, while his right held on to hers. They took about ten steps before walking through the double doors of Lemere's home. He had a foyer, some shit she'd only seen in fancy home magazines, with a beautiful expensive-ass chandelier.

"Your home is beautiful, Mere," she complimented him in awe, and she'd only seen the entrance.

"Thank you." He refused to be modest about his home. Besides the one he purchased for his mother, it was his most prized purchase. He was living in his dream home. Paid for in cash. He would always swell in pride when complimented on it.

"You're welcome."

"Let's go put your stuff away. Then I'll give you the grand tour so you can better make yourself at home. "

Amree nodded before following Lemere up the stairs. They made a left at the top, continuing down a long hallway. She counted four doors. Each he simply called a guest room.

"This is where I lay my head when I have the luxury of being here for more than a few hours," he informed her, opening the door.

Amree didn't think she could be any more impressed with the appearance of his home. His bedroom, though, was the size of her living room, dining room, and kitchen put together. He had a seating area a few feet away from his massive custom bed.

"Where are you gonna put my things?" she asked, looking around. His room was clean, so clean she felt like her one suitcase would leave a mess.

"Over here. Come on." He walked and she followed.

"Lemere, this closet is the size of my bedroom." She couldn't help comparing their spaces, because that was the best she could come up with to provide a description. Lemere chuckled at how in awe she was. It wasn't on no starstruck groupie shit, which was what made him appreciate her compliments even more.

"You can use a drawer or hang your things or both. I want you comfortable, all right?" Walking up to her, he took her by the waist, lifting her onto the dresser and standing between her legs.

"Okay," she giggled.

"I missed you," he admitted, looking her in the eyes.

"I missed you too. I mean, I know we talked every day and up until I got on the plane this morning, but I missed being near you." She wrapped her arms lazily around his neck while her legs dangled slowly, due to her feet not touching the floor. Lemere leaned into her, pressing his lips to hers, which she reciprocated without hesitation.

"Damn, I couldn't wait to do that," he spoke in between pecks.

"That's all you wanted to do? Kiss me?" She smirked, pulling back, looking him in the face.

"Hell nah, I just wanted to have some tact about myself. But shiid, I'm trying to be on some otha shit if you down." He winked suggestively, causing her to burst into laughter.

"Nah, I think you should wait a bit. We haven't been in each other's space but"—she looked at an invisible watch on her wrist—"a couple of hours, which is not enough time together for me to allow you into my pants, Mr. Webster," she spoke in a teasing tone.

"It's more than enough time. I'ma humor you, though. Besides, I want to run something by you first."

"Okay."

"I'm supposed to, well, I have to make an appearance tonight at a club in Hollywood."

"So, you want me to sit here? In your humongous house by myself?"

"No, you're . . . I mean, I want you to come with me."

"Lemere, you know . . ." she groaned. Amree wasn't feeling staying at his place. She absolutely wasn't feeling going to the club with him, where a ton of attention would be on the two of them. Him mainly. She'd be caught in the crossfire, though.

"You know I got you, right? I already know what you worried about. All I told you before you decided to come out here still applies. I'll make sure you're protected. That you feel protected, even if that means not going because you're uncomfortable."

The sincerity in his words was felt. She liked Lemere a lot. She knew eventually things would get out about the two of them if they kept doing whatever it was they were doing. She only hoped their being discreet would last a little longer. Or at least until they had a title. She found his gesture to turn down the appearance sweet. She wouldn't be the reason he reneged on his appearance.

"I'll go."

"Coo'. So, how has everything been? I know you've been busy at work, and I appreciate you pulling away to come spend time with me."

"I have been busy, so this time with you is needed. I think," she said in a joking tone.

"You got any interviews lined up?"

"A few," she stated proudly.

"More rappers?"

"I think one, but he hasn't confirmed yet. The other is an athlete. Oh, and I'll be interviewing an actress as well." She went on to mention the variety of interviews she had set up because something about how he asked if she would be sitting with another rapper made her feel a way. It was in his tone.

However, when he said, "You gotta watch out for the athletes and rap niggas," she knew the gut feeling she felt wasn't wrong. Lemere was showing a hint of jealousy, and she found it cute.

"I'm only interested in doing my job. And you and I both know I am more than capable of keeping the interview professional. Besides, I'm not interested in anything other than doing my job."

"All right."

She disliked the finality in his reply because it sounded like he either was done with the conversation or didn't believe her. She hoped neither feeling was right. She decided to place it in the back of her mind because she planned to do what she came there for, and that was to enjoy her weekend with him.

Rich Homie Quan's "Walk Thru" coincidentally was the song blaring through the room as Amree followed a few steps behind Lemere. They entered the club through the back, which she was able to appreciate shortly as the DJ announced Lemere and his crew in the building before his face was even shown. Shakil held her hand, holding Lemere's back while another guard held his front. And Mason was behind her. She hadn't cared too much for the arrangement at first, feeling like he was purposely trying to make her play the background. Though she wanted to be low-key, she also didn't want the act forced on her. Lemere's explanation did ease some of her worries. He explained how Shakil was one of the few people he trusted with his life. Since she'd become a part of his lifeline, he had to trust her with someone who'd protect her like his life depended on it. Between his guards and crew, the crowd control was on point. Though men and women were trying their best to get to Lemere, his entourage made the crowd clear space to get them to the VIP section reserved for Lemere without hassle.

"You straight?" Lemere asked, taking a seat near Amree.

Her eyes rolled in the direction of the rope they'd walked through to see random women being allowed in.

"Yep." She tried not to allow her irritation to show. However, it was difficult. She was starting to wish she'd stayed at his place with the housekeeper.

"All right. We won't be here that long." He leaned in, kissing her cheek. Luckily, the corner she sat in was dark, so no one saw their affectionate gesture. Providing a tight-lipped smile, she removed her phone as Lemere stood and walked into the spotlight. Like ants to a piece of candy, the few groupies allowed into the section flocked to him. She watched as the girls did their best to be seen as a guy passed Lemere a microphone.

"What the fuck is up?" he spoke into the mic, hyped. The crowd cheered, and for a moment, she genuinely smiled, proud to see him at work and getting love in his element. She assumed he felt eyes on him as he turned in her direction and winked as the bass to his latest song dropped.

"Y'all feeling my new shit?" Lemere asked a question he already knew the answer to. The small crowd was going crazy, dancing and rapping along with the music.

"These hoes," Amree muttered. Placing her attention back to her phone, Amree contemplated texting Erynn, knowing she would be able to help her get through the night. Erynn would talk cash shit, which would have Amree hyped and confident, two qualities she possessed with or without a hype man.

"Amree, get on your shit and relax. You got this," she said low, giving herself a pep talk. She determined that she'd rather talk about how she pushed through tonight on her own with Erynn rather than being told how to do so. Placing her phone back inside her clutch, Amree looked back toward Lemere, who was still on the mic rapping and two-stepping with a ho on each side of him. She understood the women were probably enjoying a chance of a lifetime. But selling themselves so short surely wouldn't get the results they were looking for. The Lemere she was getting to know couldn't care less about a pretty thirst bucket. At least she assumed so, because if not, what was he doing with her?

Oddly, that question really had her contemplating, due to the slim-thick female grinding her ass against Lemere's thigh. He hadn't pushed her from him, and his hand "slipped" one too many times. To the naive eye, his slip may have looked like assistance. Homegirl's dress kept rising. However, to Amree, the slip of the hand was plain ol' disrespectful. As if he could feel her eyes on him again, burning a hole in the side of his face, Lemere stepped away from the girl before looking over his shoulder at her. Amree hoped her face didn't display the level of irritation she felt. To be sure, she quickly looked down at her phone as if she were in tune with whatever was on her screen.

"All right, y'all keep partying in this mothafucka," she heard him speak, while still refusing to look up and acknowledge his next move. Her eyes on him weren't needed because she felt his presence near. Looking to her right, she saw "too-little dress" sitting about arm's length from her, Lemere next to her, and another female to his right. He was comfortably sandwiched between the two women.

"Ay, Amree," Mason yelled over the music, taking a seat next to her.

"Hey." She was completely unenthused as she looked at Mason. Her expression told him she wasn't interested in whatever he was getting ready to say.

"He just doin' his job. Them hoes ain't nothin' but props. Cuz has to—"

"Mason, thanks, but no thanks. An explanation is not needed when it comes to Lemere doing his job," she cut him off before sitting back in her chair, looking uninterested.

"All right. Well, just so you know, you look really pretty. One of, if not the, baddest females in this

room. My cousin knows it, too." Mason smiled
and extended his fist for her to give him a pound.
He knew Lemere was feeling Amree, so he would
be respectful. Not only respectful, but he would
be Lemere's angel while Mere was obviously on
his superstar thot shit. Mason also, in the short
amount of time being around Amree, could see
what his cousin saw in her beyond her beauty. She
did look amazing tonight, with her hair parted
on the left side, big and curly from her wash and
go, framing her face perfectly. And as always, her
orange tips assisted in her standing out. If that
hadn't done it, for sure, the navy blue midi-dress
clinging to her curves brought attention her way.
Though the dress was simple, Amree wore it as if
it were custom-made for her. While many of the
women in attendance were clothed just enough to
abide by the club's dress code, she was still giving
them a run for their money, leaving way more to
the imagination.

"You gon' leave me hanging?" Mason asked,
looking adorable with what she assumed was his
version of puppy-dog eyes. He genuinely wanted
to see how long she and Lemere would last. To
him, she would be perfect for his cousin. She was
laid-back and didn't come off as the jealous type.
Any other female, he was sure, would have gone off
on Lemere by now. His cousin was operating like
he hadn't brought a woman to the club with him.

Unable to hold back her smile, Amree allowed it to grace her lips as she extended her hand to give Mason the pound he asked for.

"Enjoy yourself, A. You know who my cuz belongs to. Believe it or not, you running shit. Don't tell him I told you that, though." He winked. "Now, Lemere not able to fuck off with these broads, but I am. So, if you'll excuse me." He winked once more with a crooked grin before getting up and heading toward the other side of their VIP area.

Watching Mason, who subtly had given her a nickname, walk off, she couldn't help notice a leg draped over Lemere's. He was sipping whatever drink he had in his cup, not paying the leg too much attention. However, to her, he was pushing it. She looked around, noticing only a few eyes were on their section. Where he and the females were seated, little of the club's light barely touched the area. She knew what she was about to do could bring unwanted attention. She'd eat that though to make sure Lemere knew and understood who the fuck she was. Standing, she smoothed down her dress before taking the couple of steps to where he sat, standing right in front of him, ignoring the daggers from the women who were on each side of him. It took everything in her to not laugh as Lemere's eyes grew wide as saucers.

"You're excused," she spoke as she removed the leg from his lap, replacing it with her ass. Sitting with her back to the crowd, she wrapped both arms around his neck, leaning into him so that her lips touched his ear. Enjoying the feel of her near him, on him, Lemere wrapped both arms around her waist, inhaling her scent, nuzzling his nose into the crook of her neck.

"I thought you wanted to remain low-key," he spoke, gripping her a little tighter.

"I did. Me being low-key doesn't mean for you to be openly disrespectful. I'd never disrespect you, especially not in public. I'd like the same respect. The room don't know who I am, but you do. I'd hope you'd carry it that way unless you're fine with me walking onto the dance floor—"

"I get it," he cut her off. That quick thought of her even close to another man had him in his feelings. "I'm not ever trying to be disrespectful nor make you feel uncomfortable."

"Okay." Her reply was simple yet held weight. Her "okay" was a warning.

Removing his face from her neck, Lemere looked at the girl to his right. He signaled with a nod for her to move, then did the same to the one on his left, who didn't seem to be able to take a hint, leaving Shakil to remove her.

"If it's that simple to remove your groupies, why'd you take your time?" she asked, attempting to leave his lap. His grip on her waist kept her in place.

"Having a few females around me when I'm out is what's expected of me. I don't pay them females no mind." He shrugged.

"Oh, you don't?" Her tone was full of sarcasm.

"Damn right. No reason to when I got you," he spoke, oblivious to the fact that she hadn't meant what she said the way he took it.

Truthfully, she didn't care about the women being around. She knew she was the only woman leaving with him, or he wouldn't be leaving with her at all. Her main concern was being respected. If she didn't speak up tonight, then the attention he gave to other women in her presence would only get worse. She was a cool woman and prided herself on being so. Especially since Maksym had always let her know how much a nagging woman was the worst kind of woman for a man. He assured her there were other effective ways to get through to a man, and nagging sure as hell wasn't one of them.

"I hear you. Well, I'm about to go back to my little corner while you finish working." She pulled his earlobe into her mouth, sucking it with enough force to make Lemere's dick jump beneath her.

"Nah, you can stay right here, at least until my dick go down." He hugged her tighter. "When we get back to my place, will you and I have been in each other's presence long enough for us to get to doing that otha stuff we was talking about earlier?" His hand rubbed up and down her back.

"Probably. Seriously, though. Get back to work. Watching you in your element is a bit of a turn-on."

"Rise up then." He tapped her ass, causing giggles to fall from her lips as she stood. "Nah, stay right here, though." He held her hand, tugging her gently, pulling her to take a seat beside him. Obliging, she sat, allowing him to kiss her cheek before standing and walking right back into the spotlight.

Lemere rocked the crowd for another hour before they headed out. They hadn't closed the club, but many of those in attendance left when Lemere did, including the thirst-bucket females, who did everything but strip naked as a way to get Lemere to take them with him. He obviously wasn't interested, so they accepted the hand of what they assumed was the next best thing—Mason. It took everything in Amree not to question Lemere on whether the groupies were heading back to his home. Luckily, she didn't have to, as the answer was revealed when they dropped Mason and his hoes off at a hotel. Shortly after, they were pulling into the driveway of Lemere's home.

"So, can we get into some otha shit?" Lemere asked her with a sexy smirk once they made it to the top of his stairs.

"If you can catch me." Amree took off running toward Lemere's bedroom door, only to be caught by him within seconds.

"Caught," he said as he pinned her against the door, pressing his lips to hers. Lifting her by the butt, he held her with one hand as he used the other to unlock the door.

"All right, you won. I got you. I want to take a shower first. I need to get the stench of the club off me, and you should wash off that cheap perfume that's leaking from your clothes."

"You the only woman been close enough to me for me to smell like—"

"How easily you've forgotten." She tilted her head, looking at him like he'd grown another head from his neck. "Besides, I don't have on cheap perfume. Never worn any either."

"Well, how about you come help me wash off whatever it is you think I smell like?" Not waiting for an answer, Lemere carried Amree to his bathroom. Turning on the shower, he held her firmly with one hand and eased her to her feet once the water was on. Moving quickly so she had no room to protest, he began helping her out of her dress and underwear.

"Make sure the water isn't too hot," he ordered, stepping back and removing his Armani shirt. Doing as she was told, she tested the temperature of the water with her hand, deeming it fine to step in. Slowly she entered his huge shower, never taking her eyes off him while he undressed. Lemere had looked good as hell tonight in his black-on-black Armani attire. Now that he stood in front of her in the nude with his dick swinging, she liked him this way much better. Slowly, she moved back, tucking her bottom lip between her teeth as she watched him enter. Once the water hit his body, Lemere wasted no time pulling her into him, kissing her fervently while gripping her ass.

Moaning, Amree extended her hands, placing one on the wall and the other on the shower glass, doing her best to hold herself up as his kiss made her legs weak.

"You trust me?" he asked as he broke their kiss, looking her in the eyes.

Nodding, her heart raced because she knew she hadn't told the complete truth. Lemere sensed that she wasn't being completely honest. Still, what she gave as an answer was good enough for him. As he picked her up, her legs naturally wrapped around him. He turned around, pressing her back into the wall.

"I got you, all right?" he promised before sliding inside of her.

"Shit," he hissed. This was the first time feeling Amree without a rubber between them. He knew what they were doing was irresponsible, especially since they hadn't become official yet. But he wanted her too badly to stop now.

"Ah, Mere," Amree moaned as he slowly began stroking her insides. Her pussy walls contracted against his manhood while her juices flowed effortlessly.

"Amree. Shit. Girl," he growled, moving faster, feeling himself close to his peak. Usually, he'd last longer. Feeling her without the barrier of a condom was an entirely different ball game.

"I . . . I'm cumming. Mere. Ah," Amree screamed as her entire body shuddered.

He was grateful, as his own nut had finally risen. Pulling out of her quickly, Lemere allowed his seeds to be washed down the drain.

Chapter 12

"This dress code is bogus as hell," Erynn spoke loudly into Amree's ear.

"It's not like you're new to the dress code, Erynn," she chuckled.

"So? It's always going to be a problem because their little rules and shit really messing with me, fucking shit all the way up when I walk in," Erynn scoffed, truly disgusted.

"So one: where is Tyler? Because you're cussing like you don't have an ounce of home training. And two: so you're saying that you're not about to be fucking shit up, Miss Fashionista?" Amree questioned in a mocking tone. She knew Erynn was being nothing but her dramatic self, yet still she decided to humor the conversation.

"First of all, he's right here with his headset on, not paying me any mind. Second of all, I'm still fucking shit up. I said that it's hindering me from fucking shit *all* the way up, okay? I'm fucking shit up, just not all the way like I could without the damn dress code." Erynn sucked her teeth and rolled her eyes as if Amree could see how annoyed she truly was. Laughing was the only reaction she could give Erynn's antics. She appreciated her best friend wholeheartedly, and she never was surprised when Erynn was being Erynn. Erynn was as close to her heart as Tyler and Maksym, and she was beyond grateful that Erynn, without hesitation, assisted in helping with Tyler anytime she could, because she absolutely didn't have to.

"Yeah, you love to laugh like I'm telling a joke, and I'm serious as hell."

"That's why it's funny, 'cause I know you're serious." Amree allowed another chuckle to escape her lips before composing herself and getting serious. "Dress code or not, you and I both know you're going to be the best dressed there. This is not your first rodeo."

"Girl, no, yo' friend Bekah probably gon' show me up, honey," she teased.

"Don't do Bekah. Her weave was way better last time I saw her. Hopefully, she did keep her new hairstylist. Anyway, what food are you taking my brother?"

"Barbecue, like he asked for, girl."

"I didn't know what he wanted. He didn't call to tell me," Amree spoke in the bratty tone she would take when she didn't get her way.

"Your boo make it yet?"

"Cute switch of the subject." Amree rolled her eyes, thinking of how it had been an entire month since the last time she and Lemere were together. And had he not spent the rest of her time at his home making up his shady ways from the club to her, a month would have come and gone with the two of them having no further communication.

"You know that's what I do," Erynn snickered.

"You and me both. So, let me speak to Tyler."

The sound of Erynn sucking her teeth was heard clearly before she told Amree to hold on. Seconds later, Tyler's sweet voice could be heard.

"Hi, Auntie."

"Hi, baby. Are you having fun with Auntie Erynn?"

"Yes, I always have fun with Auntie E," he giggled.

"I know. Well, tomorrow when you see your dad, can you give him a big hug and kiss on the cheek for me?"

"Um, I'll give him a big hug, maybe a kiss."

"Okay, I'll take that." She held in her laughter as best she could. She could imagine Tyler's little face scrunched up in contemplation at his decision about her request. "I love you. I'll talk to you tomorrow, okay?"

"Okay, love you too." Shuffling sounded in her ear momentarily.

Erynn came back on the phone. "Bye, ho. I'll talk to you tomorrow."

"Okay, I love you. Thanks again. Oh, and do not slip up and tell Maksym why I'm here and not there."

"Girl, who you think you talking to? I've been lying for your ass for years. I got this." Erynn ended the call, and Amree felt no way about her doing so without saying goodbye a second time. She had a few things she needed to get done around her home anyway. After placing her phone onto the charger, she went into her kitchen, removing a bottled water right as her doorbell rang.

"One minute," she called out, placing the water onto the counter as she made her way to the door. Always cautious, she checked the peephole first before unlocking the door. The smile that graced her face when the door was fully open could have lit up the entire block. This said a lot, given that the sun was already blazing over the city.

Without hesitation, she leaped into Lemere's arms, wrapping her arms tightly around his neck as well as her legs around his waist, raining kisses all over his forehead and cheeks before smashing her lips into his. Tingles filled her entire body as their lips locked and tongues danced getting reacquainted with one another. Lemere's slight squeeze on Amree's ass caused a moan to escape her lips. That same moan made his dick jump against the fabric of his jeans. Slowly, he released her ass, moving his hands up her body to her arms, which he slowly pulled from around his neck.

"I missed you too," he told her in between the kisses she was still raining on his lips and face. Amree had missed him a whole lot. She was horny, too. Phone sex and playing in her wetness had only pacified the itch she needed scratched. Her intentions weren't to jump on him once he walked in her front door. However, the scent of his Dior cologne, the fresh cut and line up, and his signature all-black attire had her pussy pulsating from looking at him. They could catch up and have small talk after she got what she needed from him.

"Good. Come show me."

Chuckling, Lemere placed his hands back onto her ass, since she'd never let her legs leave his waist, and kicked her door shut as he moved her closer to the door to lock it. Once he was sure the door was secured, he carried her up the stairs to her bedroom. Once inside her room, there was no time wasted between the two removing each other's clothing. Amree's clothes were easiest to remove due to the simple red camisole and shorts she wore. Watching her scoot back on the bed naked as the day she was born, Lemere bit down on his bottom lip, anticipating tasting her. In one swift motion, he was between her legs.

"Here." Amree placed her hand on his chest, halting him as she showed him a condom. They'd slipped up before not using one, and as horny as she was, she refused to have that kind of slip-up again. No, she didn't think he was giving in to any of the groupies he came across on tour since making it official. She couldn't be certain, though.

"I got you. Let me handle what I'm trying to do first," he chuckled. He removed the condom from her hand, tossing it onto the nightstand before taking her left breast into his mouth. His tongue circled her hard nipple as he massaged her right breast with his right hand. He gave her left breast a little more attention before moving to the right and doing the same. Amree's moans and squirming intensified as he trailed kisses down her belly, stopping at her clit. He wasted no time pulling it between his lips, sucking on it as if he were eating a New Orleans sno-ball on a hot summer day.

"Ah, Mere," Amree moaned as her hips lifted from the bed and her arms rose above her head, gripping the headboard. Lemere was doing a number on her wet mound.

"Damn, I missed this shit. You taste so fucking good, A," he admitted in between slurps. "I want you to cum for me, all right?"

"Shit," she hissed. What came out as a question was nothing short of a command, and she knew it. "Yes, Mere. I . . . I'm cumming!" The growl that escaped her at the orgasm shooting through her body was one like neither she nor Lemere had ever heard from her. The juices that poured out were also more than she had ever fed him before. To say he was turned on would be an understatement. He needed to be inside of her to feel how wet her spilled juices coated his dick. He lapped up a bit more, leaving enough to appease his curiosity. It took everything in him to reach for the condom to cover himself. After experiencing Amree with no rubber between them, putting one on almost felt like she was putting a lock on his dick. What he appreciated was that, no matter the barrier, her walls always hugged his dick and her slippery folds provided way more wetness than the condom's lubrication ever could.

"Ah, go slow, Mere," Amree moaned, halting his movements. Though she was extremely wet, getting inside her would never be an easy task.

"My bad, babe." Lowering his body, Lemere kissed Amree sensually, helping her to relax as he pushed inside of her, pushing a gasp from both their mouths.

"You gon' have to start coming on tour with me. This some shit I need daily, like water," he expressed honestly, slowly stroking her. She wanted to reply, say some slick shit that would have him considering canceling the rest of his tour to be with her. But she couldn't. The strokes he was putting on her had her breath caught in her throat. She wasn't giving him anything other than the moans escaping her lips. Between her moans and Lemere's grunts, they made music—beautiful, engaging music that kept the fire burning.

Biting his bottom lip, Lemere hoped it would assist in temporarily removing the extreme pleasure
Amree's walls provided, because he was less than
minutes away from busting.

"Babe, I need you to cum for me one more time,"
he spoke in her ear through clenched teeth as
he thrust into her harder. Nodding while lifting
her pelvis slightly, Amree welcomed the friction
caused by her movement, which had her exploding
seconds later.

"Shit." Lemere thrust into her, releasing right
after her and collapsing right on top of Amree.

Chuckling, Amree used her free hand to tap his
shoulder. Lemere's body weight had her sinking
into the mattress. The intimacy was welcomed.
Being suffocated, however, was not.

"My bad," he laughed, rolling over onto his back
while pulling her close to him in the process.

"How was your flight?" she asked, snuggling up
to him.

"Cool. Shit, the only time I get a peaceful flight
is when I travel out here or on a private jet.
Everything squared away with your people?" He
was aware Tyler and Erynn were together to visit
her brother.

"Yes. How about on your end? I know your son
misses you." Amree was also aware that Lemere
had switched some things up in his life to be with
her.

"He's straight. I'll get him as soon as I leave from out here. He'll be with me for a couple of weeks."

"That's good."

They had decided to take things to the next level, only to still be living in secret. She understood the secrecy from the media, and that's what she wanted. Keeping things under wraps from their families, though, felt weird, even though she wasn't ready for him to meet Tyler or Maksym yet. She would introduce Erynn to him in a heartbeat. She also realized everything between them was still new, so introductions would take time.

"Mere," she spoke softly, lifting her head slightly so her eyes met his. Instead, what she was met with were closed eyes. She smiled, hearing the light snores come from him. His being tired was expected. He'd sexed her like he missed her, and he'd only gotten a few hours of sleep prior to arriving. To be honest, he'd barely been sleeping, as the tedious tour schedule hadn't allowed for much rest. Slowly, she leaned in, kissing his temple before easing out of bed. Staring at him sleeping peacefully made her heart feel full. Here was this man who could have any woman he wanted, yet he wanted her. Not that she wasn't a catch. Hell, she was *the* catch. They both knew it. Still, to see the peace she brought into his life illuminating on his handsome face proved the feeling of importance he gave to her wasn't in vain.

Fear of the heartbreak she experienced with her last relationship always lingered in the back of her mind. She did her best not to compare Lemere to him because, hell, there really wasn't much to compare between them. Lemere was *that* nigga. Her ex was a nigga she invested time into who didn't know what to do with her. She was investing time into Lemere as well, so there was a similarity in that. The difference was the way Lemere accepted and reciprocated the time she invested and the pieces of her she invested without his rushing to obtain more. He openly respected how she wanted to move in regard to their relationship, even though on many occasions he expressed his readiness to let the world know she was his. Amree wasn't ready for that yet. The ridicule and the lack and invasion of privacy were none of the things she was ready to endure, especially after only being official for such a short amount of time. Maksym had taught her a lot. Taking her time with her heart was overly expressed, a lesson she wasn't taking lightly. Especially now.

Lemere slowly rose from bed, not surprised that Amree was no longer resting near him. He knew she hadn't gone far wherever she was, so he felt no need to worry. Instead, he decided to use this time to check in on his son. He thought about

Amree's tone when she asked if his junior was okay, knowing that she felt a little guilty that he chose to visit her instead of going straight to his son. By no means was he choosing time with Amree over quality time with his son. He'd only adjusted the pickup date. LJ would travel with him, giving them way more time to spend with one another. It had taken some convincing and a few thousand dollars on his end to get Kiana to agree—money and begging well spent. Although, she wouldn't receive a dime until Lemere and his son were on their way out. He knew how Kiana could be, so no way did he trust that he could give her some money and she'd still allow him to take Junior.

Sliding to the foot of the bed, Lemere leaned forward, picking up his pants and removing his cell. Sitting up, he scrolled to his son's number, hitting the option for a FaceTime call.

"Dang, man, I almost thought you weren't going to answer. What you over there doing?" he asked once LJ's handsome face came into view. He was a spitting image of his father, with a charismatic personality Lemere wished he'd had at that age.

"I was playing my game, Dad. I needed to dunk on these fools before I answered because I didn't want to pause my game midair. If you hung up, I was going to call you back, though," LJ explained, finding no issue with placing his father on the back burner to win his video game.

"You ready to roll out with Daddy in a couple of days?" he asked, suppressing the laugh he wanted to release. LJ was doing his best to keep eye contact with his father through FaceTime, yet he was failing, as his dark brown irises continued to veer off toward what Lemere knew to be his television.

"Yes, my mom said you're going to take me a lot of places and buy me a lot of stuff I like."

"Yeah, man, we're going to have fun. I miss you." Lemere decided not to even entertain what Kiana had told LJ. There was no need to. Of course, he was going to purchase his son whatever his heart desired while he was with him. Spending money on LJ would never be a problem. What he didn't like was how Kiana thought she was being slick by planting that seed in his son's head. She was using the oldest trick in the book: tell the child what his father was going to do so he expected his father to do so, making Dad the bad guy if he didn't come through as Mom said he would. She was extremely lucky that Lemere didn't care to be petty, because he too could've played that game.

"I miss you too, Dad. Wait, who is that?" LJ's eyes had grown wide as he appeared to be looking through Lemere. Not hearing anything, Lemere turned to look over his shoulder to see what had his son so intrigued. When his eyes landed on Amree, he smiled.

"I'm sorry. I didn't know you were on the phone."
Amree's cheeks were flushed with embarrassment
as she clung to the towel she had wrapped around
her. She couldn't see who Lemere was on the
phone with clearly, though the question and tone
of the speaker let her know it had to be his son.

"It's cool. Come here," Lemere spoke, halting the
exit she was so tempted to take.

Her entire face fell, as well as her shoulders,
as defeat and uncertainty washed over her. She
couldn't believe he wanted her to come closer to
him to give his son an even clearer view of her.
Granted, she was covered up, but it wasn't what
she considered appropriate covering.

"Come on," he spoke again, motioning with his
head for her to come to him. With a roll of the eyes,
she stalked over to Lemere, sitting close enough
for her leg to touch his, yet far enough to where
she wasn't directly in the camera. That only lasted
a second, as Lemere took it upon himself to extend
his arm so that his son got a perfect view of the two
of them.

"Ooh, Daddy. That's your girlfriend? She's
pretty," LJ said, sitting up, looking at Amree with a
mischievous smile.

"Yeah, man, this my girlfriend, so you can quit
staring now," Lemere teased. Amree blushed,
smiling wide, flattered by the compliment of the
young man as well as by his father openly claiming

her. Lemere not showing one ounce of hesitation answering his son's question made her feel good. Prideful, in fact.

"What's her name, Dad?" he asked, not worried about the order his dad gave about staring.

"Ask her," Lemere told him, inching the phone a bit closer to Amree, who was looking like a deer in headlights. She was nervous. Meeting his son was a big deal, even if it was only over FaceTime.

"What's your name?"

"My name is Amree. What about yours?"

"My name is Lemere, like my dad. But everyone calls me LJ. He didn't tell you?" The look he gave her pulled laughter from both her and Lemere's lips.

"He did. I only wanted to hear it from you, though." She smiled at him.

"Oh, okay," LJ giggled, and Lemere sucked his teeth, seeing how his son was putting on. It was obvious LJ had an instant crush on Amree. "You're pretty."

"Thank you. You're very handsome." Amree was smiling too hard for Lemere's liking. He was honestly getting a little jealous of his son. The boy was a charmer, like him.

"Um, are you gonna be at my dad's house when I come?"

"Uh . . ." Amree's voice was caught in her throat.

"Not this time. You'll get to meet her soon, though," Lemere spoke up, saving her from answering a question she really didn't know the answer to. Yes, Lemere had done this cute phone introduction, but she still wasn't positive he wanted things to move past it. Obviously, her doubts held no validity, because Lemere seemed to keep proving her wrong.

"Okay." The satisfaction on LJ's face from Lemere's answer brought another smile to Amree's face.

"You have a little charmer on your hands," she whispered to him.

"I see. If he don't quit coming at you with all the cute shit, he won't get to meet you."

"Jealous much?" she teased.

"Amree, when you come to my dad's house, you want to play a game with me? I have a lot of games."

"LJ, who the hell you talking to?"

Before he could answer, a woman was standing behind him. Her hair was pushed to one side, and from what Amree could tell, she was a pretty woman. It was the uninviting expression she wore on her face that did her features more harm than good. The way her neck stuck out, extended like a giraffe's, brow furrowed, and lips poked out as if she had something sour in her mouth did not flatter her features at all.

Amree was sure the woman had her hand on her hip as well, even though she couldn't see it. They were having a stare down for a good sixty seconds before Amree could no longer hide the amusement she felt and burst into laughter. She didn't laugh on purpose. However, the thought of the famous Norman from social media came to mind as Amree examined the woman's expression. As if a light bulb had gone off in Amree's head, she realized that the woman before her, in expression and demeanor, reminded her of Norman.

"Bitch. I don't know what the fuck you laughing at. Lemere, you betta tell this ol' stank groupie-ass ho who the fuck I am."

"Ay, son, I love you. I'll call you later," Lemere spoke over Kiana's antics to his son.

Once LJ said, "Okay," he ended the call.

"Whew," Amree said as she blew out her breath when he set his phone down.

"Thanks for not feeding into that." He knew it had to take a lot of restraint to be called out of her name and not respond.

"I didn't mean to laugh at her. I just . . . hold on."

She wasn't sure if Lemere was familiar with Norman and just saying his name would justify her laughter. She had to let him see what she saw. So she stood, grabbed her phone from her nightstand, and scrolled through her social media until she found the skit of Norman she was looking for.

"When she came on the phone, her whole demeanor reminded me of this." She put her phone in front of him so that he could see exactly what she was talking about.

Lemere stared at the phone, doing his best to keep a straight face. The more he could see the resemblance in Norman's gestures and facial expressions to what Kiana had shown only moments ago, the more not laughing became a losing battle.

"Man, that's cold," he chuckled.

"I wouldn't have laughed at her otherwise. I couldn't get the resemblance out of my head. To be honest, your son's mother is really pretty."

Not sure how to respond, Lemere shrugged. Of course his son's mother was pretty. Lemere didn't mess with ugly females. He wasn't going to say that to Amree, though.

"Your son is handsome. He's already my favorite person connected to you." She smiled warmly, meaning every word.

"You don't even know his little bad ass."

"I've seen enough. Besides, I'm going to enjoy him being nice to me now, because after I kick his butt in video games, he's not going to like me anymore."

"I almost forgot how competitive you were. It's coo' though, 'cause I taught my junior not to take no prisoners nor show mercy 'cause you a girl. So, if you think he gon' lie down and take a beating, you tripping." Taking her by the hand, Lemere held it to his lips and kissed it.

"Well, until we can see which of us is right, how about you show me what you can do with what's under this towel? You thought earlier was enough to make up for a whole month apart?" Standing from the bed, she allowed the towel to drop, waiting for him to do as she requested.

Lemere stood off to the side with his arms folded and a proud smirk on his face as he watched Amree's butt jiggle as she moved about her kitchen in her gray ribbed boy shorts and muscle tank from Skims. Her hair was pulled into a messy bun, and her face was free of makeup. In her natural state was always Lemere's favorite way to see her. He took one last look at her, staring at the top of her head all the way to the white polish on her perfectly pedicured toes.

"How long are you going to stand there just watching me?" she asked as she stood on her tippy toes and opened the cabinet.

"If you keep standing like that, probably another few minutes," he teased. Amree being on her tippy toes with her arms extended put an arch in her back, which made her ass stick out more and the muscles in her legs flex, and it was a sight Lemere had no problem keeping in front of him a bit longer.

"Well, guess it was fun while it lasted." She pulled the box of grits down and stood to her natural height before turning toward Lemere with a smile, which he returned as he made his way toward her. Taking her by the waist, he pulled Amree into him, kissing her soft lips.

"I hate that you have to leave tonight," she expressed when their lips separated.

"Me too, but it won't be long before we're back together. Plus, we'll be on FaceTime like always."

"Wait, that almost sounds like you have a problem with being on FaceTime for hours with me."

"Did I say that? And how could that be true when I call you more than you call me? I'm starting to think you the one with the FaceTime issue." Lemere raised his brows, looking at her as if he was really wondering if his words were facts.

"Now you know that isn't true. You call more sometimes because your schedule is crazy. I'm usually always doing one of three things: working, taking Tyler to school, or being home with Tyler. We'd talk and see each other a lot more if it were up to me."

"I was only playing with you." He kissed her forehead and dropped his hands from her waist, taking a seat on the barstool at the kitchen island. Amree knew he was joking but still felt a bit sad by his words, so she went back to fixing their breakfast.

"You mad?" he asked, noticing the change in her demeanor.

"No. Can you take the trash out for me please?" she turned toward him, smiling.

"I'm a damn superstar and you want me to take out the trash?" he teased.

"Yep, because when we're together I run things."

"Yeah, a'ight. You know you paying me in ass before I hit the road, right?"

"Wouldn't have it any other way."

Lemere chuckled before he rose and headed to the garage where she kept the trash cans. He removed the bag, then headed back toward the front, kissing her cheek first before he walked out the door. Lemere left her door wide open while he walked to the side of the house to grab her large trash cans to pull to the front of the street. He never noticed someone walking up.

Amree heard footsteps enter and was shocked Lemere had returned so quickly.

"What did you forget? Because there's no way you pulled both trash cans that quickly," she yelled from the kitchen.

"I don't know about any trash cans, but I know that you're somebody I could never forget."

The voice, how deep it was and smooth yet condescending, froze her in place. She hadn't heard this person's voice in well over a year and found it crazy how quickly it took her back to a place she promised to never visit again. Amree stepped away from the stove and took the couple steps to her living room to confirm that who she thought was speaking was in fact her ex, Troy.

"Wh . . . what are you doing here?" It was him, standing there looking as handsome as she remembered. He still had that boyish look to him, reminding her of a darker Trey Songz.

"I'm home." He said it so easily, like it was really going to be that easy for him to get her back.

"Excuse you?" She frowned, backing away as he made his way closer to her.

"I know you're not still mad at me." He looked at her with the same expression that used to have her forgiving him no matter what he'd done. Before she could respond, more footsteps were coming her way, and this time she didn't step back.

"You all right?" Lemere asked, noticing she wore a blank expression on her face. He didn't know who was standing in Amree's living room and didn't care to find out, as he gave dude his back. She was his first priority, and if someone was going to get hurt, he'd take that lick to protect her.

"Yes."

"Who are you?" Troy asked, causing Lemere to finally turn around. He saw the glimpse of excitement flash in Troy's eyes and noticed when he quickly composed himself. Lemere was too big of a star for Troy to not know who he was.

"Nah, nigga, who is you? You know exactly who I am." Lemere flexed, standing tall, ready for whatever.

Troy nodded with a smirk on his face. He immediately recognized the protective stance Lemere took over Amree. Only a man in love would react that way. He knew everyone in her small family and knew Lemere was of no relation to her, so it was obvious they were fucking.

"I'm the love of her life, the nigga she probably thinks about every time y'all fucking," Troy spoke cockily.

"Nah, my nigga. I highly doubt that, when the neighbors know my name when I'm in it." Now it was Lemere who had a smirk on his face as he watched Troy turn red and the veins in his forehead protrude.

Amree couldn't believe the two men were talking about her like she wasn't there and comparing the way they made love to her. Granted, Lemere was the best lover she ever had, but she didn't care for him to have a dick-swinging contest with her ex.

"Anyway, Amree, can we talk?" Troy looked around Lemere at her.

She wasn't sure what to say. She was curious as to why he was there. He said it was because he missed her, and a part of her wanted to know, if he missed her, why'd it take so much time for him to realize it? The other part of her knew she should tell him to kiss her ass and get out of her home. But for some reason she couldn't do either one, so she only looked at him. It felt like she was staring a bit too long because now Lemere was looking at her. And he didn't look happy.

"What do you want, Troy?" She finally found her voice, and it was apparent that the wrong thing came out when Lemere nodded and walked away, heading up the stairs and for her bedroom.

"That's your dude now?" Troy asked.

"Who I'm dating is none of your business. Why are you here? Matter of fact, you need to leave." Seeing the look on Lemere's face and how he walked away made her realize that Troy's reasoning for showing up meant nothing to her if she would lose Lemere in the process of finding out.

"You serious?"

"I am. You have to go."

"Nah, not until you hear me out."

"Leave." Her voice echoed through the house.

As angry as he was, Lemere would be a bitch if he allowed her to go back and forth with a man she clearly wanted out of her presence, so he made his way back down the stairs.

"Ay, she said yo' time is up, so it's time for you to go."

"I ain't scared of you. This used to be my shit. I done hugged, kissed, and done some more shit with her in damn near every room in this house. I got a right to be here."

"I'm not gon' tell you anymore."

"Troy, leave before I call the cops," Amree spoke up. The last thing she wanted was them fucking up her house, because she could tell they were moments away from coming to blows.

"It's coo'. I'll talk to you later." Troy left as fast as he'd come, and Amree immediately tried to explain to Lemere.

"I didn't invite him here."

"But you didn't put his ass right out either. Look, it's coo'."

"No, it's not, Mere. I—"

"And you having sex with me in spots that nigga had sex with you?"

Amree frowned. Yes, Troy had been with her in this home, but he exaggerated. They had sex but never like she and Lemere had, because Troy had nothing on him, and he wasn't that adventurous.

"No, and just so you know, when he and I broke up I got rid of every piece of furniture and started over. I even changed Tyler's bedroom because I didn't want any memories of him here."

"A'ight," was all Lemere said before walking back into the kitchen. She was unsure of what else to say, and he obviously wasn't interested in her pleading her case, so she finished cooking.

By the time she had to take him to the airport he was acting a bit better, but she was still afraid that he may be done with her.

Chapter 13

Amree looked at the date displayed on her Apple Watch and took a mental note to mark this day as the official game changer. Today, she was going to be working while also doing her best to be a supportive girlfriend. How she was going to balance the two, she had no idea. Making both work was at the top of her priority list, so it would be done. Especially because the last time they were together the bull crap with Troy happened, and she was uncertain they would come back from it. It took a long conversation that she practically had to force Lemere to have with her to fix things. She understood how her actions made him feel, and he thankfully understood she was just in shock. She wasn't sure that he had fully forgiven her, but where they were today was a start, and she was happy about it.

"Where do you want me to set up?" Johnny, her magazine's cameraman asked. They were standing outside, away from the crowd, with the perfect view of everyone walking in. The glass windows made it easy to see the comings and goings of the guests.

"Right here should be fine. Then feel free to move around. All the guests in attendance are aware that there's going to be media coverage, so there shouldn't be any issues. Plus, unlike the people here who don't care about anything other than the views they'll get on their web pages, we will let the man of the hour view the photos and approve which we can put out. So get as many as you can. Lemere will be making his entrance through those doors, also." She pointed to the area where her man would be making his grand entrance very soon.

"Cool." Immediately, he went to work, setting up his tripod and getting his camera settings ready. This was his first time shooting an album-listening party, so he wanted to make a good impression on not only the magazine's editor, but also with whoever he was blessed to have in front of his camera. He would never be opposed to doing freelance photography on the side, especially for what he knew the people in attendance could pay.

Amree's eyes moved from Johnny setting up to the throngs of people continuing to scatter around. There were a lot of people in attendance, making her proud of the love Lemere was being shown. There was no reason for her to think he'd receive anything less. It still always amazed her seeing him in his element and being praised for the work he put in.

"This is a big turnout, and we still have some time before it starts. I'm sure I'm going to get some really good footage," Johnny spoke, regaining Amree's attention.

"I agree."

Lemere rented a mansion overlooking Los Angeles. It wasn't the traditional location for an album-listening party, which was the point. His entire family were in attendance, well, all whom he considered important enough to be there and meet her. His main concern was LJ being comfortable. Had he had the party at any reception hall or club location, LJ's comfort would have been null and void. Amree had yet to meet his mother and son, who Lemere seemed to be very anxious to make the introductions to.

Not quite ready, Amree used having to work as an excuse to avoid them. So far, it bought her plenty of time. Her alarm going off on her wrist let her know she no longer had room to avoid the meeting. She was due in five minutes to the dressing room Lemere was getting ready in. The time he requested was 5:45 p.m. so that introductions could be made as well as to make sure she was on his arm when he stepped into his party at six.

"I've gotta go. After his walk-through—grand entrance, rather—if you have questions, don't hesitate to ask me. I'll find you not long after, because I still have interviews to conduct."

"No problem. You okay with me taking photos of you too? You're the date of the man of the hour, and I'm sure these other people here will be snapping whether you like it or not. At least we can keep the narrative honest."

Amree looked at Johnny as if he'd said something she hadn't known. Of course photos would circulate of her and Lemere. Hell, there were already a few out there. Yet because of her job, no one had officially put out the narrative that they were dating. It would surely be known tonight she was his girl, because Lemere was adamant that he wasn't hiding his affection toward her, nor her title. Tonight wasn't only about his album. It was also going to be about their relationship.

"Uh, I mean, yeah." There was no way she could tell him no and no way she could avoid her photo being taken anyway. Johnny was right. Every picture of her and Lemere near each other would be snapped and published.

"Hey, cousin-in-law, you need to get inside the house like now." A gentle tug on her arm had Amree looking to her left to see Millie standing before her, smiling and looking gorgeous in a navy blue Fendi pantsuit. They had become acquainted since Millie was the one who altered Lemere's calendar over the last couple of months to make sure he and Amree got their quality time in. Still, this was the first time she'd greeted her as "cousin-in-law," and it caught her off guard.

"Cousin-in-law?" she repeated, wanting to be positive she heard Millie correctly. There was loud music playing, and her nerves were all over the place, so she could've been hearing things . . . maybe.

"I got this," Johnny said as he watched Millie pull Amree away.

"Girl, yes, you heard me right. My cousin is openly claiming you, and you're meeting his son and mama. You are family, honey," she informed her as they stepped inside the mansion. People were still walking through, heading toward the backyard where all the festivities would take place. Compliments, as well as a few comments about renting or buying the place, were loudly spoken among the guests. Her initial reaction to seeing the mansion was the same, minus the desire to rent or purchase. She had, fortunately, gotten to take the grand tour with Lemere and Millie the night before, even getting in a quickie with Lemere in the master bedroom while Millie finalized paperwork.

"Can I ask you something?" Amree stopped at the bottom of the stairway. The closer they got, the more her nerves were getting the best of her.

"Sure." The look on Amree's face had her pulling her into a more secluded area underneath the stairs. "What's up?"

"Is your aunt going to like me? Is there anything I should steer clear of?" Amree fidgeted with her thumbs and index fingers. It had been a while since she met a man's mother. Not to mention, she'd never met the mother of a celebrity. So any heads-up she could get wouldn't go unappreciated.

"My aunt is coo' as hell. She'll like you. I mean, she's going to be skeptical because of who her son is. Your advantage is that he wants the two of you to meet. She knows like the rest of us that if he wasn't feeling you, didn't see a future with or trust you, you wouldn't be here. Lemere would've come with his mother as his date before having a female with him the media would've given him romantic ties to. All you have to do when you meet her is be yourself. All right?" Millie gave her a wink and reassuring smile before taking her by the hand, leading her up the stairs.

The only way to get over whatever fear Amree had was to throw her into the water and make her swim, so that's what she did. As soon as they made it to the room where Lemere and everyone were waiting, she pushed Amree inside so hard she had to catch her footing. The push was intentional, causing her to almost bust her ass. Sweet Amree had gone out the window once she composed herself. The look she gave Millie damn near scared her, causing her to toss her hands up in surrender. Millie was in no way a punk nor scared of Amree, but she also witnessed how quickly Amree could prepare a can of whoop-ass.

My kinda girl. She didn't take Amree for a weak
woman, but she also didn't take her for an outspo-
ken one. She wouldn't make that mistake again.
That one reaction from Amree told her what she
needed to know, which was that Amree could handle herself and Lemere if need be.

"You good, bae?" Lemere asked, pulling her into
him. Taking her by the chin, he kissed her lips,
hoping to relax her.

"I'm fine." Wrapping her arms around his neck,
she allowed her body to relax, getting lost in his
embrace until the sound of someone clearing their
throat interrupted their moment.

Pulling back some, Lemere looked around
Amree to see his mother with her arms crossed
over her chest and a cute smirk on her face. He
knew she was happy to see this form of affection
toward a woman other than family from her son.
She hadn't seen him this into a woman since the
day he brought Kiana to meet her for the first time.

"Babe, turn around so you can meet my moms,"
he spoke into Amree's ear.

Immediately Amree's heart fell to her stomach
as embarrassment washed over her. She couldn't
help wondering if his mom saw the look of death
she gave Millie as well as her almost busting her
ass. It was also rude of her to not acknowledge
anyone else in the room, even though she wasn't
sure how long his mother had been in there. The
whole time, she assumed.

Taking a deep breath, she slowly stepped away from Lemere and extended her hand to a gorgeous woman. She could see a definite resemblance between Lemere and his mother.

"Ma, this is my girlfriend, Amree. Amree, this is my mother, Leandria."

"Hi, Miss Leandria, it's nice to meet you." Amree took two steps forward, extending her hand, although the face before her did not appear inviting at all. The hard expression lasted only a few seconds, though it felt like minutes before Leandria smiled, taking Amree's open hand and using it to pull her into a hug.

"You don't have to be shy around me with your pretty self," Leandria complimented her, releasing Amree from their hug to take her by the shoulders, giving her a once-over.

As always, Amree did look amazing. Her signature orange tips were poppin', due to the recent dye touch-up, and moving effortlessly, due to the silk press she'd gotten for tonight. Her makeup was done naturally, only enhancing the already-flawless features of her beautiful face. Light makeup had been Lemere's request when she wanted to try something new and go bold. He'd grown to love her in her natural state and had told her to rock her face bare. A soft beat had been their compromise.

"Ooh, and you two are matching," Leandria stated, noticing how Amree's nude spaghetti-strap

Christian Dior dress matched the nude dress shirt and black Dior slacks Lemere wore. "You two look good together. I'm looking forward to getting to know you, Ms. Amree."

Amree blushed, appreciative of the acceptance she showed in only a short amount of time in each other's presence. "Same. I'm really looking forward to it."

"Daddy!" The cutest little boy she'd seen since laying eyes on Tyler came rushing through the room, stopping to wrap as much of his arms around his father's legs as possible.

"What's up little man? You ready?" Lemere asked, picking his son up, kissing him on the cheek as LJ squirmed and giggled. Placing him on his feet, he turned him around so he could come face-to-face with Amree . . . well, once she knelt down so they could make eye contact.

"Amree!" The same loud, excited greeting he gave his father, he gave to her, making her smile because his joy was so infectious.

"Hi, LJ." Her arms opened wide, inviting him into them as if it were second nature. The immediate comfort she felt with LJ didn't scare her, nor did she feel any hesitancy to embrace him as if she'd known him his whole life. Apparently, he felt the same, because he rushed into her arms without hesitation, squeezing her as tight as his little arms could.

"Ay, man, that's enough. Let go of my girl," Lemere interjected.

"Okay, LJ, your daddy is jealous because you're my favorite, so we're going to make him happy for a few short minutes, okay?"

"Okay, but are you going to my dad's house after this?" His young mind didn't grasp the jealousy Amree spoke of.

"I am."

"Good, we can play my video games."

After agreeing to play with LJ once they made it to Lemere's, everyone did a last once-over before heading to the party. Amree was blinded by the flashing lights, and her ears couldn't distinguish any of the many voices shouting their congrats and *salud*'s at Lemere. She did her best to keep her smile intact, knowing the cameras were watching, refusing to be caught looking terrible and giving people more to talk about. How devastating would it be to be called Lemere's "funny-looking date"? After he greeted the majority of his guests, Millie was on the microphone, thanking everyone for showing up, and introducing Lemere. Amree watched in awe as he swaggered to the stage.

"I want to thank y'all again for coming out and fucking with ya boy. This is my sophomore album. The pressure been real. That don't mean I don't want y'all to keep it one hundred with me. Without further ado, here's track one. This song is called 'The Definition.' There isn't a big story behind this one other than I've elevated and I wanted people to know who I am . . . well, evolved into during the process of this album." Placing the mic at his side, he turned toward the DJ, giving him the okay to play the song.

This was also Amree's first time hearing his latest music, aside from what was playing on the radio. Like everyone else, she was impressed. The lyrics Lemere spit on track one described the person she was getting to know to a T, as well as enlightening her on a few things she didn't know. By the time the song ended, everyone was on their feet applauding, herself included.

The rest of the songs played, reaching the end quicker than expected. Time was sure to fly when there was a good time being had. As he stood to introduce the last song, Amree's phone began to vibrate. Seeing the private caller display across the screen, she grinned before standing and walking as far away from the speakers and crowd as she could get. After accepting the call by pressing the numbers prompted, she was delighted to hear her brother's voice on the other end.

"What up, baby sis, where you at? Your background loud as hell," Maksym acknowledged, a tad irritated that she answered a call she wouldn't comfortably be able to take. He knew his sister though. She would accept a call from him if she were on a plane that was going down. Maksym's calls would never go unanswered if she could help it.

"I, uh, I'm working."

"Word, that's what's up. What industry party they got you at now?"

"It's an album release par—" Before Amree could finish her sentence, her phone was being removed from her hand.

"Who is this?" Lemere asked, placing Amree's phone to his ear. He knew he was tripping, having no real reason to doubt her. But the grin on her face while she walked away to take the call made him feel uneasy.

"Nigga, who the fuck is you? Matter of fact, fuck who you is. Give Amree back her phone." Maksym had received his share of disrespect, but nothing like this, especially not behind his sister.

"Don't trip. She busy with a real nigga." Lemere ended the call, placing her phone into his right pocket.

"Who was that?"

"Really?"

"Yeah, really and matter of fact, so that I don't feel disrespected at any other point tonight. You may as well axe interviewing any of these rap niggas in here." Lemere had already been feeling skeptical and honestly a bit insecure about her interviewing his peers. He just hadn't known how to tell her he didn't want her to do it. This whole situation gave him the excuse he needed to put it out there.

Frowning, she looked at him as if she had no clue who he was. At this moment she didn't. There was no way he was really this jealous, especially when she had held her composure on more than one occasion in the presence of groupie bitches. She'd never shown her hand in public, so she was surprised he wasn't doing the same. To avoid any further unnecessary drama, she agreed to humor him with an answer.

"That was my brother, Lemere." Her tone was flat, full of annoyance.

"Oh, shit. My bad, babe, I'm tripping." Remorse displayed on his face as her cell vibrating in his pocket pulled his attention. Without hesitation, he removed it, answering her phone as if it were something he did on the regular. Maksym's voice came through the phone aggressively, so much so that she could hear him clearly. Lemere's album played in the background.

"Ay, man, my bad. This Lemere. I was trippin'," he apologized.

"I don't know a Lemere, my nigga. If I did, he'd know better than to take my sister's phone while I'm speaking to her on some 'whatever the fuck you on' type shit."

"Lemere Webster, the rapper. Your sister is at my album release party. You right. I give you that.

I fucked up. It's just . . . your sister, man, loving a girl like her, then this rosé, seeing her smiling in the phone and shit . . . I blanked out. I can't even front. Out of respect though, it won't happen again. My fault, for real."

Maksym heard everything Lemere said, but still he was too pissed to marinate on the apology. He was still worried about the act, not him trying to make it right. Not only that, but Lemere was professing his love for his sister, and he didn't even know she was dating the nigga. The apology and excuses were cool and all. However, to him they were also red flags. Lemere being a rap star and a popular, rich nigga meant nothing to him when it came to his sister. Dude's music was nice. He felt a lot of his lyrics and had even dubbed him one of his top ten lyrical rappers until now. He surely had to be brought down a few notches, due to disrespect. His newfound attitude toward Lemere would no longer be appeasing until he had a serious talk with his sister.

"I feel you, bro. Let me holla at my sis though. I only have so much time left on these phones. I won't keep her long. I'm aware she has a job to do. Hopefully, you and I will get to chop it up another time."

"Most definitely. I look forward to it. My bad again. Here's your sister." Lemere extended the phone to Amree, leaning in and kissing her cheek before issuing an apology to her as well. He was sure she too was pissed at him, yet the blank expression she wore told him nothing.

In reality, her mind was racing. She knew Maksym was pissed, probably feeling betrayed. Then Lemere told her brother about loving her and had yet to say the words to her.

"Hey." Her tone was soft, almost childlike, as she greeted her brother for the second time that night. She wanted to immediately apologize but knew Maksym would have a fit if she apologized for the actions of a grown-ass man.

"You need to get up here ASAP, Am-E. Leave my son, too. You and I need to have a real-ass conversation."

"I know. I will. I love you, Maksym."

"I love you too. Get up here soon, Am-E."

"I promise. Next week."

"All right." The line went silent.

Blowing out an exasperated breath, she moved her eyes from the random parts of the crowd to a puppy-faced Lemere standing in front of her. "Why would you act like that?" To say she was irritated only described her emotions lightly. She wasn't sure if Lemere wanted to see her act out or what. "And to tell me not to do my job? What has gotten into you?" She knew the Troy situation was also probably a reason, but she wanted to act like it never happened, so she wouldn't bring it up. She only hoped that he didn't as well.

"I'm drunk, was tripping. All night, niggas been whispering about how fine you are and shit. I just forgot who I was dealing with for a second. It was wrong and disrespectful of me to react the way I did. It won't happen again, on me." Taking her by the waist, he pulled her into him, placing his forehead to hers.

"It bet' not. I see how you tried to butter my brother up, talking about love." She knew she was letting him off a bit too easy. Maksym wouldn't approve of the move at all. But he was drunk and acting out of character. Tonight was a big night for him, so he'd get a pass this time.

"Nah, that wasn't cap. Meant every word I said. Loving a girl like you got a nigga ready to risk it all." Leaning in, he pressed his lips against hers.

She wanted to resist, but his lips on hers were entirely too soothing to remove. The kiss relaxed her, something she needed to get through the rest of the night.

Chapter 14

With her hands clasped together in front of her and extended and resting on the table, Amree's left leg shook violently. Her nerves were all over the place as she tried, to no avail, to calm down. Today's visit was different. She'd gotten there first, which meant that he'd probably lay eyes on her before she did him. The last thing she wanted to show was a lack of confidence, even if that was exactly what she was currently missing. Yes, she was an adult. She could handle herself, knew right from wrong, and could make her own decisions, many of them being the right decision. And still, she knew the last time they spoke would leave all those things up for debate. Squeezing her already-clasped hands tighter, she shut her eyes and put her head down silently, reciting affirmations of strength and confidence to herself. The loud sound of clanking gates caused her to lift her head in the direction she knew the gates would be opening.

Maksym was the first guy in line. She watched as he did a quick sweep of the area before his eyes met hers. Like clockwork, they offered each other a weak yet loving smile. Regardless of the situation, they would always be happy to see one another.

"Hi," she greeted him as soon as he sat down. Though nervous, Amree looked in her brother's face, studying him to see if there were any physical changes. She knew he was upset or disappointed, probably both. Still, her guilt wouldn't stop her from checking on him or at least looking for the stress, turmoil, or physical diminishes she could see on the outside.

"Nah, get to talking. How long you been dealing with dude?"

"Since you told me to go out on my date."

"That was months ago, Am-E."

"I know. I wasn't sure where things were going to go between us, so I didn't want to tell you. Then things started moving along—"

"All them excuses, sis. What's the real reason you didn't just come out and tell me?"

"Because I didn't want to tell you over the phone. I also fucked up by making my new relationship and Tyler priorities, which prevented me from getting out here to you to tell you." She looked her brother in the eyes, being honest while feeling like shit.

"Now that the hard part is out of the way, I'm assuming the relationship is going good since the nigga talking about loving you and shit." He smiled, easing the tension between them.

Smiling back, Amree allowed what her brother said to linger for a moment. His words took her back to that night, to those words Lemere spoke. She still wasn't too sure of the validity, no matter how good it felt hearing them. Strong feelings for her he probably did have. Loving her, though? She wouldn't believe the words until he flat-out said it while not being under the influence or jealous of the attention she was getting.

"I mean, we have grown very close. I'm not going to sugarcoat my feelings, because I see myself potentially falling for him. I'm falling for him," she admitted, looking away from Maksym off into the sky as what she admitted so openly shocked her.

Instead of providing his opinion right at that moment, Maksym cleared his throat, regaining her attention and encouraging her to continue.

"My bad. Anyway, it's all still new to me. I'm adjusting to a relationship and lifestyle like one I've never had nor witnessed before. He treats me good. Respects my wishes. Has introduced me to every member of his family he's close to. Shows understanding with how guarded I am or can be, because we all know I like my privacy. I'm sure he cares, likes me a lot, even possibly is falling for me too. Loving me? I won't lie and say I'm certain of that, because I'm not a 'love at first sight, fall in love after a month' type of girl. Not that it's impossible." She shrugged.

"I don't like the way dude took yo' phone out of your hand."

She knew this was coming. She also had no words to justify Lemere's actions, because what he'd done was wrong, as well as childish. He didn't paint himself in the best light with his actions, nor did his apology change anything. It only acknowledged that he knew he fucked up. And though she knew she should probably tell him what happened with Troy, she decided against it because, though it would help Maksym understand Lemere's reaction a little bit, he still wouldn't allow that to be an excuse.

"Neither did I, which I told him about. It won't happen again."

"Look, what I'm about to say to you in no way is to disrespect you or doubt the strength we both know you possess. Still, I gotta get this off my chest, or I wouldn't be me, nor would I be respecting the foundation of honesty we've built. It only takes a man, hell, a person to be disrespectful one time and get away with it for them to feel they have a second or third time to do it again. Dude has bitches . . . women at his disposal, so to react the way he did when he should know you not that kind of woman don't sit right with me at all. We've witnessed shit like this—"

"Maksym, this isn't that. No way in hell could or would it ever be." Her voice rose an octave as sadness and anger set in. She heard him when he said he had no intention of disrespecting her. However, the comparison she knew he was getting ready to make left her feeling utterly disrespected.

"I didn't say it was, Am-E," he tried reasoning.

"You're insinuating it, though. That's not okay. I'm not okay with you even doing that," she spoke, full of emotion. Her voice cracked as tears welled in her eyes.

"That's not what I'm doing either. I'm referencing, reminding you that it's possible for shit to start off as a little jealousy only to turn into some big shit." His voice raised some unintentionally. However, his own frustrations were setting in.

"Do you really think I could ignore . . . overlook those kinds of signs? Do you know how long it took me to even forgive her? How many times a day to this day that I recite affirmations reminding me of how strong I am and not to take any bullshit and to get the fuck out at the first sign of wrong?" The tears that had been sitting, pooling in her eyes, had now filled over capacity, streaming down her face without any indication of stopping.

With his right hand, Maksym wiped the invisible sweat from the top of his head down to his chin while blowing out a frustrated breath. Her tears would always rip pieces of his heart. Right now, he had to keep his tough exterior because his sister was his heart. Protecting her would always be his first priority no matter what was at stake.

"I don't. I know you know better. Know you know how to protect yourself. That's not the point. The point I was trying to make is that we seen Auntie put up with a lot of shit. Seen her fall for the okey-doke one too many times. She mistook control for love. I know you're strong. I know you're not like her. Even know that the shit you seen from her was traumatizing. I worked my ass off instilling in you how valuable you are and teaching you the games niggas play, how to know the real from the fake. As well as how to be the kind of woman a man will love and appreciate. Anything like what he did will always present a red flag to me. I don't care who the nigga is. I'd get out this ho to come right back 'bout you. To be honest, I'm even more skeptical because of who he is. He gotta show me he deserves you."

Amree heard her brother loud and clear. She wiped the tears from her face while nodding her understanding as she contemplated if she had needed that small reminder of their childhood. Being raised by their aunt was always good until she had a man. They didn't want for anything. There was no lack of love given. Still, the lack of love they saw her have for herself was devastating, especially for Amree who, without Maksym, would've molded herself behind the woman she saw every day. Cooking, cleaning, and being responsible were a few of the qualities she openly took from her aunt. Confidence, self-assurance, and self-love were all instilled in her through Maksym, because those were obvious things her aunt wasn't able to teach her.

"I only want the best for you. You like dude, and I'm going to respect what you have with him. To be honest, he's a good catch, given he can offer you a world the average Joe can't. You know I believe you deserve the world. So, you know there's only one thing for you to do to keep me out yo' hair." He chuckled, lightening the tense mood.

Amree stared at him, waiting for his answer and questioning what it was, knowing that he would tell her anyway, would be a waste of time.

"Be you. Keep yo' eyes open, and don't take no shit. Keep it known that you are one of a kind and that he the one who lucked up, not you. Deal?"

Smiling, she extended her hand. "Deal." They shook before slapping hands for their signature handshake they'd made up as kids when sealing the deal to a promise. Though still skeptical, Maksym felt a lot better about his sister's new relationship.

"I have some good news."

"Why didn't you start with that?"

"Because we had more pressing matters to attend to. Anyway, I'm coming home sooner rather than later."

"Are you serious?" she squealed.

"Dead ass. With the laws that passed during the Obama era, I qualify to get out early. No parole, 'cause you know I'd sit my ass in here if that were the case. No dates yet. You'll know all that when I do. I see the millions of questions ready to roll off your tongue. I don't got nothing for you but what I offered."

"Fine." Amree smiled.

During the rest of the visit, she updated him on Tyler and Erynn and told him a little bit more about Lemere. By the time she left the visit with her brother, she had a whole new outlook on life and love and was very optimistic about the future.

"You're at the peak of your career, and you choose now to come out as a nigga in a relationship?" Thomas barked at Lemere while holding up his phone for him to see. "This shit right here, boy, I tell ya."

Thomas looked at Lemere in disgust, irritated with his nonchalant attitude and disregard of his arm, which had already gotten tired of holding his phone out for Lemere to see.

Sure, Thomas was aware that he'd seen the photos and blog posts circulating. Still, as his manager, he wanted respect. He wanted him to acknowledge what he was fussing about.

"Lemere." Thomas's voice vibrated off the walls of the tour bus. He wanted to gain Lemere's attention. Now he had it. Lemere's eyes cut up at Thomas, chilling the blood rushing through his veins.

"I didn't mean to raise my voice, man. I'm only trying to get you to see things from my point of view."

"You want me to say I'm single when I'm not. Fuck would I do that for?"

"Because you have a fan base of women who desire you more because you're single. Besides, you don't have to be single, only portray yourself as such."

"You've known about me and Amree for months. Sat and smiled all in her face just a week ago. What the fuck is the real problem?"

"Didn't say I didn't like her. She's a beautiful girl, probably extremely good for you on a personal level but sure as hell not on a professional one. Most artists wait until they about four or five albums in the game before letting the world know they're taken. You come out as a nigga in a relationship right before your sophomore album is due to drop."

Lemere could see Thomas age right before his eyes. Homeboy was stressed the hell out. So much so, he had Lemere second-guessing his decision. Was it a mistake to announce being in a relationship right before his album dropped? He hoped like hell it wasn't.

"It'll be fine. My music and talent speak for themselves. My fans gon' ride for me off that info alone."

"You trying to convince me or yourself? I already know what's gonna happen. Your shit gon' sell, no doubt about it. The numbers would be larger from a single rapper, though."

Thomas had seen right through Lemere's supposedly convincing speech. He was also thankful that his words were getting to him. He'd instilled enough fear to have him doubting his decision. As long as there was even an ounce of doubt in Lemere's mind, he had the ammo he needed to make him do things he wouldn't necessarily do. However, if there was one thing he'd learned while working with Lemere, it was that his ego was a mothafucka.

"I said what I said, Thom. Besides, you work for me, not the other way around."

"Cool. Hopefully, your relationship won't stop you from showing the strippers love. We'll be pulling up to KOD shortly. You know them hoes love you. They'll be all on you. Can you handle that, or will your girlfriend scold you because of it?"

"I'm a grown-ass man. I'm poppin' shit in KOD as I've always done."

"Prove it. We're here."

The tour bus came to a stop, causing Lemere to peer out the back window. Sure enough, they had arrived.

"Come on. I'm ready to go spend tens and fifties to see some ass and titties," Mason spoke excitedly as he came through the door, smiling while rubbing his hands together in anticipation.

"Give me a second. I'll meet y'all up front," Lemere spoke, looking from Mason to Thomas before retrieving his cell from the cushion beside him.

"This nigga 'bout to ask for permission," Mason said, looking at his cousin's tense demeanor.

"You got me fucked up." Lemere's nostrils flared as he balled his fists. First Thomas and now his cousin. They were getting on his nerves. "Get the fuck out." His tone was calm yet free of bullshit, so both men knew not to say anything else.

Lemere looked at his phone, contemplating if he was still going to send the message he planned to send before his manager and cousin decided to open their big mouths.

"Fuck them. I can do me and have my girl," he mumbled before sending a good night text to Amree, letting her know where he was and not to wait up. A simple okay and good night reply was enough for him to be content with his decision. Pocketing his cell, he stood, checking himself in the mirror once more before heading toward the

front. He kept going, not bothering to acknowledge anyone, knowing they'd follow regardless.

Strobe lights danced around the dark club as
they walked inside. Anytime Lemere was present,
all eyes were on him. Quickly, his crew went to
their section, and within seconds of him taking
his seat, the women were entering. Lemere's eyes
landed on one of his favorite girls, and beyond his
control, his dick stiffened.

"Fuck," he mouthed as she took a seat on his lap
as if she owned it.

Chapter 15

Amree watched Lemere's name flash across her screen, stop, then show up again. She'd been dodging his calls for the last few minutes, as that was all it took for her to be questioning him and the validity of their relationship. Ironically, everything was cool last night. They'd ended their conversation on a good note as they always did. He wasn't even supposed to have access to his phone currently, which was another reason she was dodging him. His anxiousness to speak with her during a time he was supposed to be unavailable only seemed to be an admission of guilt. The issue was she wasn't sure if he was even guilty. Feeling her phone vibrate in her hand, she rolled her eyes before looking down and seeing his name again, this time in the form of a text message.

From Lemere: I know you see me calling. Can you pick up for me, please?

Shaking her head, she hovered over the keyboard, debating whether to reply. When she exited her messages she got her answer. Right now wasn't the time for her to respond nor for them to talk. So, she was about to put his ass on ice until she figured out how she was feeling. Months ago, she spoke to him about playing bitches too close. No, they weren't together then. Still, she let him know she found his actions unacceptable. Still, she expected him to keep that in mind, with respecting her at all times at the forefront. She also couldn't help feeling like it was payback even though she knew it wasn't.

Her phone rang again. He was calling back. Like the first few calls, she watched his name flash until the missed call notification appeared. Staring at her phone, she was surprised that more than five seconds had gone by without seeing his name. Another ten, still nothing.

"He can kiss my ass," she mumbled before walking over to the end table in her living room, taking a seat on her sofa. The comfort she felt was short-lived due to someone pressing incessantly on her doorbell.

"I know he didn't." Her heart rate sped up almost instantly at the thought. Quickly, she stood. It was like her body acted in familiarity as getting to him was always an urgency. She stood fast yet moved slow. It was still up for debate whether she was upset with him.

"I'm coming," she yelled, irritated. Hoping that the noise didn't wake Tyler, and fueled by irritation, she pushed the questions to the back of her mind and headed to the door. Checking the peephole first, she felt her chest tighten as her heart skipped a beat at the sight before her.

"What are you doing here?" She snatched the door open.

"Well, hello to you too, sister-in-law." The smirk plastered on her face pissed Amree off another notch.

"Bitch. I will drag . . . You know what?" She took a deep breath, shut her eyes, and pulled together her fingers of her right hand in front of her face, pulling them down from her forehead to chin as an additional method to calm her. Between Lemere and now Colene showing up on her front door, she was a pin drop from going off.

"Number one, quit the smart sister-in-law stuff. We both know I don't like you, never have. Second, to show up at my house without asking says a lot about who you *still* are as a person. This is the first and last time you'll show up like you pay bills here. I'm going to extend you a courtesy this one time only." With her hands folded across her chest, left hip poked out some, Amree looked Colene in the eyes so she wouldn't miss how serious she was.

"So, now that you've gotten that off your chest, can we talk like adults? Not in your doorway, preferably." Colene showed her attitude as well, placing her hands on her hips, challenging Amree with her stance. Releasing a low chuckle, Amree took a deep breath through her nose, blowing it out through her mouth. Colene was really trying her patience.

"You know what, Colene, I got a lot going on today. So, you can have my number, since it seems you don't have it, due to you not calling first. You can call me in a couple of days. Then we can set up a good time to talk." She was frustrated. She wasn't sure why Colene had shown up out of the blue, especially when Colene's mother had a way to contact her. As curious as she was to know, she also was not in the mood.

"That's not gonna work. We need to talk now. I found out about the rights I still have, so—"

"What do you want?" Amree cut her off, looking to get to the point rather than bullshitting. She was getting ready to speak.

"Shall we?" Colene extended her hand toward Amree's front door, cueing that it was time for the two of them to go inside.

Not wanting to stand in the doorway going back and forth with Colene any longer, Amree decided to humor her, allowing her inside. Her mind was made up. The invitation was going to be very brief. She could take her exit when Amree requested, or she could be forced out. Those would be the only choices given.

"You got five minutes." Amree stood to the side, allowing her into her home. She watched Colene mosey inside like she was a wanted guest, taking a seat on her sofa. She was a little too comfortable for Amree's liking. Taking a seat to the far right, leaving the middle cushion to distance them,

Amree turned her body enough to face her, legs together, back straight, and hands in her lap.

"Your time starts now."

"You know Tyler is my son, right? I could take him from you. I'm being nice by—"

"See, you starting this conversation so wrong. Tyler is my brother's son. You only birthed him. I knew you were getting out, even sympathized with you. Damn near vouched that it was okay for you to want to see Tyler. Yet, you're coming at me sideways when you're the one who abandoned him."

She paused, shaking her head in disbelief before continuing. "You threaten to do anything that's not in my nephew's best interest again, and you'll see a side of me that'll have you wishing jail was still your residence. We can talk like civilized adults, or you can get the fuck out! Three minutes," Amree spoke through clenched teeth, wanting to keep her voice down, although her anger was seconds from erupting.

"You know I've never cared about your threats. However, you should take heed to this one I'm about to send your way. I need ten thousand in cash, and you won't see me again. I know you got it, or that fine-ass, rich-ass rapper you're dating can give it to you. Either pay me or look forward to seeing me in custody court for my son."

Without a second thought, Amree was on her feet with a handful of Colene's hair in her hands. "Bitch."

"Auntie, what are you doing? You said a bad word." Tyler's voice cutting through the air not only immediately called Amree, but it caused her heart to plummet to the pit of her stomach. With her hand still gripping Colene's hair, she turned slowly to look at Tyler, who was wiping his eyes.

"I'm sorry, Tyler Maksym. Auntie's talking. Go back to your room. I'll be up shortly."

"Hi, Tyler," Colene spoke. Amree's hand on her hair had loosened unintentionally, giving her the freedom to maneuver around.

"Who are you?" Tyler asked, looking at her in utter confusion.

Amree released her hair, moving out of the way so that she was no longer blocking the view. She watched as Colene's face dropped. She could almost see where her heart caused her chest to cave from hurt, embarrassment, or both. She smirked, knowing Colene felt like shit. It was good that she did, though, coming to her house and claiming Tyler as her son, only for him to not know who she was. His lack of knowledge due to no one showing him photos of her was obviously a wise choice given that, once again, she was showing she didn't give a fuck about him. $10,000 for a person who was absolutely priceless showed just how heartless and dumb she was.

"I, uh, I'm a friend of your aunt's. I was getting ready to leave." She smiled uncomfortably. "It was nice to see you." Her voice was shaky, and the confidence she showed moments ago was nowhere to be found.

"Tyler, go to your room. I'll be up in a second." Amree had taken a firmer tone that Tyler knew not to play with, so without another word, he turned, heading back up the stairs. "You got me fucked up. Do not come back here, or you're going to be the first homicide I ever commit."

"You have a week."

"Karma is a bitch. You'll get what you deserve, and it ain't Tyler. You never deserved him. Now get the fuck out." Amree practically pushed her out the door once she snatched it open, slamming it in Colene's face before putting every lock in place. As her anger soared through her body, she paced the floor, doing her best to calm down. She couldn't believe Colene's audacity. Then again, she wasn't sure why she was so surprised. The woman had never been shit. Now she was asking for money when it'd been her and Maksym's money raising Tyler. The bitch really had some nerve. Then to assume she had it because she was dating Lemere. Jail had obviously fucked up her thinking process further, because with or without a man, Amree was paid.

The stress of the day and the million thoughts playing in her head had her feeling overwhelmed. She felt tears burning at the brim of her eyes. She stalked to the side of her sofa where she left her phone. Bypassing the six missed calls from Lemere, who had to have called during her altercation with Colene, she pressed send on Erynn's number, doing her best to control her breathing, feeling like she was on the verge of hyperventilating.

"Hey, friend."

"Er . . . Erynn," Amree forced out before bursting into tears.

"Amree, what's wrong?"

"She came here, talking about taking my nephew," she cried.

"Who? Amree, I need you to calm down so that I can understand you. What's going on?"

"Okay. One second." She allowed a few more tears to fall before wiping her eyes with the back of her hand. Stepping into her kitchen, she removed a bottled water from the fridge, taking a big gulp.

"Colene showed up to my house not too long ago, wanting ten thousand dollars for Tyler, or she said she'll take me to court. The bitch gon' say because I'm dating a rapper, I can afford it," she seethed. "I'm not giving her shit, nor am I even talking to that nigga right now. I'm so mad, Erynn, and hurt. What the fuck is wrong with people?" The water-works began again.

"You can explain about Lemere later. That bitch Colene though, hell no, you aren't giving her a dime. She also signed over her rights to Tyler.

Even if she hadn't, no judge would take him from you to give him to the bitch who left him on the front porch and has a record taller than you and me if you stood straight on my shoulders. Fuck that bitch. I'm whooping her ass, period. I'm flying out there sooner rather than later." Erynn's anger had now taken on the same rush as Amree's, if not more. She meant it. She was giving Colene the ass beating she deserved on sight. She didn't care where it happened, either. Amree called her in hopes of getting help with calming down, not thinking of the obvious, which was that Erynn would be pissed too.

"I'm not sure who she spoke to. She sounded so sure. Talking about she found out she still has rights. Erynn, she is not getting my nephew. She and I will lose our lives before that happens."

"Oh, her getting Tyler isn't something you have to worry about. You and I will figure this out together. We can't tell Maksym though. He'll flip." Erynn had calmed down enough to think clearly.

"Well, she claims I have a week to pay her trifling ass, but it's not happening. I won't say anything to Maksym though. I will be contacting a lawyer to have on standby in case it becomes necessary."

"That sounds like a plan. I'll be on the soonest flight possible. Now, explain to me why you aren't talking to Lemere. We've wasted enough time on an irrelevant bitch who won't bust a grape in a fruit fight, so what's going on with you and your man?"

"I'm not sure. I don't know what I want to do with him right now. I saw some photos on the blogs of him in a strip club, and they don't look good at all. I knew he was going to be there. I know what happens at strip clubs. Maksym always told us that as long as the man doesn't leave with the strippers, trust that he was there having a good time. I don't want to be that girl, I just—"

"Feel some type of way, which is normal, friend. If your gut tells you it's more, that's what you follow. It'll never lead you wrong. What's Lemere saying?"

"I don't know. I'm not picking up his calls or answering his texts. He's calling like crazy, which is what has me tripping. Like, if it's not how the blogs are trying to paint it, why are you so gung ho on pleading your case?"

"Um, maybe he's trying to make sure you're okay and to tell you what we already know—that these damn blogs be on one."

"I know, but I'm not ready to hear him out right now. I have to get my emotions together. He's going to have to wait until I decide how I interpreted that photo."

"I mean, it does look kinda shady. *And* it also looks like all other photos of dudes in strip clubs. If this were a photo of my dude, it wouldn't bother me."

"I hear you. It's the comments for me though. Women saying how they knew a nigga like him

couldn't be faithful. Dudes saying they'd treat me
better, or I must have low self-esteem to be with
someone like him. Others saying they know Mere
had to be *real* familiar with the ho. I mean, I get it.
People are going to talk, say shit, and blow it out
of proportion. I hate that he introduced me to the
world as his woman only to turn around and have
me in a situation that's embarrassing. Confident in
myself or not, the shit looks bad."

"When you put it that way, I can't dispute what
you're saying. Fuck them people though, for real.
Who cares what they say? Half them hoes probably
sleeping with they mattress on the floor. The
dudes talking probably got miniature dicks. So,
fuck them and what they saying. Your feelings
based on how you feel from seeing the photo are
valid. It's whatever you want, friend."

"Let me know what day you'll be out here. I have
to go check on Tyler. He came down when I
had Colene by her tacky-ass ponytail. She at least
looked decent, dressed in an old-ass Puma track
suit." She didn't want to discuss Lemere anymore.
There had been enough spoken on the situation,
leaving her with another perspective to assist her
in getting her thoughts together.

"Wait, he saw her? What did he say?"

"He asked her who she was. He knows he has a
mom, but he doesn't know what she looks like. I'm
glad about that, too. No telling how things would

have gone had he known it was her. I would've been okay with it, had she genuinely wanted to see him. She only wanted to extort money from me," she spoke, becoming emotional again.

"I'm going to book my flight, give you some time with Ty, and call you later. I know today was rough, friend. Give yourself all the time you need to process your feelings. There's no rush for you to do anything other than that, okay?"

"I know. Thank you."

Amree ended the call with Erynn, feeling numb. She had no plans of letting Colene get Tyler, ever, nor plans of speaking to Lemere until she felt ready. He could call as much as he wanted. She wouldn't answer until she processed her feelings. She didn't want to be the jealous, insecure girlfriend, which she wasn't. She only wanted to take the time to obtain tougher skin. Being with him, she knew more stories than a little would continue to come out. Some would be true, but many would not. She was either going to trust him or she wasn't. Although she said she would, the blog post and photos in the strip club were making it difficult. Coming to a conclusion on whether she could handle things like this in their relationship was nothing short of complicated.

Chapter 16

Amree extended her arm out of the driver's side window to enter the passcode, allowing entry into the large iron gate. As it opened slowly, her mind and heart seemed to be trying to process fear and happiness at the same damn time. To the left of her, Erynn's eyes were wide as saucers, staring straight ahead. At least one of them wasn't having an issue processing their arrival. Slowly she drove through the gate, bypassing the long line of cars parked one after the other along the massive driveway. She continued until she stopped in front of the garage door closest to the front entrance. Lifting her phone from the middle console, she sent a simple I'm here text before setting it back down. Moments later, the door began to lift slowly, allowing her to pull in.

"Ooh, we get VIP treatment as well? Honey, you is home," Erynn teased, smiling widely. She looked around as Amree parked their rental car and the door shut. Foreign cars were parked to the left of them. Each car screamed "expensive" so loudly she wasn't sure if they were screams warning her not to touch them or to put a bug in Amree's ear to obtain the keys.

"This is *not* my house." Amree rolled her eyes as she turned the car off. She hoped she'd have a few more minutes to sit there to gather her thoughts and to speak encouraging words to herself, which would remove the doubt, worry, regret, and anguish she felt. Or to encourage herself to embrace the small boughs of happiness and the patterns her heart tried encouraging her to fully feel. However, trying to do any of the few wasn't going to happen.

"There goes your man," Erynn stated as if her eyes couldn't see for themselves.

She'd noticed him, felt him coming their way before Erynn decided to announce his arrival. She saw him walk through the door. He was smiling, happy to see her while she stared expressionless as all of her emotions were hidden beneath her flesh. Every part of her anatomy functional to keep her alive was now heightened in a way where it was all she felt, freezing her in place.

"Um, are we getting out?" Erynn asked, popping her on the leg, jolting her from her mild state of shock.

"Yes. Can you relax please?" Amree didn't mean to snap at Erynn, yet she wasn't acting like she knew Amree hadn't at one point contemplated telling him they should only be friends with benefits when necessary.

"My bad. I'm not moving until you're ready," Erynn conceded.

Instead of replying, she removed her seat belt and turned around in her seat to see a sleeping Tyler. "He's out."

"I'll carry him," Erynn offered. Turning back around, Amree made eye contact with Erynn smiling warmly. "This is going to be a fun weekend. You're not making a mistake by being here. The look on that man's face screams, 'in love,' honey. He ain't trying to lose you. Know he'd be a damn fool if he did." Taking Amree by the hand, she squeezed it.

"All right, we'd better hurry up before he comes knocking on the window. I'm surprised he gave us this much time."

"Oh, honey, he moved an inch. I put my hand up to stop him when you were checking on Tyler. Who is that little boy?" The two of them looked at the handsome replica of Lemere at his side.

"His son. How can you not tell?" Amree snickered. "We definitely have to get out now." She smiled, opening the car door.

"Amree," LJ yelled, rushing toward her. Lemere tried stopping him but missed the collar of his shirt by an inch. Amree was glad he hadn't been able to stop him as she received such a loving embrace from him. He held her as tight as his little arms would allow as she hugged him just enough to not squeeze him to death.

"Hi, LJ." She kissed his cheek before breaking up their hug.

"Hi. I'm glad you're here. Who are they with you?" He looked over her shoulder, standing on his tippy toes to see Tyler in the back seat, then Erynn, when he immediately began to blush.

"That's my nephew, Tyler, and this is my best friend, Erynn. Erynn, this is LJ."

"Nice to meet you, LJ." Erynn reached across Amree with an open hand for LJ to shake.

"She's pretty like you." His eyes were on Erynn as he spoke to Amree, causing both women to laugh.

"He's a little charmer," Amree told her.

"I see."

"Can he come play with me? Does he like video games?" LJ asked as Tyler began stirring in his sleep, a sign that he was waking.

"All right, man, back up so they can get out of the car." Lemere's voice interrupted her answer, reminding them all that he'd been standing there. He had done better than he expected, being patient, waiting for her to exit the car, as well as seeing her speak so freely with LJ, not saying one word to him. He didn't even give a nod.

"Your dad's right. We have to get out of the car first." She ruffled his curly top before he stepped to the side, allowing her to get out. She was only able to move so far, as Lemere moved in quick, taking up her personal space.

"I only want a hug. Then I'll help y'all with your stuff." He provided her with his signature sexy smirk, which she always said was hard to resist. He hoped it would work for him today. With his arms open, he waited with bated breath for her to make a move. He hadn't left that much space between them. Still, she would have to move some to feel his embrace. What felt like an eternity was only seconds as she laid her head on his chest. Without hesitation, Lemere wrapped his arms around her, holding her tightly.

Amree heard his heart beating swiftly in her ear, proving to her what she knew already: that he cared. The beating of his heart she was sure was an irregular beat. She did that to him, same as he did to her. Her heart was also beating swiftly, matching his tune. She shouldn't have been surprised, yet she was, at how in sync their beats had become. The realization was what pushed her to wrap her arms around him as well, hugging him tightly.

"I missed you, baby," he whispered in her ear.

She listened, taking a deep breath as he repeated the words.

"I missed you too, Mere," she finally admitted. Continuing to be stubborn was only doing her heart a disservice.

He pressed his lips to her forehead and held them there longer than he usually would before pulling away. "We have an audience." He smiled, looking at a googly-eyed LJ and a cheesing Erynn.

"She's worse than him," she chuckled, rolling her eyes at Erynn. "Get out of the car, girl," she yelled to her.

"'Bout time." Erynn exited the car quickly, making it to the driver's side in about three steps, stopping next to Amree. "I'm Erynn, her best friend," she introduced herself.

Lemere smiled, extending his hand while Amree shook her head. Erynn returned his gesture taking his hand, gripping it firmly.

"I've heard many good things about you, Erynn, and it's nice to finally meet you." He went to remove his hand from hers. However, she tightened her grasp.

"Likewise. Although I want you to know that I love her as if she were my sister. She is my sister, so do right by her, and you'll never have to know how crazy I can get behind her. I mean, imagine the worst thing in the world times two happening to you and multiply that by eight. It'll probably even be worse than that. You get the picture, though. So, treat my girl right"—she released his hand—"new brother-in-law." She smiled, leaning in to give him a quick hug.

Amree released a low chuckle. For her, there was no reason to defend nor make excuses for Erynn. Hell, she was a bit proud of her friend for putting it out there. She was sure Lemere knew her people didn't play about her. Maksym displayed that not too long ago. There was just something about the

way Erynn relayed her threats, though. She would
have a person sleeping with one eye open.

"Okay, move out of the way so I can grab Ty,
baby." Erynn bumped Amree with her hip lightly.

"I'll hold him if you don't mind," Lemere offered,
seeing that Tyler wasn't much smaller than LJ, and
carrying him was always a task.

"It's okay. I like carrying him. It's the only time
he allows this since he's such a big boy." Erynn
rolled her eyes, still not liking how Tyler was
growing up before their eyes.

"I like him already," Mere chuckled. "Okay, I'll
show you guys to your room." He took the bags
from the trunk, then proceeded behind Amree,
who held LJ's hand as Erynn held Tyler, who was
completely out again.

"We have to go up all these stairs?" Erynn looked
up, feeling like her legs were going to give out.

"Told you to let me carry him. But nah, we'll take
the elevator," Lemere said, chuckling.

Erynn's eyes roamed the areas of the home she
could see. She made a mental note to have a grand
tour once they were relaxed. She could hear the
music going and people laughing, as well as smell
the aroma of food, all of it blind to her eyes but ap-
pealing strongly to her senses. She was following
Amree and Lemere's lead yet couldn't wait to get to
the party for his mother that they'd come for. The
elevator ride was quick.

"LJ, can you show Ms. Erynn and Tyler the room we set up for them and show her whatever she wants to see while I speak with Amree?"

Both Amree and Erynn looked at Lemere with raised brows, noting how smoothly he separated them. Erynn could see from Amree's expression that she wanted to protest, so she gave her a look that told her she better not even try it.

"He sure can. We'll be fine. Come on, LJ, lead the way." Erynn followed LJ, who began leading the way without issue.

"We have their bags," Amree pointed out.

"Not for long. Come on."

They walked down the rest of the hall, entering his room. Lemere placed the bags on the floor before taking Amree by the hand, leading her to his bed. He sat, pulling her in between his legs, holding her by the waist, and looking up at her as she looked down at him.

"I'm sorry," he apologized for the hundredth time. This time it meant more because he was able to look her in the eyes.

She stared at him and saw sincerity in his eyes. So, why was she still wondering if they should still be an item? On one hand, she felt like she was in over her head. On the other, she was feeling a peace within her spirit she hadn't felt in a long time. Lemere was a roller-coaster ride that she enjoyed even though she was scared as hell.

"I already said I forgive you, Mere. We've moved past it."

"No, you haven't, and it's coo'."

He was right. She hadn't completely moved past it in her mind, but since she was there with him at that moment, she moved past it in her heart.

"I think we're moving too fast sometimes, and that scares me." There. She said it. Admitted a fear she had when it came to their relationship. The look on Lemere's face showed shock and a little bit of hurt, but he sucked it up quickly, because to him they weren't moving too fast. He'd take more of her if he could.

"When I first met you, I made you a promise to make sure you were straight as well as to keep you happy. I fucked up on both. Never said I was perfect. Gonna fall short a lot of times. None of that changes how I feel, though. I love you, Amree." The words left his mouth so easily. His tone was full of sincerity, and his words left a permanent stain on her heart that felt amazing to have.

The way her lips stretched as wide as they could go matched the smile she felt inside her chest. They were the words she longed to hear, the feelings she matched yet was afraid to speak first. Now, nothing was holding her back.

"I love you too, Mere." She couldn't deny it. And she wanted to laugh at how she even thought she could be anything less than his girl.

She watched his handsome face brighten. His brown skin turned red from blushing so hard. Now that the words had been said, Lemere was ready to show his feelings through actions, through being the man he knew she wanted, well, needed him to be, and through the physical. So, he pulled her down, falling onto his back, making her land on top of him, gripping her face with his massive hands, pulling her face closer to his, and kissing her with more passion than either had experienced from the other. She was pressed so closely to him that she could swear she felt his heart racing at the same pace as her own. That was the second confirmation she needed besides the sincerity in his eyes that the two of them continuing to move forward was better than them not moving at all. Besides, Lemere was spilling his heart out to her like never before.

"They say everything gets better when real love enters the equation. I know for damn sure, me loving a girl like you, things are only gonna get better. Our kisses." He pecked her lips. "Conversation." He pecked her lips again. "Sex." She raised her brow, and he chuckled. "Well, I mean, we should test out the sex theory."

"You have a houseful of guests. I'm sure Erynn has already made herself the center of attention at your mother's party."

"Then no one should miss us." He kissed her this time, not letting up. She couldn't deny him at this point if she wanted to.

My, how the tables turn, Amree thought as she looked at the notice on her desk. The pink piece of paper contained a name bright as day that she hadn't expected to see, especially requesting her services. She held the paper between her thumb and index finger as she read the comment section, letting her know what the message was pertaining to.

Singer Mary would like you to call her. Her team says she'd like to schedule an interview with you.

Amree had read over the message three times, and each time she found the words comical. The same woman who basically shit on her months ago was asking for her services.

"Hey, Amree, you have a second?" A tap at her door and the reluctant question pulled Amree's eyes from the note to Ashley.

"Yes. I was only organizing my desk and placing these messages in order of who to contact back first."

"Did you see the note from Mary?"

"Yes, and it's my least favorite, to be honest."

"Why?"

"Girl, she was rude as hell to me when I met her at the event months ago. Told me to get away from her, accused me of ear hustling, and now she wants to sit down with me? Girl, bye."

"I get it. But there is a positive to the negative here." Amree kept her lips sealed and looked her in the eyes. There was no need to ask what the positive and negative were because she knew Ashley was going to tell her anyway. "Look, she tried to shit on you the first time and now she needs you. Now, you know I am all about professionalism and can put a lot of things aside for the sake of this company. However, this is kinda different." She winked before continuing. "Take this opportunity to set her straight, and if she still decides to be a bitch, do not do the interview. She needs you at this point, not the other way around."

"You're serious?"

As she stated, Ashley was all about professionalism, and Amree could not believe what she was suggesting. She also wouldn't turn it down. Mary owed her an apology, and giving her one was the only way she was getting an interview. "Fine."

"Quit acting. Now you know you're looking forward to speaking with her."

"Maybe. So what else is going on? I know you didn't come in here just for that."

"No, I came to tell you how proud of you I am. You've been doing amazing and have become one of the most sought-out journalists, and that message on your desk proves it. You've really helped put *Extraordinaire* on the map."

The smile on her face warmed Amree's heart. Her words were pure and meant the world to Amree. Validation, though unnecessary, was something she looked for in the beginning of her career. Now she truly was the most sought-after journalist, and it felt good. Amree's approach to when she conducted interviews or wrote stories never came off as a blog post, but as a conversation between two or more people who were genuinely trying to get to know each other. She didn't care what blogs were posting or news outlets were saying. Whoever she sat with got to tell their side of the story, and she always had leading questions to keep the interview interesting and flowing organically.

"Let me know how the call with Mary goes."

"I will." Ashley left, and Amree picked the note up and looked at the number while she still had the nerve. She picked up her phone and dialed.

"Mary's World Management, how can I help you?" The caller on the other end was extremely chipper, and the tone of her voice put Amree in a slightly better mood.

"Hi, I am Amree Haylin returning a call inquiring about my services."

"Hi, yes, thank you for calling me back. I'm Monique. Mary would love to interview with you. Her schedule is—"

"Hold on," Amree quickly cut in, then released a light chuckle. She realized she had judged the direction of the call too soon, because the entitlement was showing.

"Sure."

"No, listen, you guys can't call me, telling me what someone's schedule is as if I'm expected to work my schedule around hers. Plus, she and I need to speak first before I even agree to an interview."

"You do know who you're getting a shot to interview right?"

"Sure do, which is exactly why *she* needs to call me."

"She's not available right now."

"That's fine. I'm not scheduling anything if she and I do not speak first."

"Fine. We'll be in touch," Monique told her, chipper attitude completely gone.

"Okay." Amree ended the call and got back to work. She put the finishing touches on a couple of interviews before sending them up for proofreading, a process used to catch misspelled words and grammatical errors. She organized her emails and Google calendar, and by the time she placed her callbacks in order of importance, she was ready to grab Tyler and head home. She gathered her belongings, and just as she stood to leave, her desk phone rang. She could have ignored it and allowed her answering service to keep record had the person decided to leave a message, but instead she answered.

"Hello, *Extraordinaire Magazine*, Amree Haylin."

"Hi, you wanted to speak with me?" The voice was instantly recognized, prompting an eye roll from Amree as she sat back down at her desk.

"Yes, you're requesting an interview from me, correct?"

"Yeah, and I never had to speak to the journalist first. My team has always set it up, and I show up." Her tone was as if Amree was wasting her time.

"You don't remember me, do you?"

"I can't recall us meeting."

"Well, we did at the artist event, and you were extremely rude to me. You assumed I had been trying to eavesdrop on a conversation of yours, which was far from what was going on."

There was silence on the other end, and due to being on a landline, Amree had no idea if she was still on the line, but she waited. Not long after, Mary blew an exasperated breath in her ear.

"Well, you looked suspicious standing there."

"I wasn't just standing there, and even if I were, that's no excuse to be rude."

"Maybe. Anyway, I'm sure you wanted the tea about me then and would like it now, so I can be free to interview—"

"I do not." Amree's tone was assertive, and she had to catch herself from becoming very unprofessional.

"I don't understand."

"Listen, I'm not that scared journalist you ran off. I am not interested in interviewing you and your horrible attitude. When you can remember that I am a human being like you *and* you're ready to apologize, then we can talk about maybe scheduling an interview. Now you have a good evening."

Amree ended the call, grabbed her things, and headed out of the building. She hated that things had to take such a turn, because interviewing Mary would surely be a damn good addition to her portfolio. Her follow-up questions would have produced answers from Mary that the world wanted. But if it was meant to be, it would be, because what she wasn't going to do was kiss ass to get it. At this point it was obvious that Mary needed and wanted her, so an apology should be simple for a damn good interview. She was proud of how she handled things though.

Chapter 17

"Bitch, remember when you told me to let Colene live?" Erynn asked as soon as the call connected. Amree hadn't even had the chance to say hello before Erynn spit out her question.

"Yes, I do, and I still feel that way." Amree removed the phone from her ear and placed it on speaker before looking at the time. It wasn't early by the hour of the day, but it was too early for Erynn to be calling on this kind of bull crap. She wasn't worried about Colene, and neither should Erynn be. She hadn't heard from her since the idle threat, and she felt she wouldn't hear from her again. "You cannot be waking up thinking about old shit, Erynn. You know it can shift your entire day, and Colene ain't worth that." Amree set her phone on the dresser and began looking through her drawers for some loungewear. She planned to sit around the house doing nothing besides answer a few emails, if anything.

"I ain't wake up on no old shit, honey. This is new, and I'm honestly surprised I'm the first person to call you. Well, no, I'm not, but go check The Shade Room. Do it from your computer, because I need to have immediate access to the question I plan to ask after you see this bullshit."

"Hold on." Amree picked up her phone and headed over to her bed, sitting Indian style as she leaned to the left, grabbing her laptop off her nightstand.

"You still there?" Erynn yelled.

"Now you know you still see the timer running."

"Well, it got extremely quiet."

"I just opened my computer. Hold on, let me log on." Amree logged into her personal social media account and frowned at all of the notifications coming through. She had been tagged over fifty times, and the first thing that came to her mind was that Lemere had linked her to some bullshit.

"Girl, I have over fifty tag notifications."

"Mm-hmm," Erynn sighed. "Just go straight to The Shade Room. You'll figure out those notifications later."

"Why won't you just tell me what's up?"

"Because you're online now. Just go look."

"It's loading. Hold on."

Amree looked at the first row and frowned, not seeing anything unfamiliar or pertaining to her or her man. She looked at the second and got the same result.

"Girl, I don't see anything," she expressed to Erynn.

"Go to the fourth row. That's crazy how fast new news becomes old news. Anyway, what you're looking for is on row four."

Amree's eyes quickly shifted to the suggested row, and she still didn't immediately notice anything, until she did.

"What the fuck?" she mumbled as she clicked on the photo. "This is Colene."

"Turn on the sound."

"I am. Hold up."

"So, I know y'all think little Miss Amree is a saint. Yes, I'm talking about the one dating that rapper dude. Who write and stuff. She writes about everybody else's business and acts all goody-two-shoes, but she is no saint. She and her criminal brother stole my baby and will not give him back. They want to make me out like I'm unfit when she is the one who enables illegal activities. I do not feel safe with my child being with her. She knew her brother was selling drugs, doing robberies, and hitting me. Then he goes to jail, and they take my kid. I want him back. If there is anyone out there willing to help me, I have more tea to spill about y'all little poster girl."

"What the fuck?" Amree felt like she swallowed a golf ball. Her heart rate sped up, her face felt clammy, and she felt like she was having an out-of-body experience. It didn't feel like she was living in this moment.

"So now can I beat up the ho? You can't still be trying to let her live," Erynn said, ready to book a flight and catch a case. Bail money was nothing, so Colene could catch her hands every day of the week.

"She's fucking lying," Amree fumed. "Like, she's really trying to sabotage my career." She wanted to cry. The lump in her throat made her feel like tears would be following shortly, but she refused to.

"We know she is. Which is another reason why I am going to beat her ass. I asked you as a courtesy, but I am dragging her when I catch her."

"She's not worth it. No judge would give Tyler to her and her rap sheet. She has the nerve to say shit about my brother when she just got out of jail. And he's never hit her dumb ass. Ooh, I am about to get a cease and desist out so fast."

"Get a restraining order, too. That way when I black out on her I can claim self-defense."

"You are not about to touch her. This is bullshit." Amree slammed her laptop shut, not caring to read the trolling comments she knew were a part of the fifty notifications.

"If I see her, it's on, period." Erynn meant what she said. Colene had an ass whooping coming.

"Look, I unfortunately have to run some damage control for those dumb enough to believe that bullshit. I'm going to call you later." She didn't wait for Erynn to reply and ended the call. She said a silent prayer that this would blow over, but until then she was going to get an attorney on it. If Colene kept on talking, Amree would sue her for defamation. If there was one thing she knew Colene was afraid of, it was the law. She knew once the papers were served, she wouldn't hear from her again.

Anytime they were apart, Lemere and Amree kept busy while communicating as often as possible. Today, their communications had been few and far between given the hectic schedule Lemere had to adhere to today. His sophomore album was doing really well, and almost every radio station playing his tracks from the album wanted to interview him in person. So, to keep the positive momentum going, that was what he was doing today. They'd arrived in his hometown of Lafayette about an hour ago, and he was exhausted. The nap on the private jet leaving Chicago did nothing other than reveal how exhausted he truly was.

As he sat in the back of the GMC with his eyes closed, he told himself that he needed to check in with his girl, even if only to say something as simple as, "Hey." They had spoken last night briefly, mainly to say, "I love you," and, "Good night." Having communicated with her then, no matter how little it had been, sufficed. It was enough to get him to sleep peacefully.

Not having said, "Good morning," or any other form of communication since he woke, had his day feeling off. Opening his eyes, he concluded that now was as good a time as any. He patted the pockets of his APO jeans for his phone only to remember his phone was in the car behind him with Mason and Millie. He'd given her his phone so that he could get uninterrupted rest while on the flight, with instructions to wake him for emergency purposes only.

"We're here," the driver announced as the car stopped.

Thomas, who rode with Lemere, finally looked up from his phone. "You ready?" Thomas asked, preparing to exit the car. Lemere looked at him, annoyed, opting to not provide an answer. Instead, he opened the door for Millie, who tapped lightly on the window.

"Sup, Mills," he greeted her, exiting the truck.

"Before we get in here, I told them you're pretty much open to all questions unless they link you to some bullshit. Personally, I think they want to know about your relationship more than anything else." She rolled her eyes, tired of all the talk about Mere's personal business rather than the music. She loved his relationship with Amree but cared more about her cousin being respected in his craft.

She always was and would always be Lemere's number one fan, and she only wanted to see his talents respected on the highest level.

"I'm already knowing," he spoke as they began to walk into the tall, tinted building. "You still have my phone?" he asked her.

"Yes. No one called," she informed him.

The information was hurtful, given that he'd at least expected Amree would've reached out by now since he hadn't. Entering the elevator, Millie also informed Lemere that he'd have a good amount of free time after this interview. More if he controlled the narrative and got out of there quickly.

"Damn, Mills, you be on yo' shit. I'm trying to figure out what I even still pay this nigga for." Lemere nodded in Thomas's direction, who still had his face in his phone as the doors opened.

"Lemere, glad you made it. Please, right this way." He hadn't gotten both feet off the elevator before being greeted by a petite, fair-skinned young woman dressed casually in brown slacks and a tan blouse. "Um, only one person can sit in with you. The area isn't that big. Whoever waits can sit in the waiting room next door, where you can still be seen," she informed him as they paused outside the door.

Thomas had finally taken his face out of his phone, stepping up to follow Lemere through the door, only to be halted by Mere's hand on his chest as he motioned for Millie to enter with his free hand. Thomas's embarrassment couldn't be hidden from a blind man, and Millie's chuckle didn't make it any better.

"We told y'all we'd have a special guest popping in today. So, allow us to introduce our hometown hero, Lemere. Welcome to WV104," DJ Bradley spoke into the mic as Lemere took his seat.

"What's up, everyone tuning in? It's so good to be home."

"So, let's get right into this album. Bro, you talking yo' shit. Every single track is continuously play worthy."

His compliment forced Lemere to show his pearly whites he was trying so hard to hide. There was nothing like an honest compliment to stroke his already-large ego. "Thank you, man, that means a lot."

"It's the truth, brotha. So, I gotta ask. Track thirteen seems like you got a lot off your chest with that one. Only thing is, it sounds more personal than industry rap. There had been talk about your street cred. Sounds like you used the record to set some things straight."

Lemere pondered the question, quite proud that his lyrics had been dissected in a good way. This was also a question he hadn't expected, and he was happy Bradley asked.

"I mean, it wasn't really about setting records straight. My name speaks for itself on and off the stage, before and after becoming a known rapper. I wasn't to be tried then. I'm not to be tried now. That's not to say it can't happen. Only that it shouldn't."

"I get you. Now, on track six, you sound like a man in love. We've seen the beautiful woman you've been lucky enough to call yours."

"Ain't I though?" Mere chuckled, cutting him off. It was a fact that he was lucky to have Amree.

"So, is the song about her?"

"Honestly, no. It was written before she and I met. Now that I have her, though, I like to think the song manifested her right into my life."

"That's dope. So, I'm sure your being in a relationship has been hard on the ladies. You look happy, though," DJ Silva, the only female cohost, finally cut in, getting in a word or two.

"I am. Hopefully, the ladies are happy for me too." He looked over to Millie, who smiled happily with his answer.

They spoke a bit more. Lemere had successfully moved the conversation from his relationship back to his music, announcing more tour dates, shows, and a best new album nomination.

"It was nice to have you here. Come back anytime you're in town," DJ Bradley told him.

"Thank you." Lemere stood, shaking the hand of each DJ before heading out.

Just as they came in, Lemere, Millie, and Thomas exited the building. They talked about how well the interview went as they walked toward the cars parked directly in front.

"As always, I'm proud of you, cuz. You were dope. I can tell Bradley and Silva did their homework on you, too. They damn near gave you the best interview so far. I mean, until you hit New York, because you know they do their job over there." She chuckled.

"Yeah, they did their job and didn't give me a hard time when I kept their ass from talking about Amree. Dude complimented my woman one too many times for me."

"You would've punched him over a compliment?" Thomas asked, looking at Lemere in disgust.

"Mothafuckin' right. It's called respect. Something you and I both know I don't play about."

"I see you moody again. I'll meet y'all in the car." As Thomas walked ahead, Millie took Lemere by the arm, forcing him to face her.

"Why haven't you fired his ass yet?" With her hands on her hips, she waited patiently for the answer. She was over Thomas and could do the job he was hired for better than him and for less pay.

"Sometimes loyalty keeps you in situations that common sense should take you out of. Thomas has his faults. He also has some good qualities. He does need to be demoted, though. If I did, I wouldn't have no one but Mason to yell at. Surprisingly, his dumb ass been acting smart lately." He chuckled as he and Millie began their walk toward the waiting vehicle.

"I still say he needs to—"

The loud sounds of tires screeching jolted Lemere's and Millie's heads toward the sounds. As if he were back on the block, Lemere's street sense kicked in. The accelerated beating of his heart took over his hearing, allowing him to hear nothing further. His sight, however, was still working as the barrel of a gun reared its ugliness from the minimally rolled down window of the dark blue Ford Explorer.

"Mills, get—"

The bullets began flying before he could complete the demand. Thankful he was close to her, Lemere hurled his entire body in front of Millie, shielding her as the barrage of shots seemed to be unyielding.

Chapter 18

The constant sounds of beating against a wall or door had Amree pulling her pillow from underneath her and placing it on top of her head in hopes to drown out the sounds. As she was half asleep, the noise seemed to be farther away until it wasn't. The banging persisted, getting louder as she found herself unable to drown out the sound and fall back asleep. Groaning, she threw the pillow from her head and extended her arm to reach for her cell resting on the nightstand.

"Who in the hell?" she questioned groggily as the knocks, well, beating continued while she slowly peeled her eyes open to check the time on her phone—1:30 p.m.

"Shit."

Glancing at the time, she realized she practically slept the day away. Having gone to bed late and then getting up a few hours later to take Tyler to school, she returned home, intending to nap no more than two to three hours. Hesitantly she removed the covers from over her body as she eased her way off of the bed. Standing, she extended her arms above her head, stretching as she released what she hoped was her final yawn. Whoever was banging at her door wasn't too important of a person because they hadn't called. In fact, she had zero missed calls. So, she could only assume that someone had the wrong address. Slowly she headed to the side of her bedroom that gave her a view of the front. When she peeped out from behind the blinds, she saw a work van parked directly across from her house. That was enough to keep her from panic or worry, so whoever was at her door could wait. She moved about her room, lacking the urgency she probably should've had as she put on a pair of heather gray joggers and one of Lemere's T-shirts she kept.

"Okay, okay, I'm coming," she yelled, finally heading toward her front door, taking the stairs two at a time. Without checking her peephole, she unlocked the door and flung it open, ready to tell the worker or telemarketer that they were banging on the wrong door and to remove her from whatever list she was on that brought them to her house. She wanted to send this person on their way so that she could finish a couple of things around her home before picking up Tyler.

"You have the—" Amree's hands flew to her mouth at the sight before her. Her entire body began to shake as she stood frozen in place. Fear wasn't the emotion she felt. Shock was. Confusion was. Bliss was. Bliss was actually the emotion that surpassed all others.

"Wh . . . what're you doing here?" Her words came out timidly, almost muffled because she hadn't removed her hands from her mouth. Staring at the person before her, seeing the smile on his face, had her tears cascading.

"Damn, that's how you greet me?"

Smiling amid her tears, Amree finally lowered her hands from her mouth to stretch them forward to verify the figure before her was real. She knew he was real, but because he was the last person she expected to be standing at her front door, she needed to use the sense of touch as added confirmation. Her fingertips graced his face before she practically leaped forward, wrapping her arms around his neck.

"I missed you too, baby sis." Maksym was doing all he could to hold in his tears as he hugged his sister tightly. It felt surreal to hug his sister as a free man. So, though he was ready to go inside given that she'd left him banging on the door way too long for his liking, he savored the moment for both of them.

"I can't believe you didn't tell me you were coming home," Amree spoke, head buried into his upper chest.

"'Cause I know you like surprises." He chuckled. "Can we go inside now?"

"Yes, but I'm not letting you go," she whined, lowering her hands from around his neck to his waist.

"I didn't think you would." Maksym chuckled as he wrapped one arm around her as they walked inside. He shut the door behind them. Then he looked over Amree's head at her home. Not much was different from the last time he was there. He noticed new furniture, but that was expected, because Amree didn't believe in having furniture older than three years, and before he left, her last set had been approaching its deadline.

"Can we at least sit?" He kissed the top of her head before leading her over to the sofa, not waiting for her reply.

"I'm so happy you're home." She wiped her tears, looking at Maksym. She'd been waiting for this day, for him to be free and home with her and Tyler. She planned his return much differently, wanting to have had bells and whistles waiting for him when he returned. She would take this arrival over him not having arrived at all.

"Me too. Shit feels good as hell."

"Why didn't you call me to come get you or tell me you were getting out?" With narrowed eyes directly on Maksym, she placed her hands on her hips, awaiting his excuse.

"Because I wanted to make my way home solo, sis. Regardless of how I got here, you know my first stop was going to be you and my son."

"We always said I'd pick you up and we'd celebrate." Her tone softened as she pouted like a child.

"You made those plans, sis—"

"And as my big brother, you were supposed to let me have my wish," she cut him off. She was so serious that she hadn't found the humor in her words as Maksym had. She glared at him, wanting to pop him upside the head as he laughed.

"We may as well change the subject now, because you trippin'." He laughed again briefly before composing himself.

Amree rolled her eyes before blowing out her breath in defeat. Maksym was right. They needed to focus on the more positive part of today. "Tyler is going to be so happy his dad is finally home."

"Man, I can't wait to see my little man." He beamed.

"Be prepared to sleep in his room for at least the next few days. Having you under the same roof has been the number one thing on his prayer wish list."

"I can rock with that. I still have—"

"Of course you still have your room and your man cave." She halted his question, providing an answer before he got the chance to ask.

"Thanks, sis. I don't plan to stay too long—just enough time to get on my feet."

"You were gone for a couple years too long. I'd like you here long enough to exceed that time frame."

Maksym looked at Amree, placing his fist to his mouth as he chuckled before telling her, "Hell nah. I'm not 'bout to stay here that long, Am-E. Besides, you got a boyfriend . . . I mean, a man. I know you not trippin', but I'm not trying to be in the midst of y'all lovey-dovey shit. You're grown, but you're still my baby sister."

"Your excuse is extremely lame. You're living here longer than a couple of months. Even though I *do* have a man," she snickered, watching Maksym's face scrunch in disgust. Had it not been for the giddy feeling she got from even the mention of her boo Lemere, she would have pried more into the reason Maksym was looking like he wanted to vomit.

"We'll see. So, what were you doing that had you taking your sweet time answering the door?"

"I was sleeping. I stayed up late working so that I could enjoy my day off. I've been busy with more articles than I can handle almost." She smiled, truly happy at how in-demand she'd become. She was more confident in her craft, had done more interviews, and even turned some down, Mary's included, and she still felt good about the direction of her career. She was able to go to different award shows, and not just because she was Lemere's girl, but because her work was speaking for itself.

"I'm proud of you, Am-E."

"Thank you. So, did Erynn know you were getting out?"

"No, jealous ass. Nobody knew but my lawyer and the people who let me out them gates."

"Okay. I won't pry anymore," she mumbled. "Are you hungry? There's plenty of food in there."

"Nah, I'll eat later. Right now, I want to shower and put on some real clothes."

"Well, I have a couple things to do around here before it's time to pick up Tyler. We have"—she turned in the seat, looking behind her at the clock on the wall—"forty-five minutes before we need to head out."

"Cool. I'll be ready." Maksym stood, kissing her on top of her head before he made his way up the stairs.

"Maksym," she called out to him right as he reached the top.

"What's up?" He looked over his shoulder at her.

"This is your home too. Always has been, always will be. And with you back, it finally has the piece that was missing." She thought about the times he'd come to stay with her. Maksym could afford his own place but loved being with her so she wouldn't be alone. It wasn't until he met Colene and she met Troy that he moved out.

"Nah, this is your spot, and you did good making the purchase with the money from our grandparents. It's time I make an investment like purchasing a home."

"Well until then, *mi casa es su casa.*"

The warmth of her smile radiated through to his heart as Maksym produced a smile of his own before nodding, then walking away.

The two of them completed their separate tasks and were out the door a few minutes early to pick up Tyler.

"I already have you on the list, but let's stop in here first so they can see you and know you for when you pick Tyler up," Amree said as they entered the office of Tyler's school.

"Hey, Amree, how are you?" the receptionist, Leila, greeted her as soon as they made eye contact.

"Hi, Leila, this is my brother, Maksym. He's Tyler's father. I have him listed already for pickup and emergency, but I wanted to come in and make a formal introduction."

"Hi, I'm Leila. It's nice to meet you. I see where Tyler gets his handsome looks from. You two look so much alike." Leila openly flirting with Maksym had Amree shaking her head. Her brother always had this effect on women. She just hadn't seen it up close in a while.

"Thank you. So I take it you're who I'd speak with if there are any issues?" Maksym's attempt at flirting back had Amree covering her mouth to stifle her laugh.

"Absolutely. Pickup shouldn't be a problem for you. I *can* think of other reasons you could speak

with me." Right as Maksym leaned forward, placing both his forearms on the wooden counter that
separated them, the bell rang.

"Saved by the bell," Amree mumbled before
tapping her brother. "We gotta go. Tyler expects
to see me when the teacher opens the door. We've
missed that, I'm sure."

"I'll see you around, Leila," Maksym promised
before winking at her. Leila wasn't an ugly woman.
She was very attractive if he was honest, and that
wasn't the "fresh out of jail" sight speaking for him
either. She was truly cute, reminding him of Fancy
from *The Jamie Foxx Show*.

"You cannot mess with that woman like that,"
Amree scolded him right as they stopped in front of
Tyler's classroom door.

"I'm grown."

"He hasn't spotted you yet." She changed the
subject, standing on her tiptoes to see Tyler sitting
crisscross applesauce, waiting to be called. "Let's
step inside," she suggested, not caring that they
were cutting or disregarding the other parents.
She would apologize later. Her nephew had been
waiting for this day.

Thinking nothing of her request, Maksym followed Amree inside the classroom door, stopping
right next to Tyler's teacher, who gave them both
an inquisitive look.

"This is his dad," Amree mouthed to the teacher, who beamed at the information. She was aware of Tyler's father being on vacation.

"Tyler." His teacher spoke his name in the same tone she usually would use when calling the students up, amid the smile on her face.

They all watched as Tyler turned in their direction, preparing to stand. When his eyes met his father's, he popped up as if someone lit a match underneath him. His small feet moved rapidly as he scrambled to get up and to his father.

"Daddy," he cried, with open arms rushing into Maksym's arms with tears flowing from his eyes.

Amree looked on, wiping her tears at the embrace. This was also the moment Maksym allowed his tears to fall.

"This is beautiful," the teacher spoke, wiping her tears as applause erupted behind them.

Most of the parents knew Tyler and appreciated this moment, as none had seen the boy interact with anyone other than Amree or his nanny. From the emotions plastered on Amree's and the teacher's faces, it was apparent that this was a special moment. The embrace lasted a few moments longer before Maksym got Tyler interested in showing him around the classroom. Amree stood off to the side, watching with her heart so full she was surprised it hadn't exploded. She had no idea her heart could fill with this much joy.

"Ooh, Auntie, can you cook me and my dad's favorite food?" Tyler asked as he held his father's hand, swinging it as he practically bounced while walking.

"I can."

"Amree."

Her name being called halted the trio from their walk toward the car. They all turned to see who had called Amree's name, Amree and Tyler out of curiosity and her brother out of protection. When she saw Kyle and his daughter approaching them, she relaxed. Naturally, her eyes traveled from Kyle's feet to his print then quickly up to his face as she reminded herself she was a taken woman. Still, she'd have to be blind not to see how handsome Kyle was.

"Hey, sorry to stop you guys. Ciscely wanted to catch up to Tyler."

"It's fine." She blushed. Kyle was fine, dressed in a pair of navy blue dress shoes, brown slacks, and a brown and blue shirt. She could tell he had a fresh haircut, and his smooth skin was perfectly moisturized.

"No problem. Hi, pretty girl." She knelt, speaking to Ciscely.

"Hey, I'm Kyle. My daughter is in Tyler's classroom. You have a well-mannered young man. You should be proud," Kyle introduced himself. He shook Maksym's hand firmly and kept eye contact.

"Thank you. My son has mentioned your little girl's name to me a time or two. I salute you. Tyler only says good things about her. She helps him with spelling." They all released low chuckles at the statement.

"Appreciate it. Well, we're going to go. Amree, you look nice," he complimented her before grabbing his daughter by the hand and walking off.

"That's the kind of dude I expect you to end up with. What's wrong with him? It's obvious he's feeling you," Maksym told her as they finally made it to her car.

"Nothing. We don't mesh well."

"Nah, he's not a nigga with baggage."

"Whatever." She rolled her eyes, then pulled her phone from her purse as it seemed to be vibrating nonstop. With a furrowed brow, she looked at the number of notifications on her phone. There were over one hundred linked to her social media pages. Opening the first was all she had to do to find out what was going on.

Superstar rapper Lemere was involved in a shootout that left one person in critical condition. Sources say it was the rapper. Let's send prayers his way as no one in his camp has confirmed or denied these allegations.

Amree read over the post three times, hoping the words would change or be revealed as a sick joke. But as she opened a couple of other notices, she saw that what she was reading was true.

"What's wrong, Am-E?" Maksym noticed the change in her demeanor and how she was shaking while doing whatever she was with her phone.

"They're . . . They . . . They're saying Lemere was involved in a shootout." She couldn't hold in her tears, nor was she trying to. She was scared shitless for her man.

"Exactly why I want her with a square. Shit." Maksym spoke low enough so she didn't hear him. After securing Tyler in his seat, he walked around the car to his sister, taking her in his arms.

"I'm sure he's fine, sis. Call him or someone close to him to be sure."

She nodded, still not letting Maksym go. She couldn't believe how this day had gone from sugar to shit so quickly.

"Where are you right now?" Erynn's tone was full of sympathy as she wished she could be by her friend's side right now.

"Sitting outside."

"Why are you still sitting outside, best friend?" She asked a question she knew the answer to because it was the only thing she could think to ask, knowing that Amree was dealing with a situation she hadn't been prepared for, one she couldn't fathom in her wildest thoughts. With her best friend being out of whack, she was too. They often wondered how they weren't one and the same because they always felt each other's pain.

Amree looked out the window of the car she'd rented due to turning down the offer to be picked up. She wanted time to herself to process what she was walking into. Not only that, but she didn't feel safe being with anyone other than herself, given the circumstances.

"Because I don't know if I can go in there yet. Seeing him like . . . I'm not ready yet." During the entire drive to her destination, Amree tried preparing herself for what she was about to walk into.

"I can come, like, hop on the next available flight to be by your side."

"It's okay. I have to do this by myself no matter how conflicted, scared, and hurt I am."

"What can I do to help? I feel helpless. You won't let me be there. I feel like I'm not saying the right things."

"You are helping me. Talking to me right now is helping me. I have a million things going on in my mind right now. The main thing is, how am I supposed to handle a loss like this? Being dumped by Troy because he was a selfish prick was one thing. It hurt, but I got over it. To lose someone to being shot—shootouts, people gunning for you because of who you are—is a whole different type of pain." Amree wiped the tears that were falling rapidly as she felt the pain from the words she spoke. She was trying to pull herself together so she could do what she came all this way to do.

"Aw, Amree." Erynn was crying as well. She understood what her friend was saying and wished things were different. "Best friend, things don't have to go that way. I mean, there's a silver lining in all of this."

"You're right." She wiped her face again, knowing that this wouldn't be the last time she cried today. For now, she was okay. The person standing in the door watching her was also the reason she sucked up her tears so swiftly.

"His mom is staring at me. I have to get out of this car now. I'll call you back."

"That's fine. I know you may have your hands full, so at least reply to my texts. I don't care if it's something as simple as an emoji. I'm not expecting you to call. I will check on you."

Amree heard Erynn, knowing she meant every word. She was grateful to have a friend like her. "Thank you. I love you."

"Love you too."

She ended the call and made eye contact with Lemere's mother, giving her a tight-lipped smile before grabbing her purse from the passenger seat. She wanted to pull down the visor to check herself out, knowing her eyes were probably puffy from crying. Instead, she dismissed the act by getting out of the car. The man she loved had been shot. Fuck looking cute or hiding that she cared and was hurting.

The Jordan tennis shoes she wore provided a smooth walk from the vehicle toward the stairs. She had a long night, so dressing anything other than comfortably wasn't going to cut it. With a messy bun on top of her head, she rocked a burgundy crew-neck oversized sweatshirt with burgundy leggings. She still looked beautiful while carrying what felt like the weight of the world on her shoulders.

The closer she got to the door, the more she felt like turning and running away. She hadn't felt anxiety like this since the day Maksym had to turn himself into prison. Strangely, the anxiety she was feeling also was the scale that measured the love she felt for Lemere. Love him. She did, no doubt about it. The depth of the love she had for him was unknown until now.

"Hey, baby," Leandria greeted her, tearing her from her thoughts and from the concrete her eyes had been fixated on.

Slowly, Amree rose her head. From the car, she could only see slightly Leandria's angst. Up close, she saw Lemere's mother look as if she'd aged overnight. Stress and pain were written all over her face. Her flawless brown skin, which had been vibrant each time Amree saw her, appeared dull today. Her usually lively eyes seemed to be empty. She also wasn't done up like she loved to be. She too was dressed down, wearing one of Lemere's concert shirts, black leggings, and a pair of UGG house shoes, and her hair was pulled back in a ponytail.

"Hi." Amree's voice cracked some as the women embraced. Leandria initiated the hug. She saw Amree's pain, even if she was trying to shield it. As they hugged, both women felt a sense of calm being connected to a man they loved so much who also loved them back. They unknowingly and unintentionally had taken on the role of being each other's rock.

"I'm so glad you could make it." Leandria disrupted their hug, placing her hands on Amree's shoulders, looking her in the eyes, and providing a tight-lipped smile.

"There's no other place than here important enough to be."

"He loves you."

The admission had Amree's eyes watering, filling practically to capacity as she did her best to suck up her emotions. If she didn't get them under control in the next few seconds, the water would definitely spill over.

"It's okay to cry, baby. I've been crying my ass off too."

"I know. I don't want to go in here crying. I mean, what I want probably won't matter when I see him. The least I can do is try to be strong."

Leandria chuckled. It was literally the first time she'd laughed in over twenty-four hours. What Amree said wasn't funny by far. The humor was in how she too had the same thought process until she realized the pain was more challenging to hold than the strength. She knew there was no way Amree could remain strong at a time like this. She loved her son, so once she saw him, her emotions would get the best of her.

"Baby, none of us expected something like this to happen. Hell, the last time I feared an incident like this, my son was not a famous rapper. He worked his ass off to remove himself from the life of the streets only for the streets to attack him any-fucking-way." Leandria wiped the lone tear that fell. She was getting pissed all over again at how things played out for her son in their hometown. She never claimed her son to be an angel. Hell, she knew he wreaked havoc coming up.

However, he had given back in multiples of what he'd taken. He became a role model. He was proud to be one, only for someone to hate to the point of attacking him. It pissed her off to the core. Amree wanted to respond, but she didn't find it necessary to state the obvious. She agreed with everything said and had a few opinions of her own that wouldn't do anything other than further riling up Lemere's mother. Maksym had always told her about the ways of the streets, how sometimes getting out wouldn't sit well with a person bitter about why it was you and not them. She hadn't been entirely informed on the entirety of the incident. Still, she could only assume jealousy and envy would have someone doing something so reckless.

"Let's go inside. I'll show you where he is."

Extending her hand with a reassuring smile gave Amree the courage she needed. Without hesitation, she intertwined her hand with Leandria's, following her through the door.

Amree took deep breaths to calm her nerves as her eyes shuffled around the areas she could see as they headed upstairs. Leandria stopped in front of the last door to the right, tapping it three times before motioning for Amree to go inside. Slowly Amree pushed the door open, taking one last deep breath for courage. Stepping into the bedroom, the sight before her made her heart ache. Tears reemerged, falling without mercy as she rushed to Lemere's side.

"Babe, don't come in here crying, please. My mom's hurt me with her tears already. Adding you in the mix gon' fuck me worse than the shots I took."

"Too bad, because seeing you like this is fucking with me. You're banged up, Mere. I see at least

three bandages, all in places that could have taken
you away from me, had God not been on your side,"
she spoke through her tears, wiping them.

"It looks worse than it is."

"What happened?"

"Stop crying and I'll tell you." He grinned at her
before grimacing in pain as he lifted his left arm to
pull her close to him.

"Fine," she sighed, wiping her face as she gently
laid her head on his left shoulder.

"We came out of the radio station, and a car
rolled up, and niggas started shooting. I dove to
cover Millie. That's how I got hit in the leg, my
right shoulder, and grazed across my side. Mills
thankfully had minor cuts from the bullets that
hit the ground, causing the fragments to ricochet
and hit her. But Thomas, man . . ." His voice broke.
She listened as he sucked in air, then blew it out.
Whatever he was about to tell her about Thomas,
she could feel it wasn't going to be good. She didn't
have beef with him. Though he wasn't her favorite
person, she wanted him to be okay.

"Because most of the bullets hit the car, Thomas
got hit up bad."

"He's not dead, right?" she cut him off, thinking
about the blog post she read about fatalities.

"Nah. He's barely hanging on, though. That's
the reason I haven't gone back to my spot in L.A.,
nor made any statements. I can't leave knowing

Thomas is fucked up because some pussies was gunning for me. I also can't make a statement until we figure out who was bold enough to run up on me."

"Mere, please don't tell me you're thinking about retaliating." Her voice rose an octave as she sat up to look him in the face.

"No, babe. Chill. I'm only trying to get ahead of some shit. None of that is stuff you need to be worried about."

"How can I not? Look at yourself. You were shot. More than once. I thought I lost you." Amree tried to keep from crying. It was no use. He was taking this situation way too lightly for her liking.

"I'm still here, though. Can we celebrate that? I was told by a higher power that I'm living long enough to make you my wife and watch our kids make us grandparents. You stuck with me."

The sureness he spoke with encouraged laughter from Amree's lips while decreasing her tears. Shaking her head, she stared at the man she loved and really looked at him from the crown of his head to his belly button. She would've inspected further had it not been for the cover up to his waist. His handsome face bore no worry. She didn't understand how he could be cool as a cucumber after all he'd gone through over the last twenty-four hours.

"Why are you looking at me like that? I'm not gon' break." He chuckled, grateful for her being at his side. She was everything, so he hadn't expected anything less.

"Obviously. That's a damn good thing, too. I'm also wondering how you can be so chill about all this. You don't have to hide yourself and how you feel from me."

"I know that, and I'm not. I have a lot more stuff to worry about. I can't worry about what I'm feeling when my manager is in the hospital. I'm good." It was a half-truth. He wasn't good nor was he feeling the brush with death at all. Seeing how quickly everything could be taken away from him, he vowed to live life much fuller than he had been.

"Well, I'm here now, and I'm going to take care of you so you can cast some of those worries on me to lighten your load."

"I love you too much to do that. There is a load you can help me with, though."

With a furrowed brow, she looked at Lemere. "What is that?"

"My balls, babe. They heavy than a mothafucka. We ain't had sex in too long. I—"

"I am not having sex with you in your mother's house. Which is very beautiful, by the way." Amree couldn't wait to see the rest of the home. It was smaller than Lemere's but much bigger than hers. She hated visiting a beautiful place for such an ugly reason.

"I bought this house, so it's mine. You can't say you willing to help with whatever I need then put stipulations on it. We adults. My mama knows I make love to you, and as long as you keep quiet, she won't hear us."

"Mere."

"You gon' make me beg to get some of my pussy, babe?"

Amree groaned loudly before getting up to make sure the door was locked. She would give him what he wanted because she was horny too. Walking back over to the bed, she stopped close, pointing her left index finger at him.

"The minute you say 'ouch,' we're done, whether you finish or not," she promised as she eased out of her pants, finding the mischievous grin on Lemere's face sexy as hell.

Chapter 19

Amree stood in front of Lemere's huge bedroom mirror, admiring her look for the night. Though she was a ball of nerves on the inside, she had to admit she was looking damned good on the outside. With minimum makeup, she admired her flawless skin, courtesy of the citrus detox soap she'd been using on this journey of natural body soaps, which was doing her body well. She appreciated how well her hair cooperated with the wash and go she'd decided to rock.

"You look good, babe," Lemere spoke, pulling her attention from her curly orange locks to the back of his head reflecting in the mirror. His compliment felt good. Still, it wasn't enough to ease the anxiety gradually burning within her.

"Thank you." She beamed as he came up behind her, wrapping his arms around her waist, nestling his head into the crook of her neck.

"You good?" he asked, noticing how her smile faded and apprehension followed.

"I should be asking you that. Are you sure you're ready to be around all these people?" It had only been a little over two weeks since the shooting and one week since they left his mother's house. Lemere had refused to leave Lafayette until he was positive Thomas was okay. Thankfully, Thomas was doing better and looking at being discharged sooner rather than later. He wouldn't be returning to his position as Lemere's manager for a while because of fear and needing to completely recover after taking ten bullets.

"Babe, I keep telling you I'm fine. Besides, that shit happened in my hometown. None of what happened there will happen here. This house and I are protected. There's nothing to worry about, baby. If you don't feel comfortable about tonight, maybe you can chill—"

Amree's raised brow and pursed lips caught Lemere's attention, halting his words immediately. He obviously was getting ready to say something stupid, something she noticed him doing more frequently since the shooting. Whether or not he wanted to admit it, Lemere had changed some since the shooting. He was drinking more, bossing people around more, and at times being only what could be considered a straight-up asshole.

"That was smart of you not to finish that sentence." She stepped forward, removing herself from his embrace, turning around so they were face-to-face.

"All I was gonna say was you can chill up here or go shopping on me. The party is happening, so do what you gotta do to feel comfortable."

With a raised brow, Amree placed her hands on both sides of his face. She leaned in, pecking his lips, then pulled back, gliding her hands from his face to both shoulders, when she noticed him wince in pain.

"You're okay, but I barely touched your shoulder, and it hurt. What if I touched your side?" Amree moved her hand toward it, and Lemere backed up quickly.

Chuckling, she informed him, "I wasn't going to touch you. Only trying to prove a point, Mere. You're not a hundred percent healed, but you want to have all these people around. Some you know, many are random, and I just don't get it." Her arms raised at her sides out of frustration. She loved him, so she was trying to look out for him.

Like a loving girlfriend would do.

Like his mother asked her to do.

"Babe, I'm not going to keep telling you I'm good. Me still being a little sore has nothing to do with me being able to look out for myself. I'm good. I'm having the party, and since you're my woman, I want you by my side. I also understand if you're not feeling it." He kissed her cheek, then exited the bedroom, leaving Amree speechless and pissed, so much so she contemplated leaving his home and hopping on the next flight home. Yet fear of what he would do or what could happen to him if she weren't around kept her ass right there. Blowing out an annoyed sigh, she hoped the night would go as smoothly as Mere claimed.

Lemere looked over his shoulder, seeing Amree's saddened face, not letting it affect him. He appreciated her being worried, yet he wanted her to respect when he said he had things under control. He left her to her thoughts as he made his way to the front of his home.

"You checking everyone who walks through this door, right? Bitches too? Only people I want to be strapped up in here is me and you," Lemere confirmed, walking up on Shakil.

"I got you. My thing is, if we gotta go through all these security measures, what the fuck you throwing this party for? At your home at that?" Shakil looked at Lemere, irritated but also willing to do his job.

"Because I can. Anyone give you issues, they don't get through the door." Lemere patted Shakil on the chest before walking off and lifting a glass of wine from one of the awaiting trays. It had been his second cup of wine, yet his third alcoholic beverage. Less than an hour ago, he had taken an entire bottle of Cîroc to the head.

He wanted this party because he needed to regain control. The shots he took and the way they

came at him out in the open reminded him that
he'd gotten too comfortable with his new status.
He also felt like a hypocrite. He talked big shit yet
was unable to back it up. He was caught slipping,
and that was rule number one of the streets: to
never get caught slipping. That was a mistake he
vowed not to make again. He looked around his
home, eyes checking the areas where cameras
were that only he and Shakil knew were in place.

"What's up, cuz? We turning up tonight?" Mason
put his forearm on Lemere's shoulder.

"Damn, nigga," Lemere growled, shoving Mason
off him with his good hand.

"Oh, shit, my bad." Mason flung his hands up
in surrender, feeling bad for not paying close
enough attention to Mere's injured shoulder. "Are
you good? Besides me accidentally hurting your
shoulder?"

"I'm straight, nigga. I'm not gon' be if one more
person asks me that shit." Lifting the glass to his
lips, Lemere finished the drink in one gulp.

Mason frowned, smelling the stench of alcohol
reeking from his cousin's pores. A big part of him
wanted to voice further concern because it was
apparent Lemere wasn't straight. For his own
selfish reasons, as well as a little fear, he didn't.

Lemere gave him a pointed look before shoving
the glass in Mason's hand and walking off toward
the crowd formed in his backyard. Half-naked

women paraded around in heels while a few others splashed around in his pool. He was grateful Amree wasn't the jealous type, as most women who weren't groupies would've had an issue with the flock. That was especially true when the flock wanted your man, and there wasn't a woman in attendance who didn't have her eye on Lemere. He strolled around, dapping up the few dudes who were openly enjoying the view of ass and free drinks.

A few thank-yous and the odd, "Appreciate you for letting us slide through," made him feel like the king he knew he was. Being in his presence was a privilege for those who didn't run in the same circle as or larger than his. This was another reason he'd allowed his guest list to be more open. His need to be reminded that he was "the man" had him moving in ways he would not have been had he not come so close to death.

Gradually, as he made his way to his VIP section, Lemere nodded in approval, feeling himself regain the strong confidence that usually oozed off of him. He controlled the environment tonight. Anyone looking to gain stripes by trying him would only receive a toe tag. He sat back, taking gulps of the Cîroc bottle from the many liquor varieties in front of him.

The night's sky was golden as the sun was setting. However, the figure walking toward him had a way of making any room bright. The sun always had competition when she was around. Amree was far more dressed than the rest of the women in attendance, pulling all the attention to herself effortlessly. There wasn't an eye in the crowd not fixated on Amree as she made her way to the only person she had eyes for. She made it to Lemere, sitting in his lap, wrapping her arm around his good shoulder, and placing a kiss on his cheek.

"Still mad at me?" Lemere asked, kissing her back.

Turning her nose up, rolling her eyes up toward the sky, she pretended to be in deep thought about her answer. Was she still upset? A little bit. Not enough to ruin his night, though.

"You're on thin ice." She shrugged.

"How do I skate off the ice without sinking?"

"By being on your best behavior. Have fun, but not too much fun."

"So, you saying a nigga get one of them hall pass thingies?" He smirked, eyes low and full lips moist. Lemere was feeling good. It was written all over his face.

"I said not too much fun. You must want to get fucked up in front of your guests. Do not play with me, Mere."

He knew she was serious, but it didn't change how hilarious he found her threat.

"I didn't say anything funny."

Gripping her around the waist tighter, holding her in place, he told her, "You didn't, babe. My bad. I got you, though."

Amree nodded before getting up from his lap. She placed another kiss on his lips, letting him know she'd be back in a bit. She was going to work the room and watch his home. She hadn't been feeling the party from the jump, so sitting in one spot by Lemere's side all night wasn't what she was interested in doing. She chuckled, noticing a throng of women make their way to Lemere as soon as she was less than a full foot away. She would hate to have to drag a ho, but that didn't mean she wouldn't. She did a glance over her shoulder, seeing Lemere with a ton of women in his face smiling widely. He was undoubtedly enjoying the attention. She'd give him and the whores their insignificant moment. Besides, he wasn't the only one of them in a room with fans.

Amree moved about Lemere's home as if it were her own. She opened cabinets in the kitchen, arranging glasses because she could and she knew people were watching. She respectfully gave the cooks and housekeepers orders, loudly reminding them that no one other than herself, Lemere, Shakil, and Mason were allowed to walk into the kitchen area. As she made her way back toward the foyer, she smiled at two women who were waiting outside of the door for the restroom.

"What's up, cousin-in-law?" She turned, seeing Mason head her way as his eyes made a quick detour toward the half-naked women.

"Hey. Do you know when the Porta-Potty will be here? These lines are not going to work," she spoke loudly with every intention of being heard.

"It should be here any minute. What's up?" Mason questioned, ready to accommodate Amree. They'd grown close, so whatever she needed, he had her.

"This line and the random people in the house. Not going to work." She knew she was being petty as she nodded toward the waiting women who looked like they wanted to check their outfits more than piss.

"Oh, them hoes can go outside for all I care. Y'all gotta get up out of here." Mason turned to the women, ushering them out of the house as they talked shit under their breath.

"Thanks, cousin." She grinned at Mason, who was following closely behind the women he had put out.

"What's up with you?"

Amree frowned, looking disgustingly at the hand, gripping her elbow. "Um, since your mouth works, you can take your hand off of me." She snatched her arm back, dropping it at her side.

"My bad, beautiful. I'm simply trying to get to know you." He smirked. There was nothing attractive about it either. Looking at him made her skin crawl.

"I know you." She squinted, looking at him and trying to figure out how she knew him. "Not *know* you. I've seen you around before. Which means you know I'm Lemere's girlfriend. Why are you even approaching me?"

"Aw, shit, my fault. You his broad? Bro's females are usually up for grabs. You off-limits. Coo'." The look in his eyes had lust mixed with some mischief.

Instead of giving him a second more of her time, she walked away, leaving him standing there as she made her way back to Lemere. She gave the groupies more than enough time to be in her man's face. Feeling eyes on her as she walked, she glanced over her shoulder, not noticing anything out of the ordinary. There were a ton of people in the backyard now.

"It's time for me to go upstairs. I'm over this," she mumbled.

Between the crowd of people she hadn't cared to be bothered with from jump, and the guy who'd been around Lemere at least two times that she could remember looking at her like he was ready to risk it all, Amree was prepared to finish the night in bed watching television until she fell asleep or the party ended, whichever came first.

"Babe, you were gone hella long," Lemere slurred as she walked up to him, stopping in between his legs.

The sounds of grumbling, teeth sucking, and huffing came from both sides of them as Mason, with a few other of Mere's people, kicked most of the women from the area.

"I only came back to say good night. I'm gonna chill in the house."

Lemere pulled her down, sitting her on his lap. "What's wrong? Someone say something to you?"

She noticed his eyes widen like he was ready for some sort of violent excitement. It was flattering, his being prepared to defend her if she needed it.

"No. I'm tired. Not really in the mood to party."

"Can you sit out here with me for a few more minutes? I'll even walk you up," he said, kissing her cheek.

"Five minutes, Mere," she agreed unenthusiastically. So for five minutes, she sat there on his lap while he drank and women stared.

"Ay, I'll be right back." Lemere turned to his cousin and a couple of his boys, announcing his temporary departure as he patted Amree on the ass for her to stand.

Lemere walked in front of her, unexpectedly straight, given all the alcohol he consumed. He held her hand firmly, guiding their way through the crowd.

"You know I can make it to the bedroom on my own," she told him, feeling bad for making him leave the party she didn't want him to have.

"I know. But you look good as fuck. If these clothes coming off you, it'll be me doing the removing," he told her, leaning closer so that only she could hear.

"Y'all calling it a night?" Shakil inquired, watching them approach the stairs.

"Nah," was all Lemere said as he practically dragged a giggling Amree up the stairs.

Once inside the bedroom, he wasted no time removing her shirt and pants, leaving her standing there in her burgundy Fenty bra and thong set.

"You know you shit on every female when you step in the room. A nigga lucky as hell to have you," he spoke, walking up to her, placing his hands on her waist.

"Thank you. I'm lucky to have you too."

"You damn near lost a nigga." Lemere looked her in the eyes, revealing the fear and hurt he wouldn't voice out loud.

"I didn't. That's what matters. You. Us is what matters to me. I need you to be okay, Mere. Need you to be you." Looking at him, she hoped he picked up on the underlying message in her words. No, he'd never be the same after such a traumatic event. She didn't want it to take over his life. This person he was slowly becoming was someone she was not trying to be in a relationship with.

"I'm good. I'm 'bout to show you how much, too." He smirked, then sexily bit down on his bottom lip.

"What you still dressed for then?" she challenged.

"'Cause I want dessert right now. The main entrée I'll have later." Slowly, he backed her into the bed, removing her thong once she was comfortable on her back.

The liquor had him feeling good. He wasn't concerned with his shoulder as he cuffed both her legs and started feasting on her center. Drunk or not, he couldn't fuck up eating her. It was like second nature to him. Lemere alternated between flicking his tongue across her clit and sucking it. He wanted to bring her to her peak quickly, so he moved with the perfect amount of passion and urgency to do so.

"Sss, fuck. Babe. Mere, I'm cumming," she yelled moments before her body shook.

He continued sucking until he felt her legs weaken. Kissing her pussy once more, Lemere sat up, making his way to sit beside her on the bed.

"You're going to be in pain in a few hours," she told him, eyes barely open. Whatever sour mood she had been in Lemere sucked away.

"I'll be good. I'm going to chill for a bit more, and then I'll be back. Get some rest, 'cause that wasn't it."

"All right. Can you tell someone to bring me a plate?" She rolled over to her side, getting comfortable.

"Yeah." Leaning down, Lemere kissed her cheek before pulling the covers over her body.

"Babe," she called out, feeling him lift from the bed.

"Sup?"

"Can you take off my bra?"

Laughing, Lemere did as he was asked, unsnapping the hooks and sliding down her straps.

"Thank you." She grinned lazily, eyes still shut.

"See, all that pouting you was doing could've been avoided had you told me earlier you needed a nut." He chuckled as he reached the bedroom door.

"Maybe."

Without another word, he left the room, ready to enjoy the rest of his party.

Chapter 20

Sensing a presence near her, Amree smiled lazily with her eyes still closed. The tongue lashing Lemere had given her not too long ago still had her feeling a high that only his touch could give her body. He left her feeling so intoxicated that all her previous concerns and attitude were gone. Feeling the bed dip somewhat, she continued to lie there half awake, half asleep. Her limbs were in relaxation mode, so moving to acknowledge him would be more of a task she was unwilling to complete. If Lemere called himself initiating round two, he would be doing the majority of the work.

Feeling the covers slowly move down her body, she stirred some. "Mmm," faintly and involuntarily, she released as a result. "Babe," she mumbled as his weight shifted the bed. She could feel him hovering over her as the bed sank at her head, where he used his hands to avoid putting all of his weight on her. She felt the heat of his legs against her own, and the stiffness between his legs centered at the curve of her kneecap. Still, she hadn't shifted from her side to her back to acknowledge him. Eventually, Amree was going to give Lemere what he wanted because she wanted it too. Knowing this, her initial plan to play hard to get was voided by the mild thumping in her clit. Her body was betraying her, reacting to him as if it were a necessity. At this point, she considered the reality that it was. Slowly she rolled onto her back, where she instantly noticed unfamiliarity. The scent hitting her nostrils alerted her of all the wrong surrounding her. Amree's eyes popped open, taking a moment to adjust to the dark room. She could see the silhouette of the figure over her, and it was not Lemere. Panicking, her hands flew to the male's chest on top of her as fight or flight kicked in.

"Get off of me," she pleaded through clenched teeth. Her hands were forced from his chest and planted above her head.

"Be still."

The sound of his voice near her right ear froze her movement. She knew this voice, had heard it earlier when she rejected him. Only now it was dripping with malicious intent.

"That's a good girl." He took his tongue, licking from her jawbone to her ear, taking her lobe into his mouth.

"No," Amree cried, still frozen, still in shock.

He chuckled, making her skin crawl.

"Please stop. You can leave, and I won't say anything. It's dark. I can't see you. I'm not even sure who you are. Please."

"I'll leave after I get what I came up here for. After that, I couldn't give a fuck what you say or who you tell. Yo' nigga's a bitch anyway," he laughed. His laughter echoed in her ears, and she was sure it would haunt her long after tonight.

Amree's chest felt tight, like there was a rope around her heart being tied consistently.

Think, Amree, think, she willed herself, trying to come up with a solution to get out of her current predicament. She couldn't believe this was taking place under her man's roof and with a houseful of people. It took someone really deranged to even attempt such a thing under these circumstances.

"Get off." She tried bucking her body to shift him and wasn't successful at all. She screamed at the top of her lungs. She yelled from her gut, doing her best to compete with the loud music played all over the house. She hoped someone would hear her and would come to her rescue.

"Oh, you spunky, too? I know this pussy 'bout to be fire." Forcing Amree's hands together, crossing them at the wrist, he applied pressure, keeping them in place with one hand as he took his free one to glide down her body, pausing at her pelvic bone.

"Please don't." The bravado from moments ago was gone. Feeling his hand so close to the entrance of her bare pussy left no question of who was in charge. She could only hope pleading with him brought relief. But as he snorted while continuing his act of allowing his hand to explore her body, something told her that his having a conscience didn't exist. The grip of his hand holding her wrist had gotten stronger.

"Open up." He tapped her thigh before trying to pry them open. Amree squeezed her thighs as tightly as she could, thankful he hadn't been able to overpower her with the one hand. "I'm not fucking playing with you."

He freed her hands, and that was all she needed. As he used both hands to pursue access to her center, Amree decided she was not becoming his victim. With all of her might, she swung, striking him in his temple, discombobulating him.

"Fuck off of me," she cried, flailing her arms while moving as much of her feet as possible, given the weight of his body holding them down.

"Bitch."

The backhand he landed across Amree's face, forcing saliva from her mouth, only slowed down her fight. With tears spilling from her eyes, Amree ignored the stinging of her face while reaching for the nearest item on Mere's nightstand. If she could get to her phone, she could call for help.

As she stretched her right arm to its full capacity, her assailant had gotten her legs open wide enough to have his way with her. As he ran a finger from the entrance of her vagina to the tip of her clit, Amree's body shivered in disgust right before she praised God for the lamp her hand attached to. Mustering up all the strength she could, she pulled the lamp from its resting place, swinging with all of her might, hitting him so hard that he flew off the bed. Wasting no time, Amree stumbled to her feet, rushing toward the bedroom door.

With a quick look over her shoulder, her suspicions had been confirmed. The guy who attempted to rape her was the same dude from earlier. He was disoriented, holding his head as he tried to stand. She took off.

"Lemere." Amree ran into the hall, doing her best to cover herself with her hands as she shouted at the top of her lungs for her man. Thankfully, the house was now devoid of people except for Shakil, who removed himself from the door, rushing toward the bottom of the stairs where he saw a naked and distraught Amree.

"What the fuck?" He took a step toward her then stopped, not wanting to overstep because she was exposed.

"Shakil . . . He . . ." she cried, holding on to the rail with one hand as she used the other to point toward Lemere's bedroom where her attempted rapist was finally making his way out of the room.

Shakil watched as Amree's eyes widened while she backed away from the stairwell. She was shaking. He could see it distinctly, even from his position at the bottom of the stairs.

"Amree, what's wrong?" He began making his way up the stairs, concluding that he'd deal with the overstep later.

Before he could make it to the top of the stairs, D.C., as they called him, was heading down, holding his head, walking drunkenly. Frowning, Shakil stared at him before looking back at Amree, who had now slid to the floor, crying with her knees to her chest.

"Nigga, I know you didn't." Shakil's voice seemed to sober him right up. His head shot up before he attempted to run past Shakil. Like a movie scene, Shakil lifted his arm, clotheslining D.C., putting him directly on his ass. He moved fast, grabbing him by the collar of his shirt, dragging him back up the few stairs, making sure to keep him from Amree.

"He hurt you?" Shakil asked, his voice unsteady as fear of what happened to her on his watch came to mind.

She nodded, and without hesitation Shakil raised his fist, driving it down with so much force he was sure the connection he made with D.C.'s face broke his jaw on impact.

"Amree, go into the room," Shakil spoke as softly as possible yet firmly enough to let her know it wasn't a request.

"I'm not going back in there." Knees still pulled to her chest, she shook her head defiantly.

"You don't have to. Go into the guest room. I gotta get Mere and get these people out of the house.

Slowly she stood, doing as she was told because knowing Lemere was coming made her feel better. She went into the first room, turning on the light and locking the door before burying herself underneath the covers.

Shakil, on the other hand, felt as if he was having an out-of-body experience. He couldn't believe D.C. would violate her in this way. He punched him again for good measure, wanting to keep him out cold while he got everyone out of the house. Taking the stairs two at a time, he rushed to the DJ's booth, removing the microphone.

"Everybody get the fuck out now!" He didn't care whose house and whose party it was. They had to go. Lemere stood from his spot on the sofa, damn near dropping the girl who attempted to get cozy in his lap. He was about to cuss Shakil out until he noticed the look in his eyes.

"Ay, y'all gotta go," Lemere reiterated, making his way to Shakil's side.

"Go check on yo' girl. She's in the first guest room. I'll be up once we clear the house," Shakil ordered as his eyes scanned the room, watching as people weren't moving fast enough for his liking.

"What's up?" Lemere questioned, becoming worried.

"Go to her. Me sitting here explaining shit doesn't matter. Get to her."

Shakil barely finished his last word and Lemere's back was already to him, heading inside of his home. He trusted Shakil, so he'd get to his woman while Shakil cleaned house.

Lemere had been so focused on getting to Amree that he hadn't cared about D.C. being laid out near the rail. He twisted the doorknob, not expecting it to be locked.

"Amree, baby, it's me. Open up." With his forehead against the door, he knocked, waiting for a response.

Not even five seconds later, the door was unlocked, and Amree rushed into his arms, crying. They moved away from the door as Lemere used his foot to close it behind them.

"Babe, what happened? Where are your clothes?" Lemere held Amree almost as tightly as she held him.

"I never redressed after you left the room and that . . . that guy, he came in the room." Amree sobbed.

"Hell nah," he said, shaking his head vehemently, not wanting to hear her say what his gut told him she was about to. "Who?" Anger oozed from him. Of course, he wasn't mad at her. He was pissed at the audacity of a nigga he welcomed into his home.

Knocking on the door and Shakil yelling his name interrupted Amree trying to give a reply to a question she had no answer for. She didn't know enough about him to tell Lemere who he was.

"Stay in here. I'll be right back."

"No, do not leave me." She strengthened her grip on him.

"I'll be right outside the door. Baby, I gotta go see what the fuck is going on here." He eased her hands from around his neck, kissing her forehead before leaving the room.

"What the fuck happened?" Lemere asked as soon as he came face-to-face with Shakil.

"Not sure exactly what happened. I know it has something to do with this nigga. He violated." Shakil nodded toward D.C., who was coming to.

Though no specifics were given, Lemere had heard enough. Seeing his woman in a frightened state revealed something he wouldn't have thought in a million years. He stalked over to D.C., grabbing him by the shirt before raining blow after blow to his head.

In true Mason fashion, he didn't need to know why his cousin was kicking ass. He only cared about helping. Standing to the side of Lemere, he stomped out D.C. while his cousin continued to rain down blow after blow. Blood leaked from D.C.'s face and groans left his battered lips as the men found not an ounce of mercy.

"Shit," Shakil mumbled, hating that he had to pull the men off of D.C. He wasn't satisfied with the blows he landed on D.C. earlier but knew they could only beat his ass so much. Lemere had too much to lose, and a murder charge would take away everything he worked so hard for.

"Ay, that's enough," his voice boomed as he pulled Lemere back.

"I'ma kill him! Let me the fuck go." Lemere struggled in Shakil's arms to no avail. Shakil's grip was like no other. Even with the pent-up anger Lemere tried to release, there was no match.

"He's fucked up. Mason, back the fuck up. Bro, you have too much to lose behind killing this nigga. At least here. If it's gon' be done, it can't be done here." Shakil eased the grip he had on Lemere as he felt him relax some.

"You better get that nigga up out of here, like now." He snatched away from Shakil, kicking D.C. once more before he stormed off back toward the bedroom that held Amree. With his hand on the doorknob, he turned to Mason, "Ay, you, this can't be the end result."

"Already on it."

Lemere walked into the room, and as she'd done the first time, Amree leaped into his arms, crying and shaking.

Lifting her from her feet, he carried her into the attached bathroom, holding her with one arm while he turned on the shower.

"Babe." Lemere's tone was gentle as he placed her onto her feet.

"Hmm?" With her forehead against his chest, Amree anticipated Lemere's question. She wasn't ready to talk. What she wanted was to forget today's events.

"What did he do to you?" His words came out without an ounce of confidence. Fear was the emotion overpowering anything else he felt, even the anger. If Amree had experienced such a horrible violation, he doubted that he could live with himself.

"He didn't get the chance to rape me. But he touched me. He came close—"

"Fuck," Lemere shouted, making Amree jump from his outburst.

He was angry.

Frustrated.

And he probably felt lower than low, but she was the one whose sanity was on the line. She was the person who came extremely close to losing something she would never be able to get back.

"I'm sorry, babe." Tears stung his eyes.

She looked at him, saw his pain and regret, yet chose not to say anything. Instead, she entered the shower, her back to him with her eyes shut, praying the water washed away at least some of the filth she felt.

She felt Lemere enter behind her, and though she was upset with him, she welcomed his presence.

"I'm sorry." He wrapped his arms around her waist, resting his chin on her shoulder.

"You said you and this house were protected, and look where that left me." Amree didn't want to go back and forth with who was to blame. Truthfully the next man's actions weren't Lemere's to carry. However, the fact remained that, had he listened to her, taken her concerns seriously, and cared more about her than partying, none of what she dealt with tonight would've happened. He had to understand that. She did, and she didn't know how things with her and Lemere could ever be the same because of it.

Chapter 21

With her head resting in Erynn's lap, Amree's tears trickled down her face onto her best friend's lap. The puddle her tears produced were sure to have Erynn feeling like she pissed on herself. And though the feeling would be uncomfortable, Erynn wouldn't ask her to move. Since they made it from the airport to Erynn's townhouse, this was the position they'd been in: Amree crying her eyes out, and Erynn rubbing her head. It took Amree close to an hour to explain the event that brought her from Los Angeles to Erynn's home in Missouri. When Erynn got the call at seven in the morning her time, giving her a time to be at the airport, she knew something wasn't right.

"He's calling again," Erynn spoke gently, lifting Amree's phone as Lemere's name appeared on the screen.

"Let it ring."

Doing as she was told, Erynn set the phone down feeling conflicted. Part of her wanted to answer and give Lemere a piece of her mind. The other felt compelled to let him know Amree was safe. She hadn't learned until Amree arrived that she had crept out of the bed and house while Lemere was sleeping.

"He knows I'm okay. I'm not in the mood to talk to him right now. No one other than you," Amree told her sadly.

The only other person Amree had communicated with since arriving was Shakil. He made her promise to let him know she reached her destination safely or she wasn't getting out of Lemere's house. He had been the only person awake when she called herself sneaking out. His eyes were bloodshot with a ton of worry lines on his face. He'd apologized almost as many times as Lemere had before hugging her a final time before she walked out with no interest in returning anytime soon.

"You need to eat something. You've been on the go since five in the morning. It's after two p.m. and you haven't eaten. At least let's grab something to eat. I can order takeout or delivery," Erynn tried reasoning. Amree had gone through something traumatic, and although it hadn't gone as far as it could have, it had gone far enough. No woman should ever have to fight a man off of her for any reason.

"I'm not hungry." And she wasn't. Food was the last thing on her mind. She hadn't eaten since before Lemere's party.

"You have to eat, best friend."

"I told Lemere to send the cook up with some food for me. Maybe if I had been more alert and not so trusting, he wouldn't—"

"Aht aht. You are not about to do that." Erynn raised her voice unintentionally. However, she meant every word she spoke.

Her words penetrated Amree's heart. The reality of the weight she was about to put on herself pained her, causing low sobs to turn into loud ones.

"I didn't mean to yell, but you're not about to play the blame game. Especially not directing it toward yourself." Erynn wiped her own tears. "No one is to blame except for the bitch-ass nigga who attacked you. You're brave, friend. You got him off of you, and he didn't win. He came into that room and left with a permanent reminder that you were not the one. I know it was scary, and it shouldn't be taken lightly. But you know we've always been taught to not let a fuck nigga have any form of power over us. Which is exactly what you did."

"I asked Lemere if he was sure about throwing that party. He knew I had reservations about it, and he assured me, swore up and down, that he was good, that he would be good." She sat up, finally finding the strength to do so. Her body was going through so many emotions it was no surprise she felt drained. Making eye contact with Erynn, she exhaled, knowing that what she was about to say her best friend wouldn't judge her for.

"Erynn, I'm so mad at him. He made sure he was good, and that left me unprotected." She wiped the lone tear that fell. She was tired of crying.

"You have every reason to feel the way you do. All your reasons for being upset with him are valid. He fucked up. He unintentionally dropped the ball, and it almost cost you too much. I also want you to keep in mind that his feeling protected and all the other shit he claimed were the perfect reasons to throw that party. In his mind, it meant you were safe too. You said it yourself that he was trying to compensate for whatever he lost when he was shot. Maybe that party was his way of doing that. He didn't think he'd be tried by anyone for any reason that night. Trying you would be the same as trying him."

"Exactly. Mere promised me I wouldn't be affected by his world in any way that harmed me, and it seems like that's what I've been receiving. Loving him shouldn't hurt."

Erynn heard the pain Amree was carrying, and if hearing it weren't enough, she saw it written all over her face. She was also aware that fear and anger were factors playing a role in Amree's feelings, and rightfully so. As her friend, she would listen to her vent without judgment, and whoever Amree hated, she hated them too. The same as whoever Amree loved, she loved them too. Amree loved Lemere, and as their relationship blossomed over the last few months, she didn't have one doubt that

Lemere loved Amree too. Their relationship was new to both of them because they were bringing two different worlds together, and in her opinion, the union was beautiful. She saw a man, who had women constantly at his feet, change to make sure her best friend was happy. He didn't get any additional points for that, because the moment he decided he wanted to commit to Amree, that was exactly what he was supposed to do. She just loved to see it. Amree was worth every change Lemere made, and it felt good knowing he recognized that. Staring at Amree, she tried to formulate words that were supportive yet still provided the kind of advice that only she could give.

"What I'm about to say in no way is me taking Lemere's side nor an attempt to get you to ease up on him. I only want you to be reminded of what we both know, and it's that that man loves you. Feel how you need to feel about him. Just try not to forget that. If you need space, take it. But if he is also someone you need in your life, keep him. Do what's best for you by following your heart, not the million doubts running through your mind."

Erynn opened her arms wide, welcoming Amree into her embrace.

"It's hard not to blame him, even with knowing deep down it wasn't his fault," Amree admitted.

"Do you know what happened to the guy?"

"Besides getting his ass beat, I'm not sure. Mere told me that neither I nor anyone else would have to worry about dude ever again. It's crazy because his ass has been around me on at least two occasions. The first one was the first time I went to Mere's house. He hardly looked at me that day. The second time, we weren't in the same space for more than two minutes. I'm usually good at reading people. He presented nothing."

"Well, good riddance to his ass. I know that's not the best thing to say. However, my level of empathy toward his ass . . . I have none."

Amree pulled back, breaking up their hug. "So, what did you want to eat?" She smiled at Erynn, ready to change the dynamics of the trip. A traumatic event brought her there. It wouldn't be the entire reason for it. The only way she would grow from the experience and not allow it to consume her was to be the strong woman she was taught to be. As far as her relationship with Lemere, she wasn't sure what she planned to do. Truthfully, their relationship had way more highs than lows. She just hated how the few lows in her mind were avoidable. They were both doing their best to accommodate the other, understanding that they were coming from different lifestyles. She'd be lying if she said he hadn't gone above and beyond to make her comfortable. In the blink of an eye, all of that seemed to mean nothing after being violated while in his care.

"I'm craving seafood, duh. I can order it, and we can pick it up."

"We can eat at the restaurant." The sound of her phone vibrating captured her attention.

"Still not planning to answer for him?" Erynn asked, holding Amree's phone in front of her, watching as her eyes saddened. She was having an internal battle that her pride won.

"Not right now."

"If you were avoiding him for any other reason, I would have to ask if communication was in the bylaws of y'all relationship manual. Because, honey, yo' cold shoulder is cold as hell."

"You know five minutes ago you told me to take all the time I needed, right?"

"Sure did. But he sent a text."

Rolling her eyes, Amree gave Erynn permission to read the text by nodding her head. She knew Erynn's nosy behind wanted to know what he said, and if she was honest, so did she. She was hurting, pissed, and confused and still desired his affection.

"It says that he loves you. He's sorry and to please call him. That he'll do whatever you need him to do to make things better, and that he loves you again." Erynn read the message, feeling her chest tighten. She could feel the sincerity in Lemere's words as if he were standing in front of them, reciting the words himself. The tears forming in Amree's eyes provided evidence that she too knew Lemere meant every word.

Removing her phone from Erynn's hand, she looked at the text, reading it twice herself before deciding to reply.

To Lemere: I love you too. I need time.

She sent the message, then powered off her phone. Unfortunately for Lemere, she needed to avoid any and all communication with him so she couldn't be persuaded into making a decision she may later regret.

Fighting off the effects of a hangover, Lemere didn't budge when he heard his bedroom door open. He hoped whoever it was was smart enough to leave him be, especially since the darkness of his room wasn't inviting at all. As luck would have it, his privacy being respected didn't matter to the person walking in. The blinds were pulled back, letting the sun in. Lemere groaned, pissed, "Yo, what the fuck?"

"Nigga, get up," Shakil spoke, unfazed by Lemere's attitude. It was the same attitude he'd had over the last few days. Day one had fucked Shakil up because his own guilt was already tormenting him. It was guilt that still lingered, but unlike Lemere, he knew the show must go on.

"I know I wasn't speaking Spanish when I said I didn't want to be bothered." Lemere sat up, using his forearm to shield the sunlight from his eyes. With a furrowed brow, he mugged Shakil.

"You been held up in this room for goin' on three days. You've sulked enough, and it stinks up in here. Time to get your shit together."

"You on my ass about doin' some shit," Lemere chuckled. "That's funny. You can figure out how to do your job today. Where the fuck were you when that bitch-ass nigga tried my lady?" Anger motivated Lemere to hop up from his bed and get into Shakil's face.

The bitter expression on his face didn't falter as he watched Shakil go through a wave of emotions. Shock, guilt, and then anger were all noticeable reactions from Shakil as the men stood with their eye contact unmoving and stances intense.

"Boss or not, you not about to keep blaming me for shit that could've been avoided from jump had you not had that punk-ass party. You know damn well I'm not to blame for that shit."

Lemere's nostrils flared as he did his best to appear unmoved by Shakil's words no matter how right he was.

"Yeah, I am the boss. Remember that. You came in here disturbing me and shit. What do you want?" he sneered. Lemere was sure he was misplacing his anger, but he had nowhere else to direct it. He was too selfish and prideful to run the blame on himself, where it would be correctly placed in front of Shakil.

"I came to check on you. I know we all dropped the ball that night. And even with you tryin' to come at me with this 'you the boss, I'm the employee' type shit, our bond is deeper than that. At least I assumed it was."

Blowing out his breath, Lemere watched Shakil's brow rise, giving him a look that said, "Tell me I'm wrong." Since he couldn't do that, he walked away, heading into the master bathroom to freshen up. It took less than three minutes to wash his face and brush his teeth. When he finished, he wasn't surprised to see Shakil still waiting there.

"Look, man, we are boys. Shit, family. You're one of the few people I trust with my life. Still, shit with Amree, it has me all fucked up."

"All of us. Have you spoken to her?"

The look Lemere gave Shakil would've dropped him dead if looks could kill. It also answered Shakil's question. Therefore, he chose to leave well enough alone. The reality that so many days had passed, and all his texts and phone calls had gone unanswered, minus the last one when she told him she loved him, had him crawling right back into his bed, lifting the almost-empty bottle of Hennessy to his lips.

"You gotta get ahold of yourself, mane. What you doing ain't healthy, and it ain't you."

"I'm good. I still need a minute. You checked on me. I'm breathing, as you can see, so now you can leave me be."

Shakil peered at him, full of pity, deciding to do as Lemere asked. Nodding, he made his way to the door, pausing to inform Lemere, "She's good, and she's safe. She proved she's a fighter, and you got a real one, Lemere. Y'all are going to work it out. You gotta be who she knows for that to happen." Shakil exited the room, leaving Lemere with his thoughts.

"Fuck." Lemere tossed the bottle of Hennessy, not flinching as the glass shattered against his wall.

It was crazy how things changed for him over the course of not even a full thirty days. He wasn't sure what he'd done to deserve everything that had transpired, but he knew it had to be some fucked-up shit for it to have passed on to his lady. Lemere blamed himself for slipping when the shooting happened and blamed himself for not having Amree covered at the party. It was a party he threw for the sole purpose of taking his power back. The goal was to feel powerful again because the shooting had him feeling real bitch made. Having that party only for D.C. to attempt harming his girl did nothing other than reiterate his bitchassness. For a man of his caliber, everything he was feeling was justified because the shit should not have happened.

"Ay, cuz, that situation is taken care of," Mason announced, strolling into Lemere's bedroom, frowning at the stench lingering. It wasn't until he heard glass under his feet that he realized why the stench of liquor was so potent.

"Damn, what happened to knocking?"

"Man, yo' ass been out of it. Nobody knocking on shit. Get back to yo'self, and then you can get back some common courtesy. Well, maybe not so much from me because I don't have manners and shit, but you know what I mean." Mason shrugged, stepping closer to his cousin's bed.

"Fuck you, bitch. When was it taken care of?"

"Before the sun rose. I wanted to make sure shit was in the clear before I told you. I also wanted to wait to tell you so it'll lighten the blow of what I'm about to say next."

"The fuck is up now?" Lemere sat up straight, eyes planted on his cousin. He was already on the brink of a breakdown. Any more bad news would fuck him all the way up.

"I'm what's now. Mason, get out of here so I can talk with my son."

Lemere's head whipped to the side, looking behind Mason, stunned to see his mother walking into his room.

"You called her?" Lemere's angry expression went to his cousin.

"Man, you've been holed up in this room for days and weren't answering anyone's calls, including hers. When she called me asking about you, she knew something was up."

"Get the fuck out."

"Oh, I know there is something wrong with you, talking like that in front of me." Leandria stepped in front of her nephew, folding her arms across her chest, looking at her son like he'd lost his damn mind.

With his head hung, Mason kissed his aunt's cheek before leaving them alone.

"What is going on with you? This room stinks. You stink. You're in a dark place, son. It's written all over your face. You need to tell me what's wrong, and I mean right now."

"Man," he mumbled, getting up from his bed. He took the few steps toward his mother with open arms, only to be rejected by the frown on her face.

"I told you, your ass stinks." Her frown drew a chuckle from Lemere—the first one he'd had in days.

"You came all this way and don't want to hug your only son?" He smirked.

"I see your fake-ass charm hasn't left. Now, tell me what's going on with you as you clean this shit up." She glanced around the messy room.

"All right." Lemere dragged his feet, collecting clothes and miscellaneous items off his bedroom floor.

"You can talk and clean," Leandria spoke, tired of waiting for her son to tell her what had been going on with him over the past few days.

"Nah, I can't." Tossing the shirt from his hand into the hamper to the right of him, Lemere took a seat on his bed with his mother following suit. "Shit's just all fucked up, Ma. First I get shot, and now my girl left me. I'm a strong nigga, but so much shit happening at once is hard for me to take on the chin."

Lemere had said way too many cuss words in one breath talking to his mother. It was something he would've never done had he not been going through it. That was the main reason she let him get away with having such a foul mouth while speaking to her.

"You survived those shots because you're meant to be here, baby. A few bumps in the road aren't meant to define who you are. They're there to strengthen who you're bound to become. All right?"

Lemere let his mother's words penetrate his thick skull. She was the first person to say something that had him thinking about what had been transpiring. "More money, more problems" was the saying. Oddly, it was what he was experiencing.

"All right."

"What happened with Amree? It had to be something terrible, because she wouldn't leave you for no reason. What did you do?"

Shaking his head, Lemere wasn't surprised his mother assumed he was in the wrong. Amree was borderline perfect, so it was only right to think whatever caused her to walk away was his fault. She was right in her assumption, because he was entirely at fault. Staring at the floor, he debated telling his mother the truth. He knew whatever he told her would remain between them. He also knew if anybody could help him see where Amree was coming from, because he damn sure didn't understand, she was the one. Not that she'd

experienced anything similar. Her being a seasoned woman was enough to allow her the wisdom
needed to help him navigate the situation.

"She was almost raped at my party here at the
house." He uttered the words as if they pained him
because they did. That, filled with the embarrassment, had him talking like a child confessing his
biggest sin to the one person he hated to disap-
point.

"Oh, my God, my poor baby." Tears welled in
Leandria's eyes as her hands flew to her mouth.
That was the last thing she expected her son to
say, and because of the reasoning he provided,
she felt like shit for assuming Lemere was at fault.
There was no one to blame but the sick fuck who
somehow found assaulting a woman okay.

"Baby, I'm sorry. You blame yourself?" No longer
worried about her son's foul stench, she pulled him
into her with one arm, kissing the top of his head.

"Shit was my fault, Ma. She didn't want me to
have the party, and I did it anyway. I mean, I had a
good reason for throwing the shit. I also should've
listened to my girl."

"You know better than to blame yourself. Y'all
catch the guy?" Although Leandria wanted her son
far away from street business and was happy that
he had gotten out, she was from the hood. That
meant that she knew how shit worked and knew

her son was smart enough not to get caught up in something he damn sure would not let go.

"It's handled."

"And you know not to blame yourself, right?"

"It was D.C., Mama." He ignored responding about who was to blame, refusing to lie to her.

"The fuck?"

Lemere chuckled at his mother's reaction. Mrs. Big on Grown Folks Watching Their Mouth quickly lost her religion.

"Yeah, same nigga I fed on multiple occasions tried me."

"You gotta watch who you keep around you, baby. I always told you, people only want what you got when you got something they want."

"He can't want shit but a soul and breath where he's at."

"I need to call and check on Amree. I won't say anything because I'm sure she doesn't want anyone to know."

"Can you call her in front of me? 'Cause she sure as hell not answering none of my calls."

"Don't ask me to do shit like this again, and I'm not putting it on speakerphone." Removing her phone from her purse, she scrolled until she reached Amree's name. The phone rang three times. It surprised both Leandria and Lemere to hear Amree's voice on the other end.

"Hey, baby." The genuine smile on Lemere's

mother's face could be heard in how she greeted Amree.

"Hey, Mama L, how are you?" Amree's tone was equally happy. She used the nickname she'd affectionately given her from the bond they created.

"I'm good, baby." She paused, not knowing what to say next. She didn't want to jump right into asking questions.

"How is he?" Amree spoke up. It had been something she'd been burning to know yet wouldn't call or answer his calls to find out.

"Miserable. You?"

"The same. Things are complicated right now. I love him, Mama L. I really do. Right now—"

"You have to love yourself more," she completed her sentence, or at least what she thought she was going to say.

"I can love him and myself. I've been doing it. I only need time."

"I get it, baby. Take all the time you need."

"What?"

Lemere's question had Leandria removing the phone from her ear and covering the speaker before mouthing, "Shut up."

"Mama L, you there?"

"I'm here, baby. I want you to know you can still call me anytime."

"I know, and I will be calling you, I promise. Can you do something for me please?"

"Anything."

"Tell him I don't blame him and that I love him. And if he's not ready to talk when I am, I'll understand."

"I will. Okay, baby, I'll talk to you soon." Leandria ended the call, shutting her eyes and mouthing a silent prayer for Amree and her son to work things out. She knew from the day she met her that Amree was someone special. What she just asked her to do proved her right.

"So she's good?" Lemere asked in a bitter tone.

"From what she tells me."

"Tuh," he scoffed.

"She also had a message for you."

"She can talk to everybody but me. That's some bullshit."

"She said she doesn't blame you and loves you. She also said that she'd understand if you weren't ready to talk by the time she was. However, I know when she calls, you'll be ready to talk, right?" Leandria gave him a knowing look.

"Nah, if she good, then I'm good." The words sounded good leaving his lips. The truth was that he wasn't good and probably would never be if this was how things were going to end between them. A tiny weight was lifted off his shoulders, knowing she didn't blame him. Waiting for her to reciprocate the love he was trying to give her was a task he wasn't feeling. His pride wouldn't allow it.

Chapter 22

Three Months Later

Amree beamed as she lifted the microphone to her lips, preparing to interview the gorgeous young lady in front of her. It had been a while since they last saw each other, and Amree couldn't have been prouder to be interviewing her again, for her magazine's website, during such a monumental moment.

"You go, friend."

Amree peeked over her shoulder at an overly excited Erynn and smiled. She could see the pride oozing from Erynn and appreciated her being there. The last few months had been more than trying, and she was grateful to have her family's support to get through. Their support and putting her all into working were how she kept her mind off the thing, well, person she missed most.

"You ready?" Amree asked her guest.

"Yep."

Amree nodded at the cameraman, signaling it was okay to start shooting.

"First off, congratulations on winning your first BET Award. I'm sure this will not be the last. Best New Artist is a big deal, girl." Amree was genuinely happy about her win. When she interviewed Lady Banks earlier in the year because she was getting a lot of buzz surrounding her name, she knew it would be only a matter of time before her name would be mentioned in rooms that would get her in the place they were in now.

"Thank you. This all still feels surreal. I appreciate all of it. Being recognized on YouTube was big. This is even bigger. Well, my EP remaining number one on the charts for two weeks straight felt amazing as well."

Amree smiled, aware that Bank's rambling was simply due to nervousness and riding the high of her win tonight.

"And your EP is amazing. Not one song deserves to be skipped."

"Thank you." She blushed. Her almond-shaped eyes tightened above her heightened cheeks. At the tender age of 23, Lady Banks was putting on for young women her age. She resembled a young Naomi Campbell, and her spunk and outgoing attitude reminded Amree of Erynn.

"You're welcome. So, I know you have other things to do. I only wanted to pull you to the side to congratulate you and express how proud I am. Just a few months ago, we sat across from each other, talking about a moment like this, and here you are."

"A lot changed for me after our interview. You gave me a shot that made people take me more seriously, so thank you."

"Honey, you were a star before our interview. However, I sincerely appreciate the compliment. Well, enjoy the rest of your evening. I'm looking forward to our next sit-down."

"So am I." She leaned in, giving air kisses to Amree before sauntering off.

She was proud to have gotten through the interview without a hitch. There were no interruptions, and she hadn't stumbled over her words. Her stomach had been doing somersaults most of the evening, as she was nervous someone would question her about her not-so-public breakup.

"Best friend, you are in your element honey," Erynn walked up, speaking loudly. It was taking everything in her to hold her composure. She had been excited since they took their seats inside of the auditorium to watch the awards ceremony. Up to this moment, seeing her girl looking flawless.

"You've seen my work before, Erynn," Amree chuckled. It felt amazing to be commended for a job well done.

"Girl, yeah, but not up close like this. Viewing your interviews online is nothing compared to

seeing you up close. You were made for this. I am
so proud of you," she squealed.

"Thank you."

"So, what's next?" She could see in Erynn's eyes
she wasn't ready for the night to end. She wasn't
ready to be holed up in their hotel room, no matter
how nice and expensive it was. Erynn wanted to
party with the stars, and she didn't blame her.
They both deserved a night like tonight, hence the
reason she accepted the job and demanded that
Erynn tag along. If Erynn wasn't helping Amree
through her heartache, she was working her ass off.
As for Amree, if she wasn't nursing her misery, she
was being auntie of the year, even with Maksym
being home taking the bulk of the work pertaining
to Tyler. Or she buried herself in work.

She deserved this night.

"We hit up one of the after-parties. My job is
done." This time her smile was forced, and like the
great friend she was, Erynn didn't miss it.

"I know you're offering for me. I can see it in that
forced-ass smile. We don't have to do anything
if you don't want to. You're avoiding him. I get
it. So, if it means not going out to party to keep
you two apart, so be it. I'm sure it'll be hard for
you not to jump his bones, because he was looking mighty good tonight. And he won an award."
Erynn smirked. She was still rooting for the couple
to work it out.

"I will change my mind if that's what your little reminder of why I'm not trying to go out was intended to do. Is that what you want?"

"Hell nah."

"Okay, so we're going out." This time Amree's smile reached her eyes.

"Yes! Now that's what I'm talking about. Hopefully, we'll find one that Trey is at, because look, I am ready to risk it all for that man."

"I guess that includes your life, because my brother is sure to take it if you play in his face like that."

"I'm single, and so is your brother. Now, use your journalist connections and get us to the party my future husband will be at."

Amree ignored Erynn's request as her cameraman confirmed he was finished for the night before packing up. There were still a bunch of celebrities walking around, leaving the opportunity for plenty more interviews. If she wanted, Amree could do enough interviews to have content for a while. With the photos and interviews throughout the evening, she was satisfied with what they had and was sure the chief editor would be as well.

"Do you think we should change or go the way we are?" Amree asked, looking down at the dress she wore. Both she and Erynn looked equally gorgeous, dressed better than some of the celebrity women who paid thousands of dollars for a stylist.

"I mean, we could. I don't think it's necessary, though. We look good." Erynn twirled casually, showing off her curves and dress.

The navy blue backless chiffon dress hugged Erynn's waist perfectly, displaying her Coke-bottle shape. She'd been receiving compliments all night. Her tresses were silked to perfection and parted down the middle. Her makeup was subtle, only adding enough to enhance certain areas, not adjust her entire face.

Amree too received many compliments, looking just as sexy in a long olive deep V-neck formfitting dress with a high split. Her makeup was moderate except for the olive shadow gracing her eyes. Her hair was parted on the left side with big curls set in place on the right. As always, her orange tresses gained her attention.

"You're right. Let's make our way to the car while I find which location we should hit up."

It took them less time than expected to reach their awaiting vehicle. The security handling crowd control was doing an amazing job getting people to their designated areas swiftly.

"Um, I changed my mind," Erynn spoke as soon as they were seated in the back of the limo.

"You want to change clothes?" Amree smirked, knowing it was the reason for Erynn's change of mind.

"Yeah. I barely crawled in the back of this limo without feeling as if my dress would rip. No way in hell will I be able to twerk all this ass and it not split down the middle."

"Well, you're in luck. There's an after-party at our hotel. Your boy is hosting, so—"

"Driver, I need you to step on it," Erynn squealed through the slightly ajar partition. She cut Amree off, not needing to hear anything else.

"You are a mess." Shaking her head, Amree sat back in her seat, scrolling to Maksym's name.

"What's up?" He accepted her FaceTime call on the third ring.

"I know you did not call him," Erynn mumbled, popping her in the leg.

"Nothing. What are you guys doing?"

"We're watching a scary movie, Auntie," Tyler yelled in the background.

"Now, you know he's going to be up all night scared." Amree chuckled, wondering why Maksym would even do her nephew like that.

"He'll be fine because he knows this stuff in the movie is fake."

"Yep, Auntie, it is. And I'm a big boy, not a scaredy-cat."

"You're right, baby. You're the toughest kid I know," she hyped him up.

"Everything going good?" Maksym inquired, wondering why his sister would call him on such a busy evening for her.

"Yes, we're going to the hotel to change and then an after-party."

"You see your man?"

"Ex-man, Maksym," she scoffed, rolling her eyes.

"Yeah, all right. Erynn, yo' ass betta act like you got some sense tonight," Maksym demanded.

"Boy, I always move like I got sense." She pushed Amree's leg.

"We've made it to our hotel. I will call you later. I love you guys." Amree blew kisses before ending the call.

"You play too much," Erynn noted as they stepped out of the car.

"I called because I wanted to speak to them. Had nothing to do with you. Damn, there's a ton of people out here."

The women sauntered into the hotel, heading straight for the elevators with all eyes on them. The stares were nothing unusual, so they walked with their heads high, entering the elevator. They made it to their room in no time, freshening up before changing into their final attire for the night.

The lounge area of the Four Seasons Beverly Hills Hotel was packed when the ladies stepped inside. Showing her press pass, Amree and Erynn were directed to a more exclusive area.

"Now, this is much better. Swear if I had to rub shoulders with sweaty bitches all night, I was not going to be a happy camper." Erynn leaned over, speaking into Amree's ear as she scanned the room.

"You see your boy over there?" Amree smiled, discreetly pointing toward Trey, Erynn's celebrity crush. He was dressed in all black with a microphone in hand, hyping up the crowd of people below them.

"You really got me in a room with him."

"You were in the same room as him at the awards too."

"You know what I mean. So, how do we get closer to him? I'm not trying to compete with them groupie hoes. But I am not against snatching a wig or two to get what I want."

"We are not auditioning for *Bad Girls Club*. He'll notice you, I'm sure. The way you're burning a hole in the back of his head, he's certain to feel it."

"Let's grab a drink. The bar is closer to his area anyway." With a hike of her shoulders, Erynn smirked, then turned on her heels, leading the way to the bar.

"Yo, cuz."

Shutting her eyes, Amree took a deep breath, hoping to disappear. The rapid beating of her heart came from being caught off guard by the voice behind her.

Why didn't I think of the possibility of him being here? She groaned inwardly. Turning hesitantly, Amree came face-to-face with a smiling Mason. His genuine smile was followed by her own as she welcomed his embrace.

"Man, I ain't seen you in about three summers," he exaggerated, looking her over. As much as the man in him wanted to lust after Amree, the bond they created and the respect he had for his cousin wouldn't allow him to look at her as anything other than family, no matter how good she looked in the tight-fitting black distressed Bermuda shorts and burgundy deep V-neck bodysuit revealing an unacceptable amount of her cleavage. It was an outfit she looked fire in, but it would, without a doubt, have Lemere ready to body every dude in attendance.

"It hasn't been that long."

"True. So, how you been? I mean, besides killing the magazine journalist game. Yo' ass on damn near every outlet. And rumor has it you hard as fuck to get an interview with."

"I've been good. Busy, but good."

"Damn." Mason's eyes traveled to Erynn, whom he wasn't sure how he missed. She wasn't standing far from Amree, so he wasn't sure how she hadn't hit his line of vision first, especially looking the way she was looking. Erynn rocked blue jean shorts, short enough to be underwear, with a yellow one-strap bodysuit completed with a pair of black thigh-high boots.

"Hi, Mason," Erynn flirted.

"Man, why you keep playing with me? You know I've wanted you since the first time I laid eyes on you. You missing out on a good dude not giving me a shot, Erynn." Mason placed his hand over his heart as if it hurt him.

"Maybe you are. I'll never know." She leaned in, pecking his cheek before she and Amree fell into a fit of laughter.

"You ain't right." Shaking his head, he turned his attention back to Amree. "Me and you supposed to be better than this. You really gon' laugh at my pain, cuz, when you know how I feel about her?"

"You'll be all right. There are plenty of women in here waiting to leave with you."

"Yeah, maybe. It doesn't matter, 'cause all these women in this room and I only want her." He pointed at Erynn. Partially, he meant what he said. He would be happy if Erynn decided to be with him for the rest of the evening. His eyes had been roaming for most of the night, making Erynn about the tenth woman he had eyes for that evening. She would take the number one spot if she got with the program.

"Well, Mason, we're having a girls' night out, so I'm not trying to be rude or anything . . ."

"You want me to move my ass along. It's coo'." He chuckled, leaning in to kiss Erynn's cheek then Amree's.

"He's gonna tell him he saw me here," Amree complained as soon as Mason was out of earshot.

"Sho' is. That's not for you to worry about, though. What we came to do was have fun and make Trey your future brother-in-law." Taking her by the hand, Erynn pulled Amree onto the dance floor, refusing to let the mood be brought down.

"Twerk some bih, twerk some bih. Ay!" Erynn hyped her. Without hesitation, Amree put her hands on her knees and did what her girl called for. The two women danced like no one was in the room other than them.

"See, I knew you still had it. Now, neither of us got them Meagan knees. We hold our own, though," Erynn joked, raising her hand for a high five, which Amree happily obliged.

"Best friend spin around one time for these hating-ass hoes."

Laughing, Amree humored her, feeling herself because, without a doubt, she and Erynn were the baddest in the building. Class and a lack of thirsty activity went a long way. Mid-spin, Amree realized she wasn't in the clear like she assumed. Sitting there, looking every bit of fine, was Lemere. Seeing him at this moment felt nothing like it had when watching him win his award. This view of him hurt. He was drinking, smiling, kicking it with his boys without a care in the world. Seeing him act so carefree hurt because she was still hurting.

As always, whenever it was her watching, Lemere felt it. Turning, his eyes widened when they met Amree's. He looked her over, feeling his temperature rise with jealousy. She looked good. Damn good. Too good to be in a roomful of thirsty niggas whom he'd hurt for even brushing up against her.

Amree watched his facial expression change from surprise to anger.

Is he upset to see me? she wondered, noticing the anger hadn't faltered from his face. Not until some lanky high-yellow heffa leaned into him, whispering in his ear before planting her fake ass in his lap.

"I can't do this."

"Amree, wait." Erynn stretched her arm in an attempt to stop her but was too slow. She wasn't the only one feeling a way about Amree's hasty exit. Lemere pushed the girl off of him, regretting how attempting to make her jealous hurt her. He saw it in her eyes and felt it with the way she rushed toward the exit.

Standing, he nodded for Shakil to follow him as he rushed in the direction of the women. In no time, he and Shakil caught up to Erynn, who stood with her arms folded across her chest, foot tapping impatiently, waiting for the elevator.

"Erynn, where she go?"

"To our room. You don't get to go up there to hurt her anymore." She shoved him.

"I deserve that. That's not what I'm trying to do. I want to go get my woman back."

"Oh, really? The ho you had in your face two seconds ago says something totally different."

"That wasn't shit, on my mama," Lemere admitted as they all stepped onto the elevator.

"You love her?"

"Wouldn't be stuffed in this elevator with you and this big-ass nigga if I didn't."

"We're in room 505. Cover the peephole because she might not let you in."

"Thanks. Shakil, keep an eye on Erynn. Guard her with your life."

"I got her. Go get sis back."

Lemere rushed off the elevator, leaving Shakil and Erynn behind. He studied the directions on the wall, going left as directed for him to reach their room. He'd taken about six steps before the sight before him broke him.

With her back against the wall and knees pulled to her chest, Amree sat on the dark carpeted hotel floor.

"Baby, get up," Lemere soothed, kneeling beside her.

"You moved on? That fast? You moved on?" she questioned with her head still down.

"Hell nah. A nigga ain't been right since you left me. You know it, too. I'm sure my moms told you."

Raising her head, she looked at him, teary-eyed. This man, she loved him—a whole lot. Three months, or three years, wouldn't change that. Grinning at him, she shrugged.

"Yeah, yo' ass know I was going through it." He stood, extending his hand for her to take.

When their hands joined, both felt like the part of their heart missing was put back.

Lemere pulled Amree into him, hugging her tightly, hoping the rapid beating in his chest demonstrated just how much her love did for him.

"I'm sorry, baby. Whatever you need, let me be the one to give it to you. Or know I'll die trying. You can't leave me again. Talking with everybody in my family but me fucked me up."

"I love you too."

Lemere pulled back, placing his hands on both sides of Amree's face, and passionately Lemere kissed Amree to make her feel the love he had for her.

Epilogue

From the opposite side of his backyard, Lemere watched Amree laughing and dancing with his mother, Erynn, and Millie. The smile on her face was priceless. This was what he wanted to see from her for the rest of their days—her enjoying life, carefree, while knowing he would always be in the cut looking out for her whether she saw him or not. The past few months hadn't been easy. Amree did not play when it came to him loving her correctly and respecting her. They'd gone through a series of communication skills assisting them to get to where they were now. Amree hadn't been able to speak about what happened without getting pissed. This was frustrating for him because she also swore she didn't blame him.

Yet, he was the one who received her anger. After three sessions, they learned how to better articulate what they were feeling and how to respect where the other was coming from, even if they didn't fully understand. Going through all those hoops for a woman was new to Lemere, but once he concluded he'd rather jump with her than without, he did whatever was necessary to make their relationship work.

"This a nice place you got here."

Lemere looked to his left, watching as Maksym walked up on him.

"Thanks, man," Lemere replied, greeting him with a handshake. "It's not like my last place, but it's nice."

"Yo' last spot was better or something?" Maksym asked, thrown off by Lemere's comparison.

"Nah, it's not. My last spot was the first place I purchased after getting some real money. So it has sentimental value, I guess you could say. This one is definitely better. Mostly because it makes her happy." He nodded toward Amree.

One of the ways Lemere made sure he and Amree worked was by moving out of his home. Even with redecorating his bedroom, it was still hard for her to step foot in there. Wanting her comfortable, he decided to find a home the two of them could love equally. He purchased the place they were at now, enjoying a housewarming party with their closest friends and family.

"I respect it."

"Besides, I still have my other spot. I'm renting it out for movies, videos, guest house, all that extra shit."

"That's what's up. Real estate is where it's at. I just closed on my first commercial property, and shit feels good as fuck. Coming home with a felony, wasn't nobody fuckin with me on no job shit. Instead of begging or waiting, I made something happen for myself. For my son."

"Real nigga shit." Lemere extended his fist for a pound, which Maksym obliged.

"All right, I'm about to go over here with these kids. My son and yours challenged me to a basketball game. I keep telling them they don't want this smoke. My team won a championship while I was on vacation."

Both men chuckled. "I'll have to come join y'all in a minute," Lemere told him.

"Cool."

"Ay, Maksym."

"What's up?"

"You good with me changing your sister's last name?"

"She's gon' always be a Haylin. But it's good." Maksym smiled before walking off.

Lemere chuckled. Nothing about how he asked for Maksym's blessing was traditional, nor was Maksym's reply. But real recognized real, so Lemere was satisfied with the answer he received. Even if it had gone another way, it wouldn't have stopped him from popping the question. It would've only changed the date.

After another glance at everyone important to him enjoying themselves, he glanced at his watch before heading inside of his home. He hoped no one noticed and came looking for him.

Damn near power walking to his front door, Lemere opened it, smiling at his guest as the two embraced in a brotherly hug.

"Thanks so much for doing this," Lemere spoke to his guest as they walked farther inside the home.

"No problem. This is a beautiful home you have here. Big as hell, too. Besides, I owed Thomas a favor. Your manager is a good dude. The check you wrote wasn't a bad incentive either." He chuckled.

"The plan is to fill it with babies. If everything goes as planned, we'll get started with number one tonight."

"Hopefully, my being here helps."

"My woman loves the song you're about to sing. And if nothing else, I'm sure my mom will go crazy." Lemere chuckled at the thought of Leandria's reaction. He hoped she held herself together long enough to get Amree's ring on her finger.

"All right, well, show me where I'm supposed to go."

Pointing toward the open glass doors leading to the backyard, he said, "You'll walk out those doors. She's the one dressed in the long pink dress. Get close but not too close."

"Where's my mic?"

Smiling, Lemere handed the wireless microphone to him. He sent a text to the DJ outside, telling him to turn the music off and raise the microphone volume. He peeped out the window, chuckling at how no one seemed to notice how quiet the yard had gotten because they were still in their own worlds. Lemere turned back toward his guest and nodded.

And when the cupboard's bare
There's always something there with my
love

He sang, walking out into the yard.

"Oh, my God," Leandria screamed, hands flying to her mouth. Not many people were big enough stars to have her starstruck. However, if anyone could do it, he could.

Lemere walked a few steps behind him, his eyes on Amree, who he could see was doing her best to hold her composure the closer they got. Her eyes grew when he stood beside her, singing her favorite part of the song.

"'And my love does it good, whoa.'"

"Lemere, what is this, baby?" she asked, eyes darting between the two men.

"Girl, that's Johnny muthafuckin' Gill," Erynn exclaimed, pulling laughter from them all, Johnny included.

"What Erynn said," he chuckled, taking her by the hand, pulling her closer to him.

"You know, when we first met, there was something about you that told me you'd be a permanent fixture in my life, even though you wasn't trying to give me no play. Then, I got your number, and without hesitation, I saved your name as 'my future.' At the time, my aspiration was to make you my girlfriend. So, I put that into the universe. Now . . ." He paused, kissing her cheek before kneeling.

"I aspire for something bigger. Amree Haylin, beautiful, loving, amazing woman who makes me better, I need to know if you'll do this in-love shit with me for life?" He removed the velvet box from his pocket, opening it, revealing the biggest princess-cut diamond she'd ever seen. "Will you marry me?"

"Oh, my God," she mouthed, shaking as she eased her way down. "Yes, I will marry you."

Lemere smiled bigger than he had when he signed his first record deal, as she wrapped her arms around his neck, practically tackling him onto the lawn. Cheers were heard behind them as they hugged and kissed.

"You gon' let me put this ring on your finger?" He chuckled.

"Yes," she cried, loosening the grip she had on his neck. Lemere took her hand, placing the ring on her finger.

"I love you so much."

"I love you too. This shit forever, and a nigga wouldn't have it any other way."

Through a few trials, Lemere recognized how much life was worth living loving a girl like Amree.